MW01477694

The Girl in the Mirror

Book 4

P. COSTA

iUniverse

THE GIRL IN THE MIRROR BOOK 4

Copyright © 2023 P. Costa.

All rights reserved. No part of this book may be used or reproduced by any means, graphic, electronic, or mechanical, including photocopying, recording, taping or by any information storage retrieval system without the written permission of the author except in the case of brief quotations embodied in critical articles and reviews.

This is a work of fiction. All of the characters, names, incidents, organizations, and dialogue in this novel are either the products of the author's imagination or are used fictitiously.

iUniverse books may be ordered through booksellers or by contacting:

iUniverse
1663 Liberty Drive
Bloomington, IN 47403
www.iuniverse.com
844-349-9409

Because of the dynamic nature of the Internet, any web addresses or links contained in this book may have changed since publication and may no longer be valid. The views expressed in this work are solely those of the author and do not necessarily reflect the views of the publisher, and the publisher hereby disclaims any responsibility for them.

Any people depicted in stock imagery provided by Getty Images are models, and such images are being used for illustrative purposes only. Certain stock imagery © Getty Images.

ISBN: 978-1-6632-5143-5 (sc)
ISBN: 978-1-6632-5142-8 (e)

Library of Congress Control Number: 2022912814

Print information available on the last page.

iUniverse rev. date: 03/08/2023

Working Together

The townspeople were awesome. Many would volunteer for projects that included using their own equipment. Changes were coming from the state, and towns had to be in compliance. And they walked a very thin line. April saw no reason why those who volunteered their trucks could not help with road repairs.

One day April and a state employee got into a heated argument. "This makes no sense," she kept saying. The state employee would not back down. Finally, April realized it was useless. She got up in the cab, thanked them all, and told them to go back to their shed.

That evening she called some of the council members to meet on that Friday night, along with all those who were helping on their own. Those who volunteered their time or equipment were in attendance. Many ideas were discussed. They all agreed if they were looked at as lawbreakers, then so be it. They all agreed they would keep things as they were in order to save costs. There was no need to work in the daytime either. It would be best to work at night. There would be less traffic and the temperatures would be much cooler.

One afternoon Mr. Stevens stopped by the Di Angelo's home. Miranda welcomed him in as the school bus stopped to let April off. As usual Ruby did her dance in anticipation of her best friend coming home. And that made Mr. Stevens laugh. "Hey kid, how are ya?" he asked her.

"More like middle of the road," April said laughing, holding Ruby in her arms.

"Well, I received some outstanding news and wanted to stop by and share it with you," Mr. Stevens said. April looked at the portfolio he had with him. Then he looked directly at her and said, "Sit down." Mr. Stevens opened the portfolio and in it were testimonial letters from students who had graduated from colleges all across America. These students had been in the D Farms program.

Mr. Stevens pulled out one letter and handed it to April. Her Mother leaned over her shoulder to read it with her.

My name is Toby Brown, and I was born along with my two other siblings in Virginia. When I was three, my dad decided we cost too much and took up too much of his time. He left us with our Mom who was twenty-five at the time and had no education and no job.

To say those were lean years is an understatement. Mom did all she could to clothe and feed us. She worked when she could. Mom is a fine Christian woman, but when she was away, we found all sorts of trouble to get into. At age seventeen I was heading into a life of crime when I robbed the local gas station for sticky buns and meat sticks. I was sentenced by our local judge to enter the milking program at D Farms to work and get an education.

At first, I was resentful and angry. I hated everything about it. What right did that judge have to send me away from my family? I found that answer on my own. I was thrown into a household with seven other kids about my age or older. There were two older people who were our house parents. I learned to reshape my Southern values, calling them "Ma'am" and "Sir". I remembered to say "please" and "thank you". All the kids there were learning a new kind of life.

We worked, and we were fed. Our clothing was purchased, washed, and kept clean. Those who were old enough were encouraged to attend college and church! That was something I never thought would be an option, not for me.

I want you to know this past Spring I graduated second in my class from engineering school. I had several job interviews and never would have imagined this possible without D Farms. We will be moving to New York with a new, good paying job with insurance I am taking my family with me, my Mom, my brother Will, and my sister. We are all encouraging her to apply to the New York D farms program. I am not a man of many words, but somehow thank you falls far short of my deep feeling of gratitude. I will pay back to the D Farms program for other kids like me who might not have had a chance. Thanks so much D Farms.

Letter two:

Hello, my name is Adrianne. I am a twenty-two-year-old female. Thanks to D Farms I am a registered nurse with a background in research. I am to be married this coming fall to a wonderful man who lives in Kansas. I am sure my education will help and bless many. I will forever be grateful for the parental and educational guidance D Farms set forth in their programs. I have accepted Jesus Christ as my personal Savior and am thankful for my baptism. I look forward to the future with hope and joy. I owe so much to D Farms. Thank you from the bottom of my heart.

April had tears running down her face as did Miranda. They looked up at Mr. Stevens who was looking at them. "Amazing, aren't they?" he said to April.

"Yes, I'll say. I just never could have hoped for anything better." She answered him. "What is the graduation rate at D farms?" April asked.

Mr. Stevens looked at a paper and said, "Eighty-nine percent, and the dropout rate is at ten percent. That's because a small number enter the program, don't like it, and quit."

The file was full of letters, "I am going to let these with you. You know, for those days when you are not so sure you amount to much, when life overloads you." He then put his hands on April's shoulders. "Kid, I don't know where you got this idea, but I have to say it has made a tremendous impact on people's lives. I know it has on mine. And I agree with what all of them have to say in those letters," he said. "D Farms is becoming a testimonial of doing much good for the individuals, house parents, and to the entire community. The meat stores are a huge success. I just met with the Governor of Virginia recently and unemployment is high with the coal miners. Their quotas are filled for this winter. It has been such a blessing for those families to go into the meat stores and get what they need, at no cost to them. Others who have jobs and can afford the meat are welcome to come in and purchase the beef. So the Governor was very impressed with this model."

April then asked if there were meat stores similar near all the D Farms. "Yes, by the end of this month they will be," Mr. Stevens said. "We had a tough time with compliance in some states, but often a statesman would overturn the ruling and help us out. For instance, when we went forward in Pennsylvania, we had so much trouble putting in meat stores in major cities. There were problems with city codes, permits and so on. The Governor of Pennsylvania got upset and realized there would be no profit from these models. He was more interested in tax dollars. Can you imagine that? There is undeniable greed in our country, but thankfully there are also those who know what we are doing is necessary and needed."

All the meat is donated to help the poor people, AND we also pay taxes on our buildings. So every now and then we have need of some help to push and get them in."

"It's common sense," April said with a harsh tone. "Don't they want to help the poor?"

"Yes, yes, I am sure they do, but they also want the credit. You must understand bureaucrats and politicians," Mr. Stevens said. "Well, I must be going," he said as he glanced at his watch. "It was a pleasure, as always, to see you both. Take care and call me if you need anything at all."

"How are you at milking cows?" April asked teasingly.

"Nope, gotta run," he said and with that he was gone.

Miranda moved the small suitcase into the living room near her chair. "I can read some of theses this evening," she said as she placed a tissue box on her stand.

Tina & Mel

A FEW DAYS LATER A LETTER ARRIVED IN THE MAIL, IT WAS FROM Tina and Mel from the New England area. They were at the derby races. They would be coming through sometime in July, they did not specify. They wanted to stop in and visit. It was difficult to travel with Tina in the wheelchair, but they wanted to get out and see the world again. April was thrilled, she liked Tina a lot, and Mel too. But Mel was such a big talker. He liked to boast about what he had and then complain. Tina was quiet and never complained, maybe that is why they got along so well, opposites attract?

The Captain

April would get away from everything by running and conditioning, and she found a great running partner in the Captain. He truly was a Captain of the Armed Services U.S. Army. The Captain's name was Robert Edward Lee, just like the Southern General. Having come from Mississippi, he lit out of the South at age 17 wanting more than heat, mud, and poverty. As a young man he joined the U.S. Army, and excelled with obedience, earning him an elevated rank. By the time he was thirty-eight he was a Captain.

The Captain's sweet companion in life was Adele. She was from Germany, and she still had a heavy German accent even after all these years of marriage and living in the U.S. How these two met, was always a mystery and they never said much. They were older, had lived a good life raising children, serving their country. Everyone enjoyed their company. They were so likable, and he was very funny when he told jokes. The Captain was in great shape considering he was of retirement age. April had to run hard to keep pace with him. All throughout the summer they ran on the hills and paths throughout the forests. They both loved running on the Pine Hill, where there were nice level roads and no traffic. Often Hugh would join them, and the three of them would end up sweaty and tired. The Captain would invite them to his home for a good refreshing drink of spring water. Adele would fill the glasses with a big smile on her face. She enjoyed "the kids" as she called them. Their children lived far away. They were lucky to see them once, maybe twice a year. So, the "Kids" were a good distraction for Adele.

April had her driver's permit, and she often drove to the Captain's to see if he wanted to go for a run, which he usually did. Often on those runs they would talk as they ran together. The Captain asked April if she knew what she wanted to do after High School. Did she want to enter the military or go to college right-away.

April was not sure. She said that with as busy as she was, it was confusing sometimes to keep it all straight. She was planning on entering the farm competition in her junior year, but that was still far away. And she truly felt the filly would have a good shot racing this year. April also told him that friends would be coming to stay with them in July, and she was looking forward to that.

In summer, it was time to bail hay. April loved to rake the hay into rows and then bale it. She loved the sweet smell of the cut grass and how barren the land looked when the hay was removed. "It looked like a haircut," she would say. After the hay bailer threw the bales on a wagon, April would unhook the full wagon and replace it with the empty wagon that was waiting. She drove up a bit with the other tractor and take the full wagon of bales back to the barn. She unhooked the loaded wagon while men used an elevator to take the bales up inside the barn to stack. Next, she hooked up the empty wagon, and went out to the field again. Usually there were two full wagons for the men to empty. By the time April's wagon was full, they were done with one wagon and working on the second. They worked like this from 10 a.m. until almost 7 p.m. It was so satisfying to see the barns filled with hay.

When they were finished, the men were paid. April had to clean up, which meant putting the tractor and bailer away in different sheds. She then turned off all the barn lights and closed the back barn doors. For some reason, bailing hay was so satisfying. She could smell the dry hay of clover and mixed grasses.

Often farmers would come to her to buy hay. April knew exactly how much hay they needed, and it was a huge blessing for her not to have to buy hay since it was expensive. She would sell them only half of a wagon full, if it was all she could spare, and they were thankful.

It was a matter of luck. You never knew if, or when you would get enough rain so the hay would grow. There were times it rained in another town and not in theirs.

April would stand on her front porch hearing the rain, the powerful thunder, and seeing the black clouds, but they would get just a few sprinkles of rain. Other times it would rain so hard that it looked like a wall of white.

The rain that God provided did a lot of good for the field crops. The water He gave was full of minerals and nutrients that was so good for the crops and the animals. Yes, April never took anything for granted. She was so grateful for good crops that fed her babies!

Going on a Trip

THE FIRST WEEK OF JULY CAME WITHOUT NOTICE. A CAMPING trailer entered their driveway as April was walking up her lane. It was Tina and Mel, and April ran to greet them.

It was a grand visit. They had cookouts at the lake and at home. April took Tina out on the cart with her so Tina could be with horses again. Tina loved it. She learned how to drive a cart and wanted to buy one of April's ponies for it. April discouraged her, saying that Tina needed a trained, settled-down driving horse, and April would find one for Tina.

Tina liked the idea and asked the Di Angelos if April could come back with them for two or three weeks. Their son was the Governor and wanted his parents to watch their three children while he and his wife went traveling. This was a crucial time of hay season, the filly's training. But all of them, Gordon, Miranda, and April felt that she should go. They all received a witness through prayers that April was needed there. Not like she was NOT needed here at home, but they could not ignore the impression they had. So, April left with Tina and Mel to help for two or three weeks.

April was determined to find an easy-going mare or gelding that was responsive to buggy riding or riding. She would train them herself, but she wanted more than anything for Tina to be able to get out and ride with her grandchildren.

Often Tina would lament that she loved her grandchildren and how she wished she could go riding with them. But so far that has never happened. April was not a wait kind of girl, when there was a desire that was reasonable, she would do all in her power to make that happen.

Tina had been very active with horses in the past, she was not a beginner. Tina did not need to be explained to. She knew. And that is why April was relentless in finding a suitable horse for her.

She had been at an auction and saw many buggy horses, but they were so beaten down, and that was not what April wanted for Tina. She searched and searched.

Then as God would have it, April was riding with her Dad when she saw a plain brown horse standing in a field. She asked her Dad if he knew who lived there. He said he didn't. On a whim April asked him to stop, not long, just long enough to inquire about that horse. She did not tell her Dad that she had a "feeling" about it, he just stopped.

April went to the house and knocked. No one answered. Peering through the glass of the door's window, it looked as if no one lived there. The kitchen was sloppy, and there was junk everywhere. The dishes were piled up in the sink and looked as if they had been there quite a while. She knocked again and waited. Then she looked around and she saw that the grass had not been mowed in a good while. Just then someone came to the door and opened it.

"Yeah? What do you want?" the woman said. She was standing there with a dirty shift dress holding a baby who had a nasty runny nose.

"Hi. I live nearby to you and noticed a horse in the field. Is he yours?" April asked.

"What business is it of yourns?" the woman said.

"Well, ma'am it's not any of my business, but I am looking for a horse myself."

"Well, there's no telling who he belongs to. See my boyfriend and I have split. I don't have any money for this damn kid let alone to feed a horse. I suppose he was both of ourns, but he left."

April asked, "Do you own this place or are you renting?"

"I'm renting and have not paid the rent for three months. He comes down here almost daily asking for money. In fact, I thought you were him. But when I saw you was a girl, I wondered what you wanted. I thought maybe you were my boyfriend's new gal and wanted his things back. But you are too pretty to be with him. He is a loser and he ain't getting nothin' back. He left and that's that.

April knew this was a bad situation. She wanted to help, but this woman simply had her hands full and probably wouldn't change her situation if she could.

"Well, ma'am. I sure am interested in that horse. Is there anything you can tell me about it?" April asked. She saw her Dad in the truck looking as if he wanted to get out and come to help. But April put up her hand as if to say she could handle this.

"Well, I dun know. He's ridable, and I want to say maybe three hundred dollars for 'em," the woman said.

"May I take a look at him please?" April asked.

"Go on then, git and come back with money."

April walked to the fence and found there was no electric in it. Maybe their electric was shut off. She ducked under the wire and called to the horse. "Come on, come here. That's a good girl," as she looked at the mare.

That is when Dad came over and joined her in the pasture. "He needs some feed, he looks underweight," Dad said. "Look at his feet, they have not been trimmed in a long while." He then lifted the horse's lips apart to see its age, and he let go disgustedly. "He is a gelding and barely two years old. I doubt he is even broken."

"Well, let's see about that," April said, and she jumped on sideways and straddled the gelding. He stood there blinking. April kicked him a bit and he plodded about five steps and stopped. "She wants three hundred for him, Dad. I think he'd work well for Tina. He is patient, not jittery, and he is young."

"Well, it's up to you, Sweetie, but I don't have three hundred dollars on me in cash and neither do you."

"Wait here Dad," April said as she went back to the house and knocked again. The woman came to the door right away.

"Well, ya want him or not?" she asked.

April told her the horse was underweight and needed a farrier because his feet were really bad. And the flies were not good for him either.

"Well, like I told ya, I don't have money to feed us, let alone him."

"I'll take him," April said. "But I need to go to town to get the money. Unless you'd take a check?"

"No, no paper money, I want cash." She said, "I haint got no car to get to town, anyways."

"Okay then, we will be back in about a half hour with the money and I'd prefer to wait here for my Dad to come with the trailer. If that is okay with you?"

"Suits me fine but stay out of sight. I don't want Mr. "I want the rent money" to come here."

April thanked her and said they'd be back in forty-five minutes or so.

April got in the truck, and they headed to town. April then said. "Dad you are the Sheriff, can't you do anything to get her out of there? I mean, she has nothing. Don't you think a church, or someone would help her? She needs an education, and to be taught a lot. She is living hand to mouth. I am guessing she is barely seventeen years old with a baby."

Her Dad sat there thinking and said, "I can't evict her. I can't forcefully move her out, not without the owner filing in court. The most I can do is call a charity or talk to our Bishop. But she can't stay there, I doubt she has electric or heat, let alone food."

April did not have a cell phone of her own and asked her Dad if she could use his. Gordon grimaced and said, "April you cannot get involved with this. You don't know how sane the boyfriend is. Let this one alone. We must do this properly."

Then April asked him, "Is that what Jesus would have done, do it properly with the authorities?" April knew she had her Dad but said no more.

They went to the parts store, where they were originally supposed to go and then to the bank where April withdrew three hundred dollars of her money. Gordon was so uncomfortable about that but said nothing. One the way home, Gordon stopped at the driveway and said, "I will be back in fifteen minutes with the trailer." And he was.

April waited inside the barn where she saw a pile of kittens that were starving. Four bunny rabbits that were barely alive in a cage. She spied the blanket and saddle and picked them up and put them in the eve's way of the barn. April shook her head because this was not right. You don't go and get animals and never feed them. She was not going to say one word to the woman but decided she would take the bunnies and kittens. It would be a relief to the woman.

True to his word, and she never doubted him, Dad came rumbling in with the trailer. The woman came out while her baby was screaming bloody murder behind the kitchen door. "You ain't taking that horse before you pay me," she said angrily. She marched up to the barn and held her hand out. April counted out twenty-dollar bills to the exact amount of three hundred dollars. "Then, that's that," the woman said, and she marched back into the house.

Gordon backed into the lane and the horse stood by the wire, probably hoping this would be a better life than he had here. Meanwhile April lifted the cage and picked some grass and clover for the bunnies and dropped it in their cage. They began to eat. The kittens she put in a cracked bucket, and they would be fed as soon as they got home.

The cats became Miranda's pets and were good mousers. The bunnies and kitten thrived, and they grew up friendly. The horse was perfect, calm, and steady, not nervous at all. He was perfect for Tina.

The Governor's Home

THE HOME OF THE GOVERNOR WAS A BEAUTIFUL HOUSE NESTLED in the country with acres of land and trees all around it. They had a full stable of the finest riding horses, and their children rode in competition. The children were Rusty age nine, Icarlie age seven, and Suzanne age 4 months.

When Tina and Mel arrived, they told their daughter-in-law they had a doctor's appointment and tests on the 17th of the month and would have to leave April and the children for two days. Joy had no problem with that. They had an electric security system and security guards who were also made aware that they would be needed during those two days.

As April put her suitcase upstairs, she turned and accidently bumped into a stand in one of the bedrooms and a crack appeared in the wall. She asked Joy to come into the room and began to apologize for breaking the wall.

"You didn't break the wall, dear," Joy said as she pushed on the stand. The crack opened more to reveal a doorway and a set of stairs. April looked at Joy. "You see, the life we live can be dangerous sometimes. We wanted to create a safe passageway in case we ever needed for all of us to escape should harm ever come to our home," Joy said. Joy stepped down the stairs with April following her. "Here on the wall are backpacks for each child with black clothing and food. It may be necessary for them to hide in the basement or run, but this way they have a good chance to get away if our security can't help them.

April grasped the situation "Have you ever had to use it or come close?" she asked Joy.

"It came close," she said.

"Who knows about this?" April asked Joy.

"Me, my husband, our oldest child and now you. No one else," Joy said. "Our guards don't even know because you can never be too careful. We cannot trust anyone, not really," Joy said.

April was uneasy. She never put her trust in man. She was taught to lean on God, kneel and pray then receive answers and direction as to what to do.

April spent much of the time working with a horse they had brought along. She was teaching him to lay down for Tina to get on and ride. April also wanted to teach the horse to drive a cart. Tina was so grateful that now she could ride again, and the grandchildren could ride with her. That was something they never did before with their grandmother. They would talk, laugh, and she got to see her grandchildren in a different way. They loved riding and now they could all ride together.

It was soon time for Joy and George to leave. The children kissed them goodbye, and from that moment the menu changed to pizzas, junk food, or fruit. They ate what they wanted, within reason. They made s'mores by the fire-pit. They swam until dark. They rode horses and had a wonderful time.

Before long it was the time for Mel and Tina to go. That night Mel told April that the next day they would be leaving, but not to worry because there were two armed guards who would take care of them.

April did not know why, but this did not comfort her. She felt uneasy and untrusting. April did not sleep well that night, she half slept, and half dreamt, but the dreams were frightening. As Mel packed in the morning, Tina spent time with her grandchildren. Soon they pulled out of the driveway with their big travel trailer. The kids all waved until the trailer could no longer be seen.

It was then that April noticed one guard's attitude had changed, he became bossy. As soon as Tina and Mel left, he said the kids should stay inside so he could keep a better eye on them. April did not listen to him, they swam, and she gave them riding lessons. They ate whatever for dinner too.

That night as April tucked the kids into bed, one guard kept hanging around upstairs. She told him it made her feel uncomfortable. He told her to shut her mouth and go to bed. April was shocked. He never spoke to anyone like that before.

She did go to bed, but she did not sleep, her eyes were wide open. April got to thinking she did not see the other guard for hours. She slipped out of bed and looked downstairs, but no one was there. She heard talking outside by the pool and went to investigate. She witnessed the nasty guard take out his pistol with a silencer and shoot the nice guard who had his hands and feet bound with rope. He landed face down in the pool and was most likely dead by the shot or drowned.

As fast as she could climb the stairs, April headed to the children. She roused the boy to get up NOW. She woke his sister urging her to get up and move. Then she swept baby Suzanne up in her arms and they all headed to the bedroom with the magic door. April pushed it open, and they scrambled down the stairs. April held onto the baby who was still sleeping and carefully closed the panel that hid their escape. No sooner had it closed when April heard the guard on a cell phone. He was looking for them.

Down the stairs with sleeping Suzanne. The two children already had on their black clothing. April was wearing black sweatpants and a black tank top but had to disguise her blonde hair. She put on a long-sleeved black turtleneck shirt and a black ski cap with a full face. She put the baby in a black log carrier with handles covered by a small black blanket. As they stood ready, waiting to go, they saw three sets of headlights shining into their driveway. This had all been planned, it was a set up.

April made a promise. In no way would they get these kids. They were on her watch, and she would never let them be harmed. April motioned for the kids to follow her. They had put on their backpacks. April grabbed some other things and added them to the children's bags. She put Suzanne's backpack on - it was heavy, most likely with formula or milk.

By now there were men with suits and wearing guns in holsters all over the property. April could hear them. "We must find those kids. We need some insurance," they said.

April looked at the kids and said, "We have to sneak out through the coal shuttle. I will boost you up one at a time. As you reach the top, crawl to the wood pile and go to the middle section. I will be there shortly and absolutely no talking."

First was Rusty, April lifted him, and she could feel he was anxious. "Be steady, Rusty", he nodded his head. Then Icarlie, she was a lithe girl, very strong. Not one word was uttered.

Then it was April's turn. She had to put her feet along the sides of the shoot in order to go up. At the top she almost crawled out into a man's legs. She stopped and waited, the men had flashlights and handheld radios. There were about eight to a dozen of them.

April crawled to the wood pile and motioned to the kids with her finger to her lips that there should be absolutely no talking. She used hand signals only, as best as she could. They followed her when April motioned. Soon the men were all heading towards the big bushes in the driveway, and April and the children scurried ever so quietly to the stables. Once there, April handed the baby to Icarlie to hold. She told Rusty to tack up his horse as quietly and as securely as he could. April did the same to Icarlie's horse.

Thankfully Rusty's horse was wearing Easy Boots, because his feet had been hurting on his last ride. April put a set of four Easy Boots on Icarlie's horse, so their shoes would not make any noise. Rusty mounted his horse, and April put Icarlie on the same horse behind her brother. April mounted Icarlie's horse with baby Suzanne in a backpack carrier, and they rode out of the back side of the barn. April could hear the men coming to the barn to see what the other horses were whinnying about. The gates were latched as if there were no other horses. April was smart to do that so the pens would appear to be empty. They all rode calmly and quietly away.

On the trail all they could hear were leaves, no click clock. No noses blowing, no whinnying. It was a silent ride. As they rode along the side hill April stopped. She asked Rusty to hold her horse and she handed him the reins and the baby to Icarlie. "I will be less than five minutes, wait for me."

April half ran back along the side hill to the entry of the mansion's driveway. There were four black cars, all of them with government plates. April did not see anyone, and she opened the driver's side door keeping the button pushed in so it would not turn the light on. Just as she thought, there lay the wallets on the dash and seats. April took them from all three cars. At the fourth car there was someone waiting at the front of the car. April almost did not see him. "Pass" she said to herself. She tucked the six wallets in her pockets and scooted down the driveway, over the side, and up the embankment.

April ran quietly until she saw the children safe, waiting for her. April mounted back up taking the baby Suzanne from her sister and they rode out. As it turned out, it was a lovely ride. Rusty soon forgot the trouble they had escaped from and was looking at the sky and his surroundings, thanks to the full moon. Icarlie was leaning against Rusty, asleep. They crossed streams upside hills and embankments, crisscrossed the road up another steep hill and walked along fields that seemed like miles long.

It was beginning to be light when April spied a log cabin. It was not deep in the woods, it stuck out a bit and was obvious not used in a long, long time. April dismounted and got the kids off. She put Icarly and the baby in the cabin as Rusty held the horses' reins. April took the horses and put them behind the cabin. There was a crude corral made of sapling limbs, it was good enough to hold the horses. The grass was up to the horses' chests, so they had food. There was also a barrel filled with water from the previous rain that had fell from the metal roof, so April knew the horses were going to be content.

Once inside the cabin April knew the kids would be hungry, she looked at her watch, and it was now 6:40 a.m. She opened the backpacks and decided to make them all breakfast. April made a small fire in the fireplace to make toast with marshmallow cream and peanut butter. Then she warmed a can of milk for Baby Suzanne. She made cuts in the table for the kids to play tic-tac-toe, and they spent hours playing using stones. By noon the kids were sleepy, so April let them sleep on the cots that were there. When all three were fast asleep April went outside to see where they were and if she could see anything else.

From the porch she saw nothing, so she climbed to the very top of the hill and stood by a scrub pine tree. She could see bits of the highway far down below, and some houses, but none she recognized. April guessed they had ridden a good ten miles, so she walked further along the hill to the opposite side and there in the distance she saw dozens of police cars far in the distance. It was their lights flashing that caught her eye. April walked down a half mile or so to get a closer look and where she could hear a tiny bit. The state police were conducting a highway search and screening people.

April saw enough, she headed back to the cabin and let the kids sleep till 1:00 p.m. She tacked up the horses and was ready to go as soon as the kids woke up. One by one, little heads popped up. Some had to go to the bathroom outside and they took turns. They no longer needed the black clothing and thankfully there was a change of clothing in their backpacks. After Suzanne had her diaper changed, they were ready to go.

They mounted and headed out across the field, skirting the edge, down, down, down into a small town. There April saw a grocery store of sorts and asked to use the telephone. She made a collect call to the Sheriff's office in Fresno. Her Dad answered the telephone. As much as April did not want to, her voice broke, and she almost cried. She told her Dad everything in two minutes.

"You stay right where you are, Darling. We will be there in no time at all."

April hung up and wished she had told her dad they had ridden horses. As it was, he would be coming in a helicopter, of that, she was sure. In no way would he be here in no time at all. April thought someone would take care of the horses until they could go home.

April bought the kids sodas and ice cream. They all sat on the back porch of the store. Apparently, Sheriff Di Angelo had used everything in his means to make calls and contacts to get where April was. As he promised her, Dad did come in a helicopter in two hours. It was arranged for a deputy in that area to return the horses.

Gordon hugged his daughter as if he would never let go.

April pulled him aside and dug in her pockets for the wallets. "Dad, this was a set up. I believe they were after the Governor. Since they could not get him, they were going to use the children as collateral. These are government ID's Dad, Federal Government."

Gordon Di Angelo realized the depth this criminal activity had reached, so he walked to his friend, a State Trooper Captain, and handed him the wallets. He knew this would be handled correctly.

Within a half hour April was with her Dad in a squad car approaching the estate. There were no less than two dozen State Police cars behind him, along with some high-ranking government officials. As they pulled into the driveway, April saw the scumbag guard who was acting all innocent like he did not know what happened. That is until he saw April and the kids.

April stood watching as the guard tried to approach her. Gordon Di Angelo stood between them. He pulled the handcuffs from his belt and cuffed the man while reading him his rights. He then stuffed the guard into a police car. Gordon's friend, the Captain of the State Police, slapped Gordon on his back and smiled a big smile.

Within hours the Governor raced home with his wife at his side. They were relieved their children were safe. Joy hugged and kissed her children and then she hugged April tightly. "We owe you so much," Joy said to April.

"No, you don't. I was not sure why I was to come here, but I know now," April said to her. As it turned out the guard was ordered to execute the Governor allowing the Lieutenant Governor to step in. They were all arrested, and in time they were tried, convicted, and sentenced to jail!

The Di Angelos all flew home in a helicopter, compliments of the state. They felt weary as if they had gone through a wringer. Even Miranda felt helpless. They hoped that the criminal activity was NOT in the government, but it would be foolish to think otherwise.

That night Gordon Di Angelo awoke and went into his daughter's bedroom. He watched her sleep as he had when she first came to live with them. He sat down on a chair and began to weep. He bowed his head and began to pray.

"Dear Father in Heaven, forgive me. I have tried to be a good father to her. I have tried to be there when she needed me, but as she grows and makes decisions she is pulled further and further away from us, and we are not able to protect her. Now I am beginning to understand how difficult it was for you to have a son here on earth to suffer be mocked and sacrificed. I don't have your strength, Father. I know you love us as your own children. But sometimes I don't know why. Help me Heavenly Father to be a better Father, to understand her, to be there when it is important."

Gordon felt his wife beside him, "And me too, Father. Help me be a better wife, mother, and your daughter. My tongue gets me in trouble sometimes." They held hands and continued to pray. "Father watch over our daughter, bless her with insight, to do good, not to take such risks. We know that is her nature. We pray for her to have a mind and to be aware in all circumstances and instances. Please, Father, we ask for mercy to allow the Holy Ghost to tarry with her, to always keep her aware, In Jesus Christ's holy name, Amen."

Miranda led her husband back to bed and she cradled him in her arms and kissed him. "You are a good father, Sweetheart. Your daughter looks to you in all her decisions.

Gordon yawned and kissed his wife and was soon asleep.

Miranda held onto her companion needing his strength for what she felt were her failures. Miranda felt tears run down her face and finally said, "Come on, Miranda. It's not all that bad. You have a wonderful husband who loves you, and a daughter who was a gift. Surely you know you matter to God, so be happy." With that she snuggled close to her husband and willed herself to sleep.

Later that same month Gordon was called to evict the woman where April bought Tina's horse. Now there is not much that turned Gordon's stomach but taking that woman and her baby out of that house was something no sheriff wanted to do, ever. He called Women in Crisis right there in his cruiser and told them he had a very depressing case. He explained the situation in detail.

The woman on the phone hesitated for a while and then said. "Can you bring her in. We can make sure she is bathed, has clean clothing, and we can take care of that baby." And that is what he did.

At first the woman was so afraid until she met one of the counselors and that changed her countenance all together. I'd say that is what we would all want, to be taken care of with kindness.

September, and it was back to Mutual night. Hugh was now too old, but he came anyway with Treavor. Everyone wanted them to come. Hugh would help setup equipment and tear down. He was a big help, but more than that, April really liked him. He was her kind of guy.

The filly was filling out nicely. She had several races under her belt, and she was a lot like Native Son. Wanting to kick in another gear, in spring they would put her in the Derby and see how she would do. April was excited about that. This girl could really run.

Hugh and April were regulars at Flo's Diner on Friday nights. Saturdays Hugh often came and helped April with chores. Sometimes they would take a four-wheel ride, and they always ran with the Captain. Occasionally the Captain was not there, he and Adelle took trips to visit their grandchildren.

Hugh and April took in movies, went dancing and on occasion the Marshalls came over for dinner or the Di Angelos went to the Marshall's home for dinner. April still loved horseback riding. Hugh not so much. She was often seen riding on Pine Ridge or on a backwoods trail. Those were good days, happy days. Hugh wanted to pop the question, but he knew better. He would be leaving in September for the military. He had requested a delayed entry from the Marines for this very reason.

It was not all fun and games for April. As she promised, she was at every evening meeting for their community as Mayor. She took on that responsibility as she did her others. Every Tuesday, no matter what was going on with her life she was there. April made them aware of the Farm Competition. She had talked in depth with the committee, so they knew exactly what to do when she had to leave. She left an outline for the next year and added if they needed help, call Mr. Stevens as he was very much aware of her concerns.

April would also be leaving in September for the Farm Competition, both April and Hugh would be leaving about the same time. Hugh was not sure which one of them would be leaving first.

April often wrote to her grandfather and birth Mother. She always handed them to her Mother since she did not want the letters to sound stupid or sappy. Miranda loved April's letters and told April so.

One day right there on the kitchen sink, as she was doing the dishes, Miranda noticed a letter. She finished the breakfast dishes and sat down opening the letter. It was from April and in the third line Miranda had to get up to get tissues. She fanned her face and read some more. She cried and read more dabbing at her eyes. Miranda loved her daughter as all mothers do, but there were times that she felt April was either deliberate or stupid!

Yes, there she said it! April could manage an entire farm on her own but could not make up her mind to put only whites in a washing machine, she had to add colors too. That was why Miranda "inherited" farm clothing. On a brighter note, it gave her opportunity to buy new clothing for herself. But she loved that girl, and needed her, just as she needed the air she breathed.

It seemed every day was an adventure with April. She was always looking for more, something more to do. Miranda had April tested for OCD (Obsessive Compulsion Disorder), but it turned out April was negative. She simply loved being busy. Miranda was not upset or complaining. All the things April did were good. Miranda just wanted to know. By no means was April upset with her Mother. In fact, she laughed at her, "Take me as I am," April said teasingly to her Mom.

April simply liked being busy. If she had to sit still for any length of time, she would become sleepy. And she did not want that one bit.

She admired those in professions that were in a class all by themselves. Emergency crews, emergency room nurses and doctors, the busiest people ever, and that was her in a nutshell. April could think much better when she was busy and overloaded. She liked doing two to four projects at one time. It was just who she was.

In school she was no different. The teachers were a bit concerned when April had a full plate at home and then volunteered for most anything at school. They soon understood that is what made April excel. To limit her would not do her well at all. April was one who was always looking ahead, at what was next. In time they understood her.

Because of that April did not have many very close best friends, three at most, and April was fine with that. They were good girls, who were even better with April around them. That's what their parents said. April loved her three BFFs so much.

She had known them since fourth grade, and they felt the same way about her. To April they could have been her sisters and she would have loved that. They were not the same, but that was the interesting thing about them to April. To say she loved them is an understatement, they were inseparable.

Christmas at Church

That year as usual all the Churches were preparing for the Holiday season. Much to April's surprise she was asked by the Lutheran Church if she would be willing to sing for them.

Now April never announced or advertised her singing, but with the summer fair contests, she got to be fairly well known. But in this instance, she was overheard singing by one of the ladies' guilds from the Lutheran Church from the Flower Social. The women from the guild had her sister and husband with her when April sang a song in preparation for a Sunday Service.

The letter came, and well, April felt she should be neighborly and kind. So again, she and Miranda went to the church on Sunday on their way home from their church. They inquired with the Guild what song they wanted April to sing. They settled on "Oh Holy Night".

April needed to practice. She practiced in the barn to get every sound out of her throat and lungs. She practiced in the shed. Miranda's nerves were on edge, but she encouraged her daughter to keep practicing. As her vocal cords grew stronger, her tone was on pitch, and she was able to reach notes she had never reached before. She was ready, as ready as she could be. April had practiced in the church six times and the song sounded amazing.

Miranda asked the Marshalls if they would like to attend with them. Mrs. Marshall readily said "yes". She said she was excited to hear April sing in that beautiful church.

Miranda bought April a beautiful dark blue crushed velvet dress with a darker blue bodice. She looks stunning wearing that with her blonde curly hair pinned up.

They came early and sat near the front. April was slightly nervous as she looked around and then adjusted her seat. She pulled at her gloves and Miranda gave April a hug that seemed to help settle April down.

The congregation began singing Christmas songs followed by an address by the Pastor. Then they read from the papers that were handed to them as they entered the church. And then it was April's turn.

When she first stood up, she was nervous. Her hands straightened her dress, and she adjusted her gloves again. As the prelude music began, she looked up at the choir in the balcony at the back of the church and you could watch her slowly slip into the song.

April was completely lost, the song showed emotions on her face. You could see the words clearly gripped her. As she sang about the Savior tears rolled down her cheeks. The emotional words and the strains of music of the song touched her inside. Many of the people were also moved to tears as well. When the song came to the Emanuel, she hit the high notes and held them. It gripped hearts of those there. It was a beautiful rendition of the song. April had given her all. This was talked about in such a kind way, in the streets and in homes. Many said it was breathtaking! And Aprils thought? Well she was just happy to have helped.

Christmas at Home

CHRISTMAS WHEN YOU ARE YOUNG CAN BE A CRAZY TIME, YOU don't want much, and you have very little to no money to spend on others. That's how it is.

Gordon and Miranda had ordered tickets to a Christmas Ball at their firehouse. April spent many hours there decorating for the theme of *Winter Wonderland*. There were sprays of tinsel looking like snow. Someone offered to do an ice sculpture, and well, it was beautiful. Hard to imagine there in Fresno, but it all came together.

That night Miranda dressed in red with her hair swept up, she looked quite beautiful. April had worked at several jobs during fall to purchase her Mother a pearl necklace with a diamond stud in the center and matching dangling earrings with the diamond stud at the top next to the ear - they were so dazzling. April knew her mother would love them. In order to earn the money to buy them, April baby sat, picked and sold produce, and gave private riding lessons in all her limited spare time.

The night of the ball as Miranda dressed, April knocked on the door. "Come in," her Mother said. April held the wrapped square box in front of Miranda. "For me?" Miranda asked.

"Yes, for you, for Christmas and I felt you could use this tonight," April replied.

Miranda carefully tore open the paper and revealed a blue velvet box. She opened it and began to tear up. "Oh, my make-up, "she said, using a tissue to dab at her tears. "Oh my, how did you do this?" "Gordon! Gordon, please come in here," she said.

Gordon came in with his face half shaven in boxer shorts. He looked at the jewelry and Miranda's tear-streaked face, and he leaned over and kissed his daughter leaving shaving cream on her face.

"Dad," April said loudly while Gordon laughed. Miranda swiped at her husband with her tissue and then they all laughed. April helped her Mother with her make-up and Miranda put some on April and she wrinkled her nose. "You look so pretty with some paint." her Mother said to her daughter smiling.

"Mom, this is so not me," April said disapprovingly. "Maybe when I am older, but for now, I like how I am, curly hair and all."

When her parents walked out of their door, they looked like royalty. April had been in town the day before and picked up a video movie to watch from the "clearance" bin. As she picked it up to pop into the player, the telephone rang.

"Hey April, is the coast clear?" Hugh asked.

"Well, my parents just left for the Ball, and yours?"

"Yeah, they left about ten minutes ago, so what are you doing tonight?" he asked her.

"I picked up a video yesterday and was going to pop it in," she told him.

"What is the name?"

April cringed inside, "It's a romantic comedy, *You've Got Mail*."

Hugh said, "Nah, I'll pass. Have a good time."

"I hope to, you take care," she said and hung up. April almost felt relieved. If Hugh did come over, she felt she had to change her clothes, then comb her hair. Tonight, all the chores were done. She was tired and never ever really relaxed or did just nothing.

But tonight, was planned and that was her plan to do absolutely nothing but watch this movie, eat popcorn, maybe laugh and cry, and go to bed early. Ruby could not agree more!

Christmas came and they had chosen a family to spend on rather than themselves. It was a good family, a Mom and three kids. They were trying hard to keep up. She walked to work at the hospital and the kids hustled to do odd jobs. So that year, without them knowing, a tree, gifts, just the right size clothing, and toys they wanted magically appeared. The funny thing about being the recipient of good is you have no idea who did this. You had to be nice to everyone, which they were anyway!

The best part was when the salvage yard was told about this by one of the deputies, they decided to also do something special. They had received a decent car which had been stolen and was only three years old. They decided to fix it up, shine it up, and donate it to the family as they had no car. Gordon was elated, it took a bit of work to get the title and transfer the registration from bad to good he said. This little family was overjoyed and very humble.

Christmas evening, they sat around their decorated tree. April had four packages, Mom had four and Gordon had four. Mom got a new cardigan sweater, a certificate to get her hair done and two gift cards for dinner. April got new boots, a skirt and dress set, a new watch, and a gift certificate to get her nails done. Gordon got new socks, a new tie, and a nice cardigan. The fourth gift for Dad was not going to arrive until tomorrow.

That thought tickled April inside. She was the only one who knew, this was going to be great! She was depending on Rodger who worked at the Garage and if the manager would be reasonable with her. She decided to pray about it, and hopefully everything would turn out.

They all had eggnog and homemade pretzels and Gordon commented many times how good they were. Manny called and spoke to his daughter, Gordon, and April. By the time April was to talk to Manny her head was drooping, she was nodding off to sleep.

Gordon touched her foot and said, "Hey, Pumpkin, it's time for bed." April did want to talk with her grandparents, so she waited a bit longer. Her conversation was not very long. She was tired and she did not protest.

Soon all of them were gathered on the floor for Family Prayer. April was asked to say it and she did. Then she kissed her father and Mother good night.

April headed off to bed realizing tomorrow was going to be a very exciting day! As she lay in bed, she was tired, but the thoughts of what tomorrow would bring had her smiling and she had to settle down to sleep. Her faithful companion was with her and that gave April huge comfort. Ruby was without a doubt the most dedicated dog April ever had. She was more human than a dog to April.

The Christmas Pickup Truck

April woke up extra early. She did the milking, fed the ponies and calves, and waited by her driveway for a 6:00 a.m. visit. Along came the truck she was waiting for, and she hopped in. "Hey, Roger," she said.

"Hey to you, too," he answered her. They drove to the local car lot where there sat a truck Dad had looked at for the past four months.

"So, when do you want me to drive that truck?" Roger asked.

"I will let you know, and I will be borrowing Dad's truck in the morning around eight. You park the new truck in front of the Police Station, and put the key in this," and she handed him an envelope with Dad written on the front.

"Okay, I'll see you shortly then," Roger said.

Gordon Di Angelo had noticed the light turquoise blue Chevy pickup truck over four months ago. The silver and chrome screamed beauty. It had a V8 engine and had all the whistles and bells. April asked Roger about the truck a week ago and he told her Reggie the dealer got the truck for $10,800. But now was asking $15,000. Roger also told her in Newman they were selling the same truck for $10,800 and tax. He told April to keep that in mind if she did not want to deal with Reggie.

The day after Christmas April walked into the car dealership showroom bright and early and asked to see Reggie.

Reggie came out all roly-poly as he was very overweight, and his eyes lit up when he saw April. Reggie was very talkative with a lot of personal questions and April wanted to end this conversation.

"Say Reggie, what are you asking for that blue Chevy out there?" she asked him.

"That is not blue, its turquoise and the sticker says $15,000."

"Awe, come on, Reggie, you can do better than that. I know for a fact I can get one for $10,500."

That made Reggie a little nervous since he thought he had money in hand when April walked in. "Yes, you are right, but this beauty is sitting right here, in your town," he said.

"Yes, you are right about that, but my Dad, he likes to drive around, you know that. So, if we drove and he saw the same truck knowing he paid more, he would be an unhappy Sheriff," April said.

"Here is my offer, I will give you $6,800 in cash and a full-grown steer, pasture raised. You can sell half if you want, but it's a great deal. And that is all I will offer. It's been sitting here for four months." April stood there waiting.

Reggie went to retrieve a calculator and punched in some numbers. "I am not sure I can do that," he said.

"Oh, sure you can. You did not pay $10,500 for the truck, it was less. So, either we deal, or I will go to Newman and get one for $10,500 or less. I am sure they would appreciate one of our beef steers to enjoy. And . . . having the Sheriff driving one of their trucks through town.

By now Reggie was wiping his brow, "I am not sure. You know Mr. Thompson was in looking at the truck," he said.

"Wow, good for you, but if he had made an offer, we would not be talking about that truck now. Would we?" April said.

Reggie knew she had him in a corner. It was a cash deal for more than half and he knew he could easily sell half of the steer to someone for two grand. And it was for their town Sheriff. He imagined he would be looked well upon for giving the Sheriff of their town a small break. "Okay, it's a deal," he said.

"I don't want more than ten miles on that truck. Do you understand me?" April said to him. April signed some paperwork and handed him the envelope with the $6,800 cash.

April agreed the steer would be at the butcher the next day. April walked out of the showroom, went to the garage, and made the arrangements with Roger.

At 9:00 a.m. the day after Christmas, Gordon De Angelo was bored out of his mind. There were no accidents, not even a cat stuck up in a tree. And then April walked in being her cheerful self. "Hey, Dad, may I borrow your truck for a half hour. I have an errand.

Her Dad flipped her the keys. "Be careful" he said to her.

April got in her Dad's truck and drove to the dealership where Roger had the new truck washed, cleaned, waxed, and ready to go. April made sure he had the envelope to put the key in, and he did. April watched Rodger park the truck in front of the Sheriff's office, get out, lock the door and upon entering the building almost bumped into Sammy the newest deputy heading into work.

"Oh, hey there, Sammy. How are ya?" Roger said to him.

"I am doing alright, just fine. How are you?"

"I'm good," Rodger said, "but I need a favor. Would you be so kind as to drop this envelope on the Sheriff's desk, where he will see it?" Rodger asked.

"Oh sure, no problem at all," and they both parted ways.

Rodger walked back to the garage with his hands in his pockets. "That was too easy" he said smiling. "Okay then, I will be around 4:00 this evening and pick up that steer, it's at the Jones barn, right?" he asked.

"Yes, it is. I will have him in a separate pen, with easy loading access. And if you need help call me," April said.

"Nah, I can do it. I helped my Grand Pop lots when he farmed."

"Okay then, I'm off for home," April said, as she hugged Rodger. He felt her put something in his pocket. April got in her Dad's pickup truck and left.

Rodger put his hand in his pocket and pulled out a $50 dollar bill. That April, she was always such a crazy good kid, and Roger knew her Dad would be delighted with the new truck.

It was almost 9:30 a.m. and Gordon Di Angelo did not know if he could make it to noon. He saw someone had pulled up in that pickup truck he had been watching and realized it must have sold. A nice gift for someone he thought, and he felt a bit disappointed.

He did not need another truck, he had one. It was a bit old, and the seat coverings were well worn and some tares in the seat, but it served its purpose. That new truck sure was nice though. Someone was going to be happy he thought.

The clock was not moving, he checked to see if the battery was any good, and it was. So, he pulled out a magazine to read, looking up every now and then. No one was in the street, and that truck sat there. He got up and walked to the front window, he saw no one. So, he sat back down and did paperwork.

Sammy the new deputy had been assigned from 12 noon till 6 p.m. at the station, unless there was a problem. Sammy had Gordon's number and knew to call if there was any trouble. Sammy had been in earlier and brought in gifts, they all did a gift exchange. His wife brought candy for the police station. Gordon cut a piece of nut roll Miranda sent in, there was not much left.

Ten minutes to twelve, Gordon stood up to straighten his desk getting ready to leave for home. He looked outside for his truck, but April had not brought it back yet. Sammy came in and they exchanged pleasantries, and Gordon got his hat and stood by the door. "Are you waiting for someone?" Sammy asked.

"Well, yes my daughter borrowed my truck and said she would be back, but she is not here yet," Gordon answered him.

"Oh, that's right," Sammy said as he pulled out the envelope from his shirt pocket, handing it to Gordon. Roger asked me to give this to you earlier. I forgot to put it on your desk."

Gordon looked at the front of the envelope, it said DAD. Then he opened the envelope and found a key inside. He held it to the light and the key said *Chevy* on it. He stood there briefly and then it hit him. He went outside and put the key in the lock, and it turned unlocking the door. He was excited, overwhelmed and on the verge of tears. That daughter of mine, "I swear," he said out loud.

He got in the truck and looked around to familiarize himself with the controls. He put the key in the ignition and turned it. The engine started and purred. Into reverse, backed up and then forward to home. What a feeling, the truck smelled new, the odometer had ten miles on it. Never in his lifetime had Gordon owned a new truck.

As he drove some of the townsfolk waved at him, the drive was so relaxing and he was enjoying a ride home for a change, instead of rushing. As he turned into the driveway, there stood his daughter with a large poster that read, "Merry Christmas, Dad."

Gordon parked the truck in the driveway, got out, and walked over to his daughter. They were both crying. He hugged her lifting her in the air. "You should not be spending money like that on me," he told her.

"Are you kidding me?" she said, "Dad you do more work for D Farms without pay than anyone I know."

He took her by the hand and called to his wife. "Momma. Come out, Momma," Miranda came out on the porch to see what was going on, and he stood by April pointing to the new truck.

"Oh, after lunch we are going for a ride," she said.

And they did, it was such a happy feeling to see her father so thrilled with his new truck. It was like a new toy, but he had genuine feeling for his trucks, he always kept them clean and well cared for.

How awesome it would be for her Dad to drive this truck to work, it was safer, and more reliable. He did not care about looks, or newness. Her Dad was not like that. And April made a small wager that her Dad would drive his old truck from time to time, and he did, he truly did.

Yes, it was a Great Christmas! They were a small family with a lot of love for each other. They openly expressed love and showed love by example. If only these moments could last forever, to stay in them. Wrap yourself in the warmth of them. But life is not stagnant, if it is, there would be no growth.

A Very Late Birthday

It never rains in California, but when it rains, it pours as the song says, and boy are they ever right. It rained so much that it was damp and chilly.

One evening April came home and the house was decorated with banners and the table was set fancy. April wondered who was coming. Mom and Dad were not home and there was cooked chicken in a pot on the stove. April put a fork in the pot and lifted some out, mmmmm, delicious. They must be having chicken tacos, one of her favorite foods.

April put her backpack at the stairs step and changed into chore clothing. She went out and fed the ponies and started her rounds of feeding all the animals, before ending up at 4:00 p.m. at the milking parlor. She was not scheduled to work tonight, but with no one at home it was a quick stop to say "Hi" to everyone and then go home. It was Friday, and there was no hurry. Mrs. Adams was at the living room window waving to April with a hanky to come into the house. April went in, but Mrs. Adams and Lois were there and had a card for her. "Happy Birthday," they both said.

"Wow, how nice of you to remember," April said. Both women just stood there grinning. April stepped forward to hug them both and said, "I appreciate the effort, it was very kind of you both," she said.

April was wondering what in the heck was going on, her birthday was in April. But she went with the flow. She would never say anything to make anyone feel bad for doing good. So, then she said "Goodbye," and left. April drove the gator to the Jones' farm. It was like heaven out here. She took her time and as she drove, she began to sing a song she loved. It was a song that was sung at church, she did not sing loud, but the song gave her comfort.

As she rounded out the ride heading down the hillside, there had to be fifty or more cars and trucks at the barn. There were large party tents erected, and they were heated. She knew because she could see steam coming out of the top of them. They were all lit up and there was a party going on.

She put the gator away and walked up her driveway from the barn. Her Dad and some other men she knew were on the porch.

When he saw her, Gordon ran to her. "Now, Pumpkin, I want you to sneak in through the basement. I will help you. Go up and wash and change your clothing into something nice. Your Momma has a big surprise for you, and you don't want pictures taken with you looking like this," he said.

April did not ask why. She just did as he told her or both of them would be in deep do-do.

When she came downstairs Miranda met her on the steps all excited and sweaty. "Now, April, you know that we were not able to do much when you turned sixteen. You were working, helping, and so much more. You got your permit to drive, and we did not do anything special for you. So today is a big surprise for you.

April felt trapped. She loved her mother dearly, but she always went overboard for her. So, April was determined to enjoy it all, not utter one word, and just enjoy everyone and everything.

April knew her Mom meant well but sometimes!!! April sighed and went up to change. She put on Christmas attire. A pretty, purple dress with purple shoes and a nice hair piece, she even put on a puff of blush on her cheeks.

April came downstairs and led by her Dad to the tents. Once inside April was stunned, everyone she knew was there. A huge, decorated Christmas tree stood in the corner and there were over two hundred seats with tables. The rooms were packed.

April was overjoyed and overwhelmed. Then her Mother had a microphone in her hand asking her to say something to the crowd.

Now April was used to giving talks at church, but this was very different. She took the mic and said, "I want to thank everyone for coming. Many of you know my birthday is in April, but with me being away, my family could not plan a birthday party for me." April laughed. "But I never would have imagined this. And I have to say, Mom, this is awesome. I want all of you to know I love you and I encourage you to talk with each other. You all have one thing in common, each other. I am sure many of you already know one another, and if you don't know a person, talk to them, and you will soon know them. I want you to eat a lot of food and cake and most of all have a great time, talk, and enjoy yourselves."

And then April saw someone she had to talk to and went to her. Nora stood up with tears in her eyes. April hugged her for two minutes. They stood back wiping eyes. "Sixteen now," Nora said.

"Yes, Ma'am, sixteen," April answered her.

"You know I have been counting the years too and was hoping to see you," and she handed April a box.

"Oh, you shouldn't have," April said.

"Yes, I felt I had to. It is who you are, and I want you to never forget where you came from. I am hoping you stay humble. You are an amazing young woman, and I could not be prouder of you." Nora learned forward and kissed her cheek. April had that big lump in her throat and thanked her and asked where she was staying. "With Mrs. Adams and Beth," she said. "So maybe we can visit again. Now you go and see the others." And she shooed her away.

Next was Grandpa. He stood up to kiss her and she threw her arms around him. He too had a box for her, and April stood there speechless with tears. "You okay, April?" as he patted her shoulder.

"Are you staying a couple of days?" she asked him.

"I stay with you," he said. "You go now, we talk later," and he too pushed her away.

April talked to everyone. It was after 10 p.m. and she was still going, and so was the party. April saw Hugh talking with her grandfather, sitting on a chair near him. Mrs. Marshall was with Nora, hugging her.

Everyone truly did talk with everyone else. It was more than she could have hoped for. April was sitting with her Mom, Nora, Mrs. Marshall, and Beth when she realized people were leaving. She looked at her watch, it was 11 p.m.

"Oh, my gosh," she said. She got up and said goodbye to all of them and thanked them for coming. Since it was Christmas, sort of, each person that left was given a small token from a bowl – restaurant gift certificates. They did not expect anything, but they all left happy.

Grandpa John had left a while ago and April was sure he was in bed. She asked her Mom about cleaning up and she said they hired people to do that, and not to worry about it. The company who brought everything was Action Party Rental. Her friend Ava's parents had this business. She did see that truck earlier in the day, but never expected that they would set up at her home.

When April went into her house, she saw the light on in Grandpa John's room. She knocked on the door and he said, "Open, come in."

April saw him sitting on his bed holding a picture. It was one of her jumping hurdles with Old Roger. It was a clear picture of her face looking sideways where the next jump would be when that photo was taken. There were eight smaller photos on each side of the large picture. There was one just like it on her bedroom wall. Her Grandpa John wiped his hand lovingly over the picture. He looked up at April with the rim of his glasses had tears on them. April sat beside him and just listened. It took him a while to gain his composure when he said, "I wish I could have been there to see this," he said. "I feel I have missed so much of your life. I wanted to be there, and this, this is something!"

"I know Grandpa. That is my favorite picture too. We do have a video of that day if you would like to see it. I am sure we can copy it for you to take home and watch at home," she said.

"Oh, my April," he said, and he hugged her close.

The feeling of love was so evident April was happy and at peace, something that had eluded her for many years. Something she had not felt for a long, long time. No more questions of her past haunting her. The answers had all come. One big blessing was sitting right here beside her. She loved Grandpa more than the father she had. Before long Grand Pa yawned and April kissed him on his forehead and said, "Would you like to have prayers?"

"Yes, you say them, April." So, they both knelt together on the floor by his bedside and had prayer. Then he went to bed.

April said good night to her parents, hugging them both and went to her bedroom. Ruby was there waiting for her yawning, as if to say, "Where were you?"

April had Nora and Grandpa's boxes with her. There were many more gifts downstairs, but she was curious what the boxes held. Her Grandpa gave her four rubies sewn onto a piece of linen and some photos of him when he was a young man in Portugal. There was also one photo of his wedding day. April was so grateful.

The box from her birth Mother Nora had many items. There were pictures of her as a baby and growing up, and some of them included her brothers. Now April had many questions, but they would be saved for later. There were also recipe cards with blue ribbons attached, a small quilt that April thought may have been one of her baby blankets, a tiny bracelet with pink blocks that spelled her last name, and footprints in ink of her first day on earth.

April closed the boxes and flopped on her bed. She lay there and began to cry. She was so grateful for parents with open minds. She was so glad her birth Mom Nora and her sister Lena were here to be with her too. That was a huge blessing to her.

It seemed to April that when Miranda did not understand her, her birth Mother did. But she loved her parents dearly. They were receptive to her past and the people from where she had come. It made April so very happy that she had tears of gratitude. She felt so blessed, she could barely take it all in.

April realized how blessed she truly was. She had horses and animals of all sorts. She was able to help many people with their animals and especially with D Farms. She believed with her whole heart that D Farms was a revelation from God. He put that in her brain to help so many. It was not planned, it just happened. There was no other explanation. And you know, the more people that were helped made April so happy, she could not help but giggle.

All these people in her life were kind and loving. Why can't people be happy? Why? April truly believed it was a choice. Even the poorest person in ill health was happy, she herself witnessed that. It was just an excuse and a poor one.

To be happy and appreciate things around you is a blessing for you! To be unhappy and unappreciative is what you do to yourself.

God's love is everywhere, in the smile of a child, in the eyes of a dog looking at you. It is in the beauty of the flowers and in the chirping of the birds. It is everywhere. You only need to let yourself be open to see it and hear it, and then you will understand.

The Books

THE NEXT DAY MR. STEVENS POPPED IN. HE HAD TWO LARGE books for April to give as gifts to her Grandpa and to her birth Mother, but he wanted her parents to see them as well. Grandpa was in the living room talking with Manny and Gordon when Mr. Stevens came. Mr. Stevens brought one book to Grandpa John and told him, "This is what your granddaughter has accomplished with her bottom in the saddle on Native Son." The book held photos of each farm that had been bought over the years. Inside each flap were letters from workers, giving thanks for the opportunity to work and get an education."

Grandpa paged through the book, there were many pages, and he asked, "How many farms are in this book?"

"So far, there are one hundred eighty-five and counting," Mr. Stevens said. Grandpa was stunned as was Manny and Gordon. Mr. Stevens explained, "I hired a topical land guide company in the beginning to advise us what land was the most fertile in each state. As farms came up for sale in those areas, nearby, and some others connecting to them were bought with April's racing money. Each year the farms were quickly transitioned into milking facilities under D Farms. They produced good incomes."

"This was your granddaughter's idea to help others out of poverty or difficult situations and to end hunger in America. When I took this job, I could only see a small part of what April saw. I never thought it would grow so big, this fast. She is an amazing young woman with a big heart. She is worth a lot of money, but you would never know from knowing her. She is the kindest, giving, and humble person I know. And I believe that is why she is always happy."

Manny and Grandpa poured over that book. Gordon asked Mr. Stevens if he could have two more books made, one for him and his wife and another for Manny.

"Sure, but this one goes to someone else, and I believe you know who. She has a right to know what April has done as well." Gordon agreed. "I will get them to you yet this month. They are all on file on the computer. It is just a matter of printing them and putting them in a book," Mr. Stevens said. Gordon thanked him shaking his hand.

"I have the best job in the world, traveling, seeing the many places, and buying farms I never could have imagined. My wife has been able to go with me on some trips flying, and she loves every minute of it. I believe one day our son Cole will continue this job for your family's legacy. He is familiar with everything, having come along with us over the past years. He will graduate in four more years, and he is interested in taking the application for D farms to earn his education. Like I said, I am blown away by her vision and offering me the chance of a lifetime," he said. "Okay, I am leaving now. I want to deliver this one."

When Mr. Stevens arrived at the Adams' farm, all four women greeted him. They had him sit down and offered him something to eat and drink. He felt like he was five years old again.

Nora sat down and he gave her the book. Beth was sitting beside her with Mrs. Adams on the other side. Lois was taking a nap upstairs.

As Nora paged through the book as Mr. Stevens explained to her the same things, he had said to Grandpa John. All the women oohed and awed at the farms, and some were so pretty. One insert was pulled out of a Wisconsin farm page and Beth read it. It had all the women in tears. The letter was put back in its place. And everyone was amazed at the number of farms in the book.

Nora hugged the book to her chest, "My little girl did all this?" she asked.

"Yes, with her derriere in the saddle. She earned the money to buy these farms. One hundred eighty-five of them and counting. If you notice this farm is in the book, as is the Jones' farm. Your daughter had the foresight to help end poverty in the United States."

Nora sat there. She could not wrap her mind around what her daughter had achieved. While Beth said "Amazing." and Mrs. Adams said. "What an achievement." Nora said nothing. She was very proud of her daughter but could not understand how she achieved so much. She herself was in a bad situation and had no clue how to get out. Clearly her parents had taught her good coping and management skills, as she had none.

Her marriage was over, all he wanted to do was sleep and run around with other women. She had found women's under clothing in their family car several times, and she knew what that meant. She never would have cheated on her husband. But the stories in town were no secret. She clearly wanted out but had no means. She had no land of her own, no money. She had nothing. She did not voice any of this to anyone. This was not the time.

Mr. Stevens left and in the coming days, April had a lot of time to spend with Nora and her Grandpa John. She was relieved that Nora and John got along. April was not sad that her Dad did not get along with either of them. Well, that was then, and this is now she thought to herself. I am so lucky to be here with the parents I have, I love all of them.

Both books were mailed instead of flown home with the recipients. Grandpa wanted his mailed to another address, not his home. Nora was fine with the book coming to her home. She would tuck it away in a safe spot just for her to look at. He would not have any interest whatsoever. In fact, she believed he would be angry about her having been successful and he was not.

But the truth was he was sick and tired of working and farming. They boys could easily handle the farming, but he treated them like "little boys." and that angered them.

Nora has watched both boys tear down the tractor motor and repair it. They were not little boys, they were men. Men who were proud that they could do things. It was the same with cars or trucks.

Once when their grandfather wanted to put another engine in his old pickup truck, the boys said they'd do it, but their grandpa said he'd take it to his garage. Four hundred dollars later, Grandpa still had the same problem and drove the truck slowly to their farm. It sat parked under the eaves of their barn, the engine up on a hoist and little by little the boys combed through the engine and what was wrong? The intake valve, which was an easy fix, and their grandfather said from now on he'd bring it out to them if he had trouble.

A New Home for Nora and Lena

JANUARY CAME QUICKLY, FOLLOWED BY WINTER MONTHS OF dreary weather. In March the decision was made for the filly to run in the Derby. She was officially named Mony Mony. The DJs loved to play that song when she won.

Most of the time Mony Mony was in training, and she loved to run. She had many of her father's traits. Her Mom had the sweetest temperament which Mony, Mony also had, such a good personality. She danced and lipped anyone nearby.

In late March, unbeknownst to April, her birth Mother Nora called to speak to Miranda. She asked if there was someplace for her, for her and her sister. Both of them were in loveless, abusive marriages. After forty years, they were both broken down with nothing left. They had no money, nothing!

Miranda spoke with Gordon, they had to be careful. They did have several rental homes and could easily put up the two sisters. They did not know them well and they wanted to be careful. They did not want trouble having the exes come after them or having them charge April.

It was Gordon who spoke with Nora. He got all the information he needed, and he felt strongly that the two sisters should come. He would make the arrangements to put them into a nice home in town, near the grocery store and other amenities. He also assured them when they were ready, he would send them a check to travel.

Nothing was said to April, until the final arrangements were made. Both sisters were older, afraid, and unsure. They wanted to work, and they wanted to pay their own way, but for now, they had nothing.

Gordon found a nice, good condition automatic sedan for them. The car was put in the garage at their home. The house was furnished adequately with good, gently-used furniture. Miranda supervised the home furnishings. She made sure the refrigerator was full, the freezer full, pots and pans, dishes, everything they would need.

It was late March when the two sisters arrived. Each had only two suitcases, that was it. They were grateful for the home. It was more than they could have hoped for. They set about to make the home theirs.

They sat down one evening and discussed a job they could do on their own. They learned there were no cleaning women in the town. It was not an easy job, but one they could do together. They could wipe, scrub, cook, vacuum, and run errands if needed. They made a crude ad and took it to the newspaper. It was made cleverly showing two women with mop, broom, and a cleaning cart. They started the ad for one week. Miranda called them and said she would be happy to put their ad on the radio at no cost for them. She arranged a small group to sing a jingle for their cleaning service which both Nora and Lena loved. That radio spot played every day, six times a day.

In no time they were getting calls and had jobs lined up. Some were for elderly folks to clean their home once a week. Some were for business offices to be cleaned at night. Others were for after parties or before. The women met many of the townsfolk and were accepted and loved. The sisters were happy they had found a way to take care of themselves.

They spent many hours together working and could often be found on their back porch having lunch or tea in the evenings. They preferred to walk to the grocery store with their hand-held pushcart. They did not buy many groceries and the walk was enjoyable. Often, they walked through the park and sat down to watch the children play. Sometimes they had an ice cream cone as they rested. They got to be well known for their good work cleaning, happy attitude, and their kindness. They were always willing to work even when schedules were changed.

April liked to stop in on evenings. The old TV would be on, and the two women yacked to each other and would laugh. In all of April's short life, she had never seen two sisters as close as these two were. As she would watch them often April wished she had a sister, but that was just wishful thinking. It did not mean they would get along. Truthfully, April was happy.

The Di Angelos often invited the two sisters to dinner, but they did not come very often. They were tired from their jobs of cleaning during the day or at night. Miranda understood. If they could not come, she would wrap up the meals for them and drop them off. Giving the ladies a night off from cooking, that always made the women happy.

The end of March came around and April birthday would soon arrive. They had April's birthday early due to the impending race in May. She just wanted a small get together and begged her Mom to keep it small. Miranda did. She had April's favorite meal and invited the ladies. They had chicken tacos, a large salad, and home-made baked beans.

Nora insisted she be allowed to make the cake. In no way would Miranda deny her. April's cake was not traditional, she loved fruit and here is the recipe for April's favorite.

Take a large seedless watermelon and cut out a nice slice, two inches wide from the rind. Lay it on a tea towel and covered the top and side to absorb the moisture. Do the same with a cantaloupe and a honey dew. Make sure to remove all the seeds. Take a plate and cover them with parchment paper. Put the first layer, the watermelon, on it. Cover it with Cool Whip and then add the second piece, the cantaloupe. Cover that with Cool Whip, add the last piece, the honey dew, and fill the center with Cool Whip with pistachio nuts crushed or slivered almonds. Cover the entire "cake" with Cool Whip, sprinkle crushed pistachios or almond slivers on top, and refrigerate for two hours.

Baked Beans (in a crock pot)

1 pound of hamburger cooked, 3/4 pound of bacon cooked, 1 cup of chopped onion, 1 two-pound can of Bush baked beans, 1 pound can of Chili beans (her Mom used red kidney beans) 1 pound can of Baby Lima beans drained, 1 cup ketchup, 3/4 cup brown sugar, 1 tablespoon liquid smoke, 3 tablespoons white vinegar, 1 tablespoon of salt and a dash of pepper. Cook on low for 8 to 9 hours. Serve hot.

These beans were loved by so many people. They could not get over the good taste, *just like their Mother used to make*, the old timers would say. April loved them, she was making a cookbook of her favorite foods, and this was in the beginning of her own cookbook.

All of April's gifts were small and personal, which made it extra special for April. From her Aunt Lena she got a homemade certificate to cut and style her hair. But since April had long curly hair, she thought a trim would be best.

From her birth Mother she got a certificate to teach her how to cruel, knit, and embroider. April wanted to learn, so that was awesome. There were some small kits included for April to try, but if she needed help Nora promised to help her.

Her parents got her a beautiful set of racing silks with "Mony, Mony" on them to wear. They were a turquoise color with black. April thought they were beautiful and loved them.

How wonderful it was to live in peace and harmony, no one picking on anyone, always kind tones of love. What a wonderful way to live. It reminded April of the song "Love at Home", which she sang a lot.

April was content and happy, however there was something still bothering her that she did not feel whole. She could not name it and could not fill that hole. She felt that perhaps as she got older, she would find out what that was.

She never took anything for granted. In the Bible it says, "Man was created to have joy," and that was what she aimed to do every day. Even when she served people, she felt great joy.

And then April had an epiphany, a mind-blowing thought. She realized the reason she was so happy when she served others was that it was ordained from God. *When ye serve others, ye serve me.* She got it and clung onto that scripture. Well, it was in her own words. But never would she complain about helping others, it was a joy.

In January the filly had her papers filed and the fee paid to run in the Derby. She was ready. There was no doubt of that. Again, that would be on the first Saturday in May. She had a soft mouth and was extremely responsive. April was excited at the thought of letting her run.

April realized racing would be here before she was ready. She knew that Mony Mony was ready, but she was not. April realized she was doing more for others, which she loved, but she needed time to get ready as well.

So again, April was working out, running, lifting weights and all she could do to prepare. She cut down on her eating, which upset her Mother immensely.

Nora knew, as did Lena, they encouraged April to do what she thought was important. Of course they both loved Miranda Di Angelo, but April could not eat all Miranda made, and they felt April should eat only what she needed. You cannot serve two masters. So that was that!

April appreciated her Mother's efforts and to please her April ate all the vegetables and fruit they had in their home. April realized she lost twelve pounds by eating, sweet!

This was not an out and out dire to lose weight. April was eating, and the foods she ate, and the exercise she was doing, working, and running, all contributed to her losing weight. She was young and it came easy for her, for her Mom, eh' not so much.

Miranda tried, she joined at the fire hall where women worked out, she had all she needed but the pounds refused to come off. All she wanted to lose was ten pounds. That's it! And it seemed impossible. But she was determined.

She ate less and increased her fruit and vegetable intake. She had all the housework to do, laundry to hang outside, and so on. But after three weeks of that, she still had no weight loss.

In frustration she stood in front of the mirror and said, "Do I cut off my head?" She looked and then she looked closer. Her face was not as round, it was thinner. "Ah," she said, "it comes off from the top first," and she laughed.

She did indeed keep up her routine and you know she did it. It took her a long time, but she did it. She wanted to lose ten pounds to get into a beautiful dress for Christmas and she was determined to do it. She went out later that week and paid a good sum of money for the dress. She came home and said out loud, "Now Miranda, there it is, if you want to wear it, you must not give up"!

The Farm Application

THE APPLICATION FOR THE FARM COMPETITION HAD BEEN MAILED and April watched the mailbox every day. If the mail was already taken out, she always asked her mom, who replied, "Nothing yet."

Then one long tiring harrowing day as she walked up the steps to the porch there was her Mother swinging an envelope. "I think this is what you have been waiting for," she said.

April grabbed the envelope and held it, wanting to rip it open, but she wanted her Dad there too. Good or bad, she wanted both of her parents there as the envelope was opened. She was not scheduled to milk until later that week, and she was so, so glad that they instituted the milking program that D farms had in their program. It sure was nice to have a day or two off every week.

April kissed her Mom and said, "I have to finish chores," and off she went. She had to feed the calves, steers, and ponies. She even stopped and called Hugh from the barn to see if he wanted to come over and hear the results. He said he could be there around 4:30. When April got home, she told her Mom to put on a little more for dinner. Miranda really liked Hugh a lot, he was such a good guy and inside she wished that her daughter and Hugh would become a couple someday. They were so much alike and then in other ways, so different. But they always got along with each other. Neither one of them had a spoiled attitude. Both had common sense, both were kind and willing. She just sighed, "Maybe, just maybe."

Dad came home ten after 5:00 as usual, he wanted to change and shower before dinner. Hugh was in the living room reading the newspaper and Gordon shook his hand before going up to shower. "Reading my paper, eh?" he teased Hugh.

"Yes, Sir. I don't get a chance to read ours, either Dad has it or Mom drags it around in pieces, some here and there." Gordon just laughed. He knew just what Hugh meant.

They were all waiting in the living room when Gordon came down. "Okay, what's going on?" he asked. April handed him the envelope and asked him to open it and read the results. Gordon sat down in his chair and opened the envelope carefully. He waited a few seconds and handed the envelope to Hugh.

"Here, Hugh, you read it for us. I don't have my reading glasses."

"Are you sure, Sir. I mean this is family business."

"You are here anyway, may as well make yourself useful," Dad laughed.

Dear Ms. April Di Angelo,

We received your application papers which were filled out correctly. They were reviewed by our committee. We are pleased to announce you have been entered into the business farm competition to begin in September. We will be contacting you personally to let you know which farm to report to as your beginning first farm.

There is a rotation of (four) allowing three months at each farm. We will be in touch in the month of May to finalize plans . . .

So, there it was, they all began talking as April sat there, quiet. "What's wrong?" Hugh asked her.

"Nothing" she answered. "I was just thinking. I don't know where I am going. It could be a cold region or very hot. I guess time will tell."

Miranda added, they offer a big grace period before calling us. It's only the month of April right now. I guess some will drop out before they start. Sometimes life can change your decisions. As far as we are concerned, we know how long you have been looking forward to going, and you will."

Dad stood up to hug his daughter and congratulate her, as did Miranda kissing her forehead. Hugh stood up and looked at her parents, asking, "May I kiss your daughter too?"

Dad said, "If she allows you to, it's fine with us," and he laughed. Hugh gave April a kiss on her cheek, and April pulled him back to her to kiss his lips. April felt it was time to let her parents know her decision. This was the man she chose. Not right now, but in her future. Not one eyebrow was raised, not one word was said.

April was content, she had time as did Hugh. A year apart would surely test them both, it would be interesting to see the outcome. To April, Hugh was for her, and from what she felt from Hugh, he was on the same page she was. But often, time changes things, and April only wanted to be sure. They were both young and there was no hurry. They were both committed, Hugh to the Marines and April to the farm competition.

Besides there were many other things in April's life to keep her busy. April was still Mayor of the town. She was still very active in her church with Mutual Nights and helping as much as she could. She was still milking on her scheduled days. And she had others to help and maintain relationships with, like Nora and Lena.

Believe it or not, her hands were much better, and April was thrilled. She hated taking medication and watching her hands. She did not know of anyone who had the condition she did. Of course, there were other issues with her friends, and in the long run she thought that if all problems were on the floor, she would take back the one she had. She had become used to taking care of her "problem" hands.

Much to the chagrin of her Mother, April did sometimes forget to take along her hydrocortisone cream that helped her immensely. Even if she applied it at night, that seemed to help her. April was not one for pills. She often forgot to take her vitamin every morning so how would she remember to take a tray of pills. Nope that was not for her. April was very empathetic to those who had to take volumes of pills. She was always kind and considerate to others.

Many times people have "problems" others are not able to see. That is why April decided if she had to have a "problem", she would take what God had given her. She knew how to handle it and what to do about it when there was an outbreak. April sat there and said out loud. "God is good, and God is great," and she meant that with all her heart.

The Kentucky Derby

As they arrived at the racing venue in Kentucky, Mony Mony was curious about everything around her. She was not afraid, just curious.

To April, not much had changed at the track. It was the same people, and the same reporters that loved to harass her. During one interview a reporter asked if she would like to go out to celebrate and have drinks with him. April cut him off "I don't drink alcohol, not for any reason. I don't like it and I am on a strict diet with the race. You should know that."

Many of the other reporters laughed at him, "She sure got the best of you," one said. They all left in good humor, and nothing was taken personal. They all knew April was underage to drink and she was under tremendous stress with the race.

The papers were filed, and Marty did not foresee any problems. April was scheduled to ride and was ready. Her weight was not a problem, and everything was good. Too good! April thought if everyone is so good, why did she have a foreboding feeling about this race?

Her Dad joined her, and they both talked about it. "Did you pray about it, honey?" he asked her.

"Yes, I have. I just don't know, maybe its jitters," she said.

Race day April had on the new turquoise silks. They were bright like Mony Mony's. They matched the only way they could. Mony Mony was a tall girl. She had long legs. She was red like her dad with a very wide blaze that made her eyes look enlarged, like a lady. She was very striking to look at, but the truth is once she was on the track to run, you did not see her long, she was a streak of speed.

Typically, April did not have a companion rider, but one was assigned to her, it was a new regulation. That was no problem for Mony Mony, she had the sweet temperament of her Mother, she did not care.

At the gate Mony Mony loaded like a princess prancing into place. April placed her goggles over her eyes and re-adjusted her seat in the saddle. She looked at her stirrups, grabbing the reins at Mony Mony's neck. She leaned forward, she was ready.

The mare looked around a bit and April patted her neck, "It's your turn girl, you go and do what you do at home. Have fun!"

Every horse was loaded in the gate and in seconds the gate opened. Mony Mony was every bit like her father with the opening gate, she came out like a bullet. She immediately rode the rail because she liked it there. They were sailing along when another horse came beside them bumping them purposely, outright. April looked over and saw an unknown rider. She moved Mony Mony out to the outside and let her go. In less than ten seconds a horrible accident occurred. Another rider was also bumped knocking his horse off stride. The horse tried to catch himself as he went stumbling. His rider was sent sprawling across the track.

April saw this happen and reined in Mony Mony. April knew if she did not that rider would be crushed in seconds. April turned the mare, leaned over as far as she could and grabbed the man's silk shirt. April dragging the rider off to the rail on the outer side where he would be safe. His horse had run a few feet but was safe at the outer rail. The strain on her left side hurt her knee but she was determined to turn and run because the mare was pulling.

The pack of horses running were a good turn away from them and the race seemed out of reach. But the mare broke free and ran like she knew what she was up against.

By the next turn they were at the end of the pack of horses, and to the three-quarter turn they were in the middle. Mony Mony gave it all she had and blazed forward winning by a nose. It was an incredible race, it seemed impossible, but Mony Mony did it! She truly had the heart of her father.

The reporters were beside themselves. This was quite the upset. This filly really had speed, and no one expected her to be so far behind and come up and win.

April did not want to get off. Her knee was hurting so bad she did not know if she could walk. Her Dad saw her grimace and he knew something was very wrong. His daughter never ever showed pain.

After the photos, after the award, after it was all over, Byron led Mony Mony to the paddock area where both Dad and Marty helped April get off.

"Please don't make me bear weight," she begged and began to cry with pain. They placed April on the seat of a pickup truck and her Dad raced her to the local hospital. It took a while to be seen, but it was revealed she had torn a meniscus in her knee.

"Oh boy," she said with tears falling, "This screws up everything."

"Now don't go jumping to conclusions," her Dad said. "It will all work out, it always does. Your health is important, so just relax and take it easy."

After a CT scan a doctor came to them to explain what should be done. He told April the surgery was minor, she would wear a brace for a while, have physical therapy, and in 2 to 3 months be as good as new. April sat there with her teeth clenched. Her Dad knew her well enough to know what she was thinking. "Is this the only option?" Gordon asked.

"Well, yes," he said. The doctor got up to leave saying, "I'll send someone in for you to sign the surgery papers."

April looked at her Dad and said, "Have you had enough, because I am leaving." She stood up and hobbled out of the room, down the hall, and left the hospital.

April needed help to get in the pickup truck and they headed back. As they drove along April saw a sign at the prosthetic shop. "Stop here," she said loudly to her Dad. Her Dad pulled the truck over and helped her inside.

An older woman came to them, and April sat in a chair and told her what had happened. "He did not understand that I am going to race again in two weeks. I can't be out like that. Sometimes you have to do what you have to do," she said.

"I have no intention of suing anyone, but I am going to make my own brace if I have to so I can get through this."

The woman understood completely her father had racehorses and still did. So, they looked around for a brace that would hold her knee in place. Something she could fashion tight to give support, but not cut off blood supply.

"Now you must understand this is just temporary, you must have that knee fixed soon," she said.

"I am going home to my doctor and this brace will help me get there. If I must have another rider for my horse, I will. I want the best option for her too," April said.

"Oh my, a typical horse racer, how often have I heard that same song from my Dad," the woman said.

The brace fit, it was tight enough to keep the knee stable to get her home. Now the pain was manageable with Tylenol, Advil, or Aleve alternating them, but April did not take much of anything. She could keep her mind off the pain if she had something to do.

At home April did see the hometown doctors in the hospital. They ordered an MRI. They said the meniscus was torn but not through, and the brace certainly saved the tissue from ripping. They encouraged April to keep wearing it. They also told her that surgery might not be necessary. April was relieved. No surgery was an awesome thing. She did get another blessing from her Dad and that comforted her.

Miranda wanted to wait on April, but April was not having it. She knew if she sat, she would become stiff. Sure she hobbled a bit on crutches, but the more she walked carefully the better her knee felt.

Hugh understood the pressure April was under. He also was very much aware she was leaving in September for a full year, and by the end of June, he too would be gone.

That evening they were alone, and Hugh had to say what was on his mind. "April, you know how I feel about you, in fact I think it scares you a bit," Hugh said.

"Well not scares me, but I" and she stopped.

"You what?" he asked her.

"Hugh I am going to be blunt. I am not one for fancy words and, well, I love you. I love you more than any guy I know. And I know it's real because I think of you more than I should. But we both know we are on different paths right now. I think that maybe we are to take our routes to be sure, really sure, what we want. I want to be married in the temple. I don't want anything less. That is a commitment for eternity, and forever is a long time. I need you to understand."

Hugh almost gushed, "Sure I understand. May I kiss you, please?" He asked her.

April blushed and said, "Yes."

Hugh leaned forward and kissed her lips. It was April's first real kiss, and she leaned into it. April wanted to experience what it was really like.

Hugh pulled back and was breathless. He was wide-eyed and excited, almost nervous.

"Now do you see what I mean, Hugh?" We are new to each other in this way. As comfortable as we are with each other in every other way, this way is different, and I want it to be right."

"Oh, I thought it was all right," Hugh said. "Didn't I kiss you right?" he asked her.

April pulled at his arm to pull him back for her to kiss him again, saying, "I am not sure, let's do that again and I'll let you know."

Hugh believed her at first, but this kiss was not like the first. She wanted more and he felt it. He stroked her hair back and kissed her deep putting his arm around her back. They separated and he kissed her three more times like pecks on her lips.

April was smiling and he knew she was teasing him, and he liked it.

"Will you wait for me?" he asked her.

April looked at him stunned, "Hugh, I am so busy. I feel as though I am in a whirlwind most of the time. Yes, I will wait for you. Will you wait for me? No matter what, I do not have a choice as to where I am going. It is all planned out for me, the place, the time, how long and that is my life for a year. I will not have any time to "be with" anyone else. The rules are very strict. I may not call anytime I want either."

"I am not complaining but times goes, and I am here, always here in my heart. Sure I travel, I will be racing and then on the Farm Competition, but I always come here, this is home. And when you come home, I will be here, I promise. You are not someone I want to be with. You are someone I don't want to be without. We must give each other time, yes?" She asked.

Hugh was almost speechless, he had hope, but this went beyond more than he could have hoped for. "Yes," he said.

Then his Mom and Miranda came into the room laughing about something they saw in town. Miranda knew that something had happened between these two but only time would tell. They were tight lipped.

The next race was two weeks after the Kentucky Derby this was the Preakness. It was held about May sixteenth. April was ready, the new brace was not bulky it fit under her silks. The new brace was fashioned like a boot upper. It was leather with soft lining. It had eyelets and strings to tighten the boot as needed. She did not want to bend it much in the saddle or weight bear without a firm support. April was determined to race. She had no foreboding feelings this time.

Mony Mony was ready for the Preakness. She had been ridden often by another rider who was a longtime friend of Byron's, their groom. The right-hand man for all their racehorses, his name was Russ. Russ was a small-framed man, very muscular, almost wiry guy. Russ was 26 but could easily pass for 15. He had red hair, freckles, and the lightest color skin which he inherited from his Irish Ancestors.

April truly felt she could ride, she felt strong, and her knee did not hurt with the brace. If, however, she was hit hard on the track, she might not be able to finish. It was a risk she was willing to take. Mainly because Mony Mony was such an amiable mare she rode hard and fast for anyone.

It did not matter to her who rode her. She did her job and did it well. However, in a timed race Marty and Byron both noticed Mony Mony was faster in 10ths of seconds with April aboard. Maybe it was the fact she had raised her. Who knows, but the time clock did not lie.

There was not much to say about the Preakness, that race Mony Mony ran just like her Dad, out like a streak. No one ever caught her. She came out of the gate, took the rail and was like a locomotive. Her nostrils flared and she had a long stride that was fast. She started out ahead at two lengths at the first turn she was ahead by five lengths. At the three-quarter pole she was out by eleven lengths. The crowd went wild. All the loudspeakers broke into the song "Mony Mony" by Tommy James and the Shondells. The entire stadium was singing and dancing.

April's knee was fine, a little tender but no worse than when the race started. Her eye shields did not work very well. Her eyes were watering. There was no mud or dirt in her eyes because she was so far out in front. It was an amazing race. Mony Mony sure made her Dad look even better. He had the genes to pass on to offspring for Derby winners.

Marty wanted to sell Native Son's semen to breed other mares. April did not want to spread him all around. They had a selective good thing, and she wanted to keep it that way.

With the second Derby in the books, Mony Mony had one more race to compete in. That would be the Belmont. That was in two weeks after the Preakness.

They headed home to rest. Mony Mony was pampered at first and then her schedule of keeping in shape continued. Russ was her only other rider. He really liked that mare and did anything around the grounds to help out. He breezed other horses and fed them. He spent time with the mares, fillies and stallions that were born. He had his eye on a roan stallion that Marty noticed when it was born. The roan had the sleek look of a runner, but time would tell.

April often stopped by to look at the babies. April had her eye too on that roan stallion. He was only two months old and already was taller than the rest of the babies. He was gentle and willing. The first to the gate, not afraid to leave his Mom and that was a good thing.

All the babies had hands on as soon as they were born. Marty felt imprinting was crucial to taming and training. Both April and her Dad agreed.

Many people asked to work at the grounds of the racehorses. Marty always had final say. The grounds crew were few, but important to Marty's program. He knew everyone by their first name. He included them in all his plans including what was for dinner. Marty was insistent, they all worked there, they ate there as a family to keep peace.

The next and last race of the Triple Crown was the Belmont. That was Mony Mony's next destination with the Di Angelos, Marty, and Byron.

By now it was evident April might have to go for minor surgery. There was a constant black and blue mark at the outer side of her knee. April tried but realized she might not be able to mount and ride Mony Mony. At times the pain she had was almost unbearable with the wrong twist of her body.

It was decided Russ would ride Mony Mony in this last leg of the race because April was not one hundred percent. Russ was elated for the chance. Marty felt doubtful Mony Mony would win this race. She had a lot of competition, including two wild cards that were from the United Kingdom.

Marty said, "Hell, I don't care. Win or lose I know this mare will give it all she has. I know how it is, every rider will go after the winner, trying to upset the cart." He walked away grumbling. April knew Marty was not angry, he was stressed out.

Marty gave all he had in training and to know that wild cards without much workload would enter, did not sit right with him. But that is racing. They all knew Mony Mony had it in her, but anything can happen in a race.

They all arrived three days ahead of time giving Russ time to adjust. He was to learn the track and most importantly of all, listen to Marty. Russ was no beginner, and he had raced in Mexico and in the United States since he was sixteen. He felt at home with Marty. He liked the criticism that helped him learn and Marty was liberal at dishing out criticism when he saw someone doing other than what he told them.

On race day, Mony Mony was calm. It was Russ who was nervous. "It's just a ride," April said to him. "Just like at home on our track. If you are nervous, she will pick up on your vibes and be nervous too. You know that!"

"I know. I just can't help it. My Dad was like this too! I think sometimes if I just had a drink to calm me down," he said.

"Oh, no you don't. You do that and you will not be on the back of any of our horses. If you have that attitude and want to drink alcohol before a race, you will not sit on our mare." April was livid, she did not tolerate excuses. If you are that nervous, go for a walk, exercise, do something to expend your energy. Don't take the easy way out," and she stormed off to find Marty.

Marty already knew, he had found Russ in a pile of horse blankets one evening, totally passed out from drinking. He sobered the man up and gave him a stern talk than he shook him by his shirt. Alcoholism is not a whim. It is a disease, and that disease ran through Russ's family for generations. If he wanted to kick that habit, they were willing to help him. This was a fine time to announce you need a drink to race.

April started to dig out her silk racing uniform when her Dad found her. "What are you doing? You can't ride. You know you can't," he said.

"Dad, I'd rather be hurt on her than have him rein her wrong and have her go down. I don't want a broken leg on her or for her to be injured because he needs a drink or has the shakes or jitters. I deal with my problems. Why can't he?" she asked.

Because we are all different. You have a strong moral compass that guides you, Sweetie. Not everyone is like you. Russ never was taught different, he watched what his family did to cope, and it was alcohol. I will go out and talk with him, you stay here. You are not in the frame of mind to uplift or encourage anyone. Let me handle this," and he left.

Dad and Marty were outside with Russ as the riders began to mount and be led or companioned away. Russ stood there nodding and shaking his head. April was super angry. He hid this from them. Never ever would they have hired an alcoholic to work with their horses. It was too dangerous, a disaster waiting to happen. Later April sought out Byron and jumped him about Russ. Byron was an honest man and he outright told April he never ever saw Russ drinking. What more could April do?

Soon Dad and Marty helped Russ mount Mony Mony. He was off taking their prized mare to load in the gate. April had a sick feeling in her stomach. This was not a hobby. This was their lives. This is how D farms bought farms to help educate people and feed the poor. It made April angry and as she thought about it, she got angrier. She felt like all of this with Russ was a mistake.

April walked to the rail beside her Dad and Marty and they said absolutely nothing. She was aware they knew exactly what she was thinking. Russ out and out lied to them, not verbally, but by keeping this a secret. Inside April was grieving, she knew Mony Mony's ability and with Russ on board she knew beyond a shadow of a doubt that the mare was on her own. She could not count on Russ. Oh, he will ride her, but might not have the ability to make the moves she would need on the track to win.

And April knew that mare could win. To say she was thoroughly disgusted was an understatement.

Marty looked at her and said, "She will come in at second or third, no matter who is on her. That mare is not stupid. She has a mind to run, but if either wild card is more rested than she is, then they might have a chance to take away her title."

At this point April could do nothing but pray, and she did. To have Marty admit the mare was not rested and to have a drunk aboard the mare, all described disaster. Had she known any of this, she would have confronted both Marty and Russ. They worked for her, not the other way around.

April left her Dad and Marty at the track. At this point April did not care. All she wanted was for the ride to be over and for Mony Mony to come in safe. She had already won the crowds from previous races, and they all loved her. There were toy companies who wanted to make a likeness of Mony Mony to sell. She was that beloved. That mare had given rides to invalids with down syndrome near their home track. She also gave rides to kids with Parkinson's disease or those with Parakinesia, she was that patient. All the kids loved her. They were so excited when Mony Mony came to see them. Their eyes lit up and they could barely control themselves. Sitting on that mare, their infectious smiles were mirrored to all those around them. The kids loved sitting so high on such a tall horse. Yes, Mony Mony was already a winner.

They loaded and the gates opened. Mony Mony grabbed the rail as she always did. She held her own until the last stretch.

In the end of the race, it was determined a photo finish was necessary, the race was that close. They determined it was by half a nose. That photo was looked at over and over by several different angles, many times. There was an announcement that Mony Mony had won by a nose. April was thrilled! It did not matter anymore. Mony Mony had her chance, and she was awesome. She did all that was asked of her and more. She would continue to race and have babies. Mony Mony was a keeper on D Farms.

Russ was talked to and encouraged to go into a rehab program. It took him ten months, but he kicked the alcohol habit. Well, it is a lifelong struggle, the longer you stay away, the easier it gets. Russ realized alcohol was a disease and that he would never be free from the nagging want of it. But he was in control now, not the alcohol in control of him. That all happened when April was away at the farm competition.

April knew Russ would have this problem his entire life. D Farms helped him at every step. Yes, April was angry, but you don't throw people away. While April was away, she took the time to write a personal note to Russ to congratulate him and let him know they would always help him if he truly wanted to change. Russ treasured that note, he knew how busy April was, but she took the time to let him know. That meant a lot to him.

Shortly after they came home, Miranda was on the telephone to their family doctor. She wanted to know what to do next with April's knee. He advised her that April needed an MRI, which is short for magnetic resonance imaging, to see if there had been any changes. Then they would make a decision based on that test.

Within two days April was in the MRI listening to the pings and pangs and weird noises, not moving at all. She opted to listen to music luckily, for her they had a George Strait CD that April liked a lot. The one about cowgirls was one of her favorite songs. She told the tech she was just concerned she might fall asleep and twitch. The tech advised her not to and smiled.

As it turned out the surgery was minor. She only needed a few stitches to repair part of the tissue of the meniscus and wear a brace for a few weeks. After that would be physical therapy and it would heal as good as new.

Hugh is Leaving

THE GOOD-BYE SEND OFF FOR HUGH WAS THE LAST WEEKEND OF June. April still wore her light brace for support, but she knew this was not going to be easy for her, or for him.

The Marshalls knew how Hugh felt about April. His Mother, in particular, was concerned. Young love can be so difficult. All she could do was to be there for him if he wanted to talk to her.

The party was at the Marshall's home. The cake was awesome. It had Hugh's picture on it in full Marine uniform. It was evident Hugh was excited and nervous. He greeted as many as he could, but it was mechanical. He was trying not to show his feeling and emotions. There were a lot of people who came, most were from his high school. Some came from church including the Bishop, his counselors, his recruiting officer, and the school chaplain. Everyone April knew and a few she did not.

April watched Hugh and wanted to talk with him, but knew this party was for him, it had nothing to do with her. While she had been down with her knee surgery, April gathered a lot of photos that had been taken over the years. Most of them had both her and Hugh in them, and some were of just Hugh.

As per April's request, her Mom had the pictures copied at their local store. April made a scrap book of photos and comments for him. She also put a CTR ring (Chose the Right) on a sterling silver chain for him to wear. There was a deep pocket in the back of the scrap book that worked out nicely.

April was never one to sit around and do nothing. She got up from her chair and went to the kitchen to help Mrs. Marshall, "I can't sit here and do nothing," she said to her. "Please let me help."

"You are an invited guest. Go out and mingle," Mrs. Marshall said.

"I'd rather not," April said as she pulled Mrs. Marshall to the doorway of their big living room. There they saw that there were girls all over Hugh - some laughing, some pulling at his sleeve, some were asking for kisses, some did not ask, they just went for it. Hugh's face was full of lipstick.

Mrs. Marshall understood, on both parts. Hugh was good natured, and he would comply as it was a party, nothing more. She also knew if the roles were reversed and that was April with boys all over her with Hugh watching, he would not be happy either.

She put April to work to keep the bowls of whatever full. Just take the bowls from the kitchen counter and fill the others. There were more bowls in the refrigerator if she needed. Mrs. Marshall wiped her hand on her apron and walked into the living room clapping her hands. "Girls, girls, are you little girls or are you ladies?" she asked them. Most of them laughed at her giving a stupid answer, they were so immature.

Mrs. Marshall made it clear there would be no kissing unless it was in "hello" or if they were leaving as in a "goodbye". They were to behave themselves, they were adults, and should act like adults. Keep your hands to yourselves. She did not want one thing to lead to another. All that was needed was for someone to throw something and then all HE Double Hockey Sticks would break out. She did not want that or to have to clean up an unwanted mess made by invited guests. They were to act appropriately.

The hours went by quickly, some guests came and went, but some were pesky and got to April. Particularly one girl who kept hanging on Hugh. She had been a friend of Vicky's. Vicky was the former Mayor's daughter who had died in that accident years ago. The girl hanging on Hugh was from another school and had been in the gymnastic competition that year. April had not seen her since, but it was definitely her. April was sure of it.

April made it a point to walk up to her, tap her on the shoulder, and ask her what her name was.

"Who's asking, the hired help? she said.

That irritated April. How blatantly rude, how ignorant, and snobby she was.

April went to Hugh and took his hand in hers and said, "Hugh, can you please tell me why I am here? Am I the hired help?"

"Oh, hell no. You are my girl. You are the most important person here, besides my Mom," and he hugged her. Mrs. Marshall watched all of this and felt all was good.

The "girl" got up and left, but before she left, she made sure to call out to Hugh, "See you later, Huey. I promise to write."

Hugh did not hear her. He was talking to the Captain at the time in an in-depth conversation.

April was ready to growl, she wanted to know about her. April learned from another girl at the party that girl was Sandra Fetterman.

Sandra was from another town and had been in the gymnastic competition, but she never placed. Her parents wanted their daughter to be a debutante. They were a wealthy family from oil stock. Sandra had no manners at all, and not many friends either. She could buy anything she wanted including people. Sandra had a very loose reputation at her school and was proud of it. She enjoyed fighting and arguing. She bullied girls who were smarter than she was or poorer than she was, and that was just about every girl. The school had little power over since her parents would hound the school or teachers at 2 a.m. to get what their little girl wanted, including changing her grades to passing.

Oh, if Hugh only knew. April hoped that someone would be kind enough to clue Hugh in. She spoke to Donny who was one of the varsity players who had played football with Hugh. They also biked, hiked, and swam together. Donny laughed and said Sandra was the kind of girl every guy wanted to meet and winked at April. Sandra was not "bring home to Momma material" but a fun time.

April wrinkled her nose and said, "Fun, you call that fun? How much fun would it be to have a child with that?" and Donny backed off like he saw a ghost.

"I would not wish that on my worst enemy, she can be evil," Donny said. "Hey, Hugh is a big boy. He can do what he wants. If he makes a mistake, it's his own fault. I am not going to say anything." Donny said.

April looked at him with surprise and said, "Well, you just came down a few notches in my eyes, Donny. If it were me, I'd want to know." Then April asked, "Would you please clue Hugh in on her, she seemed like she was making Hugh her next target."

"I'll see, but you know Hugh does not like being told anything," he said.

April kept things going in the kitchen, chips, pickles, and potato salad. She refilled lunch meats, the crock pots, and lastly the hors d'oeuvre tray. Later she filled the ice buckets and sodas. April kept this up for almost three hours when Mrs. Marshall came behind her putting her arms around her. "Stop, Dear, just stop and come with me," she said.

She took April by the hand pulling her along to the back of the house. There was a very large back cement veranda. Standing there all alone was Hugh, all by himself, lost in thought. Mrs. Marshall pushed April out there to join him, winking at her.

April walked silently behind Hugh putting her arms around his waist, "Hey, there!" she said.

Hugh pulled April around, so she was standing right in front of him. He lifted her up onto the porch side which was two feet wide with cement. Hugh looked at April directly into her eyes for a moment and said, "Well here we are, the time has come, and all I need to know is where you are."

April touched Hugh's chest where his heart was and said, "Right here, I am right in here."

Hugh pulled her close to him to kiss her and she melted in his arms. This was it! This was the man for her. She knew it as well as she felt the beat of her own heart against his. She knew him and he knew her. They were not only compatible, but they were also like soul mates. So often she would say something, and he would complete her sentence, and she could do the same with him.

When Hugh stepped back, they both had tears in their eyes. "Don't cry," she said and wiped away his tears. "This is temporary we both will be busy learning and in time we will come back together again. I will be here. I promise you this, and I will wait for you. There is no one else for me, this I swear to you."

Hugh's tears began to trickle down his cheeks again. "I hope so. I have loved you since the first day I met you. I remember hiking those trails at the lake holding your hand, and all those years of Trevor teasing me. He was right, it was you, it was always you. I need to do something, please come with me," he said to her. They walked out to the stables, and the horses nickered to them.

"Hey there," he said as he gently touched his horse's nose. "I am going to miss you too," and he patted the horse's neck. He reached up into a dusty saddle bag and pulled out something. He had his back to April, and she could not see what he had.

Hugh turned around with a box, he bent down on one knee and said, "April, I felt I should do something, give you something as a token of my love, and for you to remember me by." He opened the box and there was a stunning opal, ruby, and diamond ring. Hugh said, "I don't want to scare you. I am scared. I don't want to leave without a promise to you. I have prayed that you would wait for me. I want to go to the temple with you to be married for all time and eternity as well. I am hoping that by you taking this ring, it seals our promise to each other for a later time in our lives."

April was stunned "Hugh, this ring," and he finished the question she had.

"This ring belonged to my grandmother. My grandfather gave it to me, for you. April, I wish this was an engagement ring, but it's not. It's a promise ring. One my grandfather gave to my grandmother over seventy years ago, when they were in Ireland.

She wore it with pride reminding everyone she was saved, waiting for the man she loved.

Hugh slipped the ring onto April's finger, it was a bit snug, but it did fit. He stood up and embraced her and they kissed a long lingering kiss. They came out of the stable hand in hand, happy, relieved, and feeling they would be all right. A commitment had been made and at the end of their journey they both knew they would be right here waiting, one for the other.

Mrs. Marshall was with Miranda on the back of the veranda when they saw Hugh and April walking up the steps. That is when she spied the ring and she immediately walked up to April and embraced her, "Welcome to our family," she said.

Miranda began to cry tears of joy. A wish of hers had come true. How very grateful she was. These two were like two peas in a pod. They were so much alike, and each uplifted the other. It truly was a blessing, and she went to find Gordon and Mr. Marshall. They all came out in a short while to congratulate them both. What a rush it was for April, a feeling of complete and total peace.

The six of them stood together and talked for a while. April's and Hugh's lives were set for the entire next year, Hugh in the Marines and April in the farm competition. April would graduate the following June, so they were okay. They all prayed these two would be all right, that they would settle into their new lives, and keep busy. That way both would keep their eyes on their goal, each other.

Hugh was prepared to leave, the sooner the better. He wanted to get going and get started. He did not want his parents to drive him. He bought a bus ticket and within two days he was gone.

On his way to the bus station, he wanted to stop by the sheriff's office. Hugh stepped inside. Gordon was sitting at his desk. It was very early. Gordon looked up, stood, and reached out his hand to shake Hugh's.

"Well, this is it," Hugh said. "I wanted to talk to you before I left. First, I want to apologize for asking your daughter to wait for me without asking your permission. It was wrong of me. If I had to do it over, I would have asked you first." Hugh hung his head.

Gordon slapped him on his should and said, "That's okay, Hugh. I understand. I was a lot like that too."

"Well Sir, I am not like that, and I am being honest with you, sir. I am in love with your daughter and hope to marry her someday, in the temple of course."

"Hugh, I would be delighted if you would be my son in law someday. The temple is the only way we want to see our daughter married." Gordon said.

With that the two of them embraced, it was not awkward. Gordon remembered well what this moment was like when he made up his mind to do the very same thing years ago. He wished Hugh well and out the door Hugh went.

Meanwhile April was at home in the middle of packing to take her trip to wherever. Not typical packing, just throwing something in every now and then, so she kept the suitcase open. She would not know details until near the end of July.

With Hugh gone, she had time on her hands. April wanted to go swimming but had no partner. It was the same with movies or a run. April realized how dependent she had become upon Hugh. "Well, I can't keep this up," she said to herself, and she got up to go out for a run. Before leaving she checked the milking schedule. How great it was to have the same schedule for all D Farms. She no longer had to milk, but always kept a check on who was. She left a note for her Mom who was out, and headed off for the Piney Hill run.

April was feeling lonely at the halfway, so she sat on an outcropping of rock and looked out. This was a beautiful place, piney scrubs but the land was not barren. Often deer came to ear here and drink at the many ponds and streams on this hillside. The plateaus were a welcome relief to many of the wildlife. She soaked it in and while she did, she could see Hugh running with her. Hugh had an easy smile and way about him. She shook her head and then got up to push on.

Olympics Again?

When April got home, she took a quick shower. When she came downstairs, she noticed there was a message on the answering machine. It was for her, or rather her parents, it was from the Olympic Committee, and she thought, "Here we go again."

As it turned out Miranda already had gotten that message. Since she went to pick up some clothing from the dry cleaners, she stopped in to see her husband. He kissed her cheek, and she handed him a cinnamon roll that she'd baked at home.

"What do you want?" Gordon asked her.

"I don't want anything but to discuss something with you." Then she handed Gordon the message.

As he scooped another bite into his mouth he stopped and looked at Miranda. "You do know she is leaving in September, and this is now June. I can't imagine her getting ready this fast and performing with them in such a short time."

Miranda asked if he would make the call and take care of the details for her. She was on her way home to put the dry cleaning away and start dinner. She herself did not want to deal with anyone from the Olympic Committee anymore. Too many were pushy and wanted what they wanted.

After she left, after he had scraped, spooned, and licked his plate clean. Gordon washed his hands and then picked up the telephone and dialed the toll-free number. "Hello, Stacy Saunders, please," he asked.

"Just one minute, who is calling?" The voice on the other end asked.

"Di Angelos are calling," Gordon said.

"Beep, boop, beep, boop," the waiting signal continued for about three minutes. Gordon was about to hang up when a woman's voice come on the other end. "Hello, this is Stacy Saunders, how may I help you?"

"Hello, Stacy. I was wondering the same thing. You called our home asking about our daughter April Di Angelo, and we are wondering how may we help you?"

"Oh, yes, Mr. Di Angelo thank you so much for returning our call. We would like very much to speak to you about having your daughter represent the United States in the swimming events here in Florida in August for the Olympics," she said.

Gordon told her April was leaving in September not sure of the date and was afraid that the timing would be too close.

"Oh, don't worry about that," Stacy said. "I will e-mail you the information and send someone to speak to you and you wife about the schedule. Will the end of this week be all right?" she asked.

Gordon sighed, "I guess it will be. Do you know what time?" he asked her.

"Ah, I'd say about 3:00 in the afternoon," she said.

"Could you make it at 5:00. I am not off work till 5:00," he said.

"All right. I will pass on the information, and you have a good day, Mr. Di Angelo," and she hung up the phone.

"Good day, humph! Now Gordon knew April was an avid, adept swimmer. In his opinion she swam like a fish. But this would be totally up to her. They would discuss this at dinner.

At dinner that evening Gordon brought up the conversation.

April knew Stacy Saunders. "She was the coordinator for the other events in the last Olympics. She was also coordinator for the Equestrian Summer Olympics. Don't you remember her, Dad? Stacy is about 5' 4" tall, with short reddish blonde hair. She talks faster than she can walk or do anything else, and she never stops," they all laughed. "Stacy really is a nice person though. I wonder why they thought about me?" April asked.

Gordon kept his thoughts to himself. We always pay more than our fair share, we liberally offer our daughter every time they ask, so why wouldn't they ask about April!

"The representative is going to be here on Friday. They will bring the information with them. What I got online was just an overall of the Olympics," he said, "Momma will you make a little more of something for dinner so we can share with this representative. We are all hungry at 5:00?"

"Oh, you know I can, and I will," Miranda said. She was a bundle of nerves again. She was excited and loved the Olympics. She knew that April would do her best and no one could ask more than that.

Friday came and there was a guy knocking at their door. He was very young looking although he said he was twenty-five, but he looked like he was seventeen and he hated that. No one said it verbally, but you could see he looked about nervously.

Miranda said, "Young man you are such a good-mannered, well-rounded person. We appreciate you taking the time to talk to us and explain all this gobbledygook to us," and he laughed, from that time forward he was at ease.

He did explain April was to report to the Florida camp as soon as possible to see if she would make the team. If she did, then she would go to Germany with the team and would be there until the end of July or into August. He thought the games were the second of August for two weeks. But of course, she would not be required to stay the entire time.

April looked at her parents. The truth was April loved to swim, and there was no pressure. She was in great shape from swimming and lifting weights with the Captain after Hugh left. She felt ready, and she wanted to at the very least try out.

The papers were signed, a check was made out, and that evening Miranda secured a flight for April to head to Florida. Mom would come along just to see if April made it through the trials. Gordon was fine with it. "I can eat cereal and be happy he said."

Miranda was not having any of that. After she secured the tickets and called Stacy for her to reserve a hotel room near the complex, Miranda hauled out chicken, a small beef roast, sausages, bacon, and ground turkey. With these meats and other things Miranda made eighteen meals for her husband, all cooked, sealed, and placed in the freezer. They were all marked, and he could pull out what he wanted each night.

"Just pile them up in the dishwasher," Miranda said.

"I do know how to do dishes, Dear," Gordon teased his wife.

"I know you do, but you have enough to do every day," she said.

Off to Florida

Within two days Miranda and April were off on another adventure, they were flying to Florida. The flight was good, no problems other when Miranda got a slight earache from the cabin air pressure. April did give her mom some gum to chew, but that did very little for her.

On the ground there was someone with a sign "Di Angelo" to meet them. Off they went to another place through streets, past channels, and river ways. Miranda loved the water, inwardly she thought April loved it because she did, and maybe this was true. In Mexico as a child Miranda was always begging to go swimming in big water.

At the venue the swimmers were already holding tryouts. April asked where to go and she was told to change. In a few minutes she came out with a full swimsuit, her goggles, and head cap. She waited for her turn and as she waited, she stretched and bent this way and that to relax her muscles. Then her name was called, "Di Angelo." She stepped up on the podium and waited for the whistle. It blew and off she flew off the stand as low and as far out as she could go.

April maneuvered her feet to go as far as the water would take her and then she began to swim. This was six laps, and when the laps were finished, she placed first in that heat. The heats kept going, that day April was in six of them. Her stamina was good, and she was not tired. She was getting hungry!

By 7:00 p.m. all the heats were finished, the postings would appear on the outside door in the morning. If your name was on the list, you were to wait until 9:00 a.m. Then be there for signatures and eventual departure.

Miranda wanted to take April out to dinner for a good meal. Something April liked and they did not usually have at home. Miranda found a nice seafood restaurant, knowing April loved seafood. Miranda did as well, but Gordon, eh, not so much. It was a nice place to eat, it was clean, and the waitresses looked happy. April loved shrimp, scallops, and lobster. April was so happy she knew her Mom liked seafood but did not make it often if at all. There were other options on the menu as well.

April's plate came out and it reminded her of the time when she came through Tennessee with Barbara. She wondered how she was and what she was doing. She mentioned this to her Mom. "Oh, I don't know, Sweetie. I do still have her address and I can write a letter to her if you like," Miranda told her.

"Yes, that would be nice. She was so good to me, the entire trip she was with me. I honestly don't know what I would have done without her. Gone hungry I guess," April said, and Miranda winced.

A little before 6:00 a.m. Miranda woke up just like she did every morning.

She realized she was not in her own bed and saw her daughter sitting quietly looking at a magazine. "How long have you been up?" she asked April.

"Oh, just a little while," April answered her Mom. But she lied.

Miranda got up, showered, and dressed. In no time they were carrying their suitcases to check out and head to the trials area.

When they arrived at the parking lot, there were many girls there already and some parents. Some were crying, some were jumping up and down. April came to the list and started at the bottom, going up when on girl said, "You name is up there" and she pointed to the top.

"How did you know who I was?" April asked her.

"Are you kidding, you're April D. You were in the Olympics before, and you were famous. Don't you know that?" she asked.

April laughed and said, "Famous? No, I did not know that I was famous, and I am glad I didn't know, or I would have a big head." As she held her hands to the side of her head in exaggeration and they both laughed.

April found her Mom and hugged her with her thumb in the air. "I figured you'd make it," Miranda said. "Okay, let's wait and get things started for you. I guess you won't be flying home with me after all."

At 9:00 a.m. the doors opened and the eighteen or so girls went in with their parents. Papers were signed, some ran to go, some were clingy. April turned to hug her Mom. "I remember when I would cry like that. I still love you, Mom, and I appreciate all you do for me. I don't even know all you do for me. But that's why I love you so much. Thanks, Mom!" April had a big goofy grin on her face and hugged her Mom. April lifted her Mom squeezing her. Miranda hissed. April laughed at her, hugging her one more time, she kissed her Mom and then she was gone.

They all loaded the bus heading towards the airport, all their neck IDs had to be stamped along with their air transportation cards. It was an exciting thing for most of these girls. Only six were returning, the others were new. It was their first time.

April sat with a young girl who was about 13, she was long and lean, full of muscles. "Hey, I'm April. What's your name?"

"My name is Jamie Gardner, and I am from New Jersey," the girl said.

"Well, hey there New Jersey. Good to meet you and I'd like to be your friend." April held out her hand to shake Jamie's and they laughed.

The flight from Florida to Germany was a long, long flight. The girls slept, some watched TV. Some listened to music or read books. April just enjoyed the flight. Transatlantic flights always amazed her, such a long distance. April loved to look out of the windows. Granted, sometimes it was just clouds, but sometimes you could see towns that looked like they were made of micro sticks and sometimes bodies of water. It interested her, all of it.

When they landed, it was all business. There were already girls chosen to be on the team, and those who were just arriving would be either fill ins, alternates, or standbys. April did not know where she would be, just like all the other eighteen girls.

They all put on their swimsuits and entered the swimming pool area. There the coach spoke with them as a group, the woman was stern. She was thorough, clear, and concise. No one had a question.

The youngsters were expected to swim and show what times they could pull. It was all work. As time went on, the younger girls and alternates worked with those who were already on the team. April was singled out to see what she had. She was not thirteen, she was sixteen now. They expected production and she delivered. When it was all said and done, April was clean up on the team, she would be the last swimmer in the lanes.

April had tremendous arm and leg strength. She was able to hold her breath for an amazing length of time without becoming panicked. In other words, she enjoyed being in the water and performing for whatever stroke they asked of her. When she finished her lane, she would always look up at the clock to see what her time was. She would throw her head back and laugh. She was improving with each lap, each practice.

The events were starting in a few days and the United States Team was ready! The girls were anxious to get going. April took it upon herself to talk to them individually and sometimes in groups. She reminded them to stay grounded. They were with friends, and they were not alone. If they needed a hug, it was just a shoulder away. The coaches appreciated her kind efforts to keep the girls calm. April had great leadership skills to pull this group together as a solid team.

The coaches were not only happy with her efforts, but they also began to eye her as a team leader. There were individual events after which April would massage their shoulders to settle them down. If they did not do as well as they felt they could, she would hug them, reassuring them to wait and see. Yes, there was no doubt about it April quickly became the one that the girls went to for whatever they needed.

The team event was quite the match up, there were twelve countries vying for medals. April stretched while she listened to music. She put her arms over her head, hands clasped and pushed them forward and back. Then she stretched her legs and hugged whoever was near her.

Then the moment arrived, as the teams came in many cheered for them, but the loudest cheering was for the United States team. It warmed the hearts of all the team swimmers.

The first swimmer was on the podium, all twelve lanes were full, and the whistle blew. It was exciting to watch and nerve wracking to see your teammates fall back to other competitors. As the U.S. team swam, some when ahead and some lagged behind. Some were afraid and some were full of adrenaline.

Each lane was either swimming or jumping in. In this race the swimmers were required to go four laps. April was ready, waiting on the podium as her teammate came barreling in. This swimmer discovered that she was behind in the second last lap, so in her final turn she tried to catch up but was still behind.

Now it was up to April. As the swimmer touched the wall, she was poised to leap, and she did. She pulled her arms hard and controlled her movements as much as she could. "Mechanics, mechanics," that is what the coaches drilled into their heads.

As she swam, she concentrated on her breathing. She was steady, strong, and kept going. Flip and go some more. Change the stroke for another lap, flip. April did not look at the other lanes, she concentrated on her lane, her breathing, and swam. She gave it all she had.

April did count the laps and paid strict attention to the type of stroke she was to be doing. Other than that, she was like a porpoise, blazing through the water. On the last lap as she flipped, she looked over her right shoulder, and did not see the swimmer. However, she could be under the water and come up later for air. As she turned her head to get air, she could hear the swimmer coming on. April surged forward as strong as she could. She poured on all the strength she had. This was her favorite stroke, the free style.

As she touched the wall, she was there alone for seconds. She put her head back and realized she not only came in first, but she also broke a world record with her swim. As she came out of the pool the team came running to her and hugged her. Some had tears of joy, and some were laughing, or jumping up and down.

The crowds in the stands erupted with cheers and shouts for the United States swim team. And a reporter with a headset and microphone came to her. April had her arms around four girls as she spoke with the reporter. April refused to make it sound like she won the race. "This has been an amazing opportunity to swim with the strongest team in the United States. I have been blessed to be part of the team and so grateful to have become friends with all those on the team," she said. "During my leg of the race, I gave it all I had. This is what I promised each of the girls and what I asked of them. I was blown away when I realized we had set a new world record. This is the greatest group to swim with," and she put her head down as she began to become very emotional. When she raised her head there were tears coming down her cheeks, the girls hugged her and held on.

The reporter respectfully let her alone. She and the girls headed back to the dressing area to change for the awards ceremony. Then they stood on the podium with the other two teams who earned the silver and bronze on either side of them. They were all excited as they waited, and then something unexpected happened.

A group of men who were Native Americans came into the medals ceremony area after the medals were awarded. Before anyone could leave, they wanted to pay their respects to April.

They had a staff that was curved at the top which was their flag. Some had on headdresses, and some were wearing animal heads to represent that animal. They were here in peace and called out to April. They wanted to recognize her heritage. Her birth Mother was Chippewa, and these men were Chippewa warriors. They gave a speech, then respectfully asked April to come forward and they presented her with an amulet for her to wear. This was so special. It was such an amazing event for April to experience. She was humbled by the strength and power of these men.

And then it was over. April was not required to stay, and she wanted to go home. Without April knowing her birth Mom and her Aunt Lena were at the venue with Miranda. They all were able to watch April and had an amazing time! Those three were her cheerleaders, whooping and hollering for her.

They headed out with the help of security, boarded a bus, and headed to the hotels. Miranda told April the three of them would meet at "her" hotel and to wait there. April entered her room, packed her suitcase in minutes, and sat down to wait. She waited, and waited, and almost fell asleep when she heard a knock on her door. It was Miranda, and they were ready to leave.

The bus headed to the airport where they boarded and headed to Georgia. That was a layover, then onto California, and finally home. It was an amazing trip, full of memories and good times. Miranda, Nora, and Lena became such good, dependable friends, they were like three sisters. That made April's heart happy. They all talked with each other. The differences between the four of them faded away. They talked and laughed. They munched on food, and it was such fun, all four of them together. April soon fell asleep with her head on her auntie's shoulder. Lena looked at

April and said, "She looks so much like our grandma. Don't you think so, Nora?" Nora just nodded her head, but Miranda wanted to know more about April and her great grandmother. They promised to give Miranda a picture. One of their grandmother's which was April's great grandmother.

As April lay against her aunt's shoulder, Lena began to think back about April when she was a little girl. She was so delightful and funny. She would talk gibberish on the telephone for hours and they would catch her and holler at her to put the phone down, repeating, "No, no!" When they walked up on April, she would put the receiver down and point her finger at the telephone and say "No, no". She was a cute little thing, as was her own daughter. Sadly, she had no contact with her, by her son-in-law's request. Lena was not one to argue as ridiculous as this was, but she obeyed what he said. So, she agreed to stay out of the way.

Yes, she had missed much of her sister's life and this little one's too. Now her life was good, they were happy. The peace they enjoyed was not with them for much of their lives. But now it was time to thank God for all his good care and showing them the way.

She stroked April's hair and said an inward prayer for God to always watch over her and it seemed she was the key for all of them. She saw that with April's grandparents on both sides, they were more receptive to Gordon, he said it one night and Miranda agreed with him.

Yes, all the days of their lives both she and Nora would pray for God to watch over April and keep her in his care.

Heading Back Home

They arrived at the airport around 2:00 a.m. Miranda needed bus tickets for the four of them. When the woman at the counter saw April and realized who she was with these three women, the woman asked, "Who are you, Ma'am?"

"I am Mrs. Di Angelo, and I am taking my daughter home with her dear family," she said.

"But isn't that the girl who just was in the Olympics and helped the United States win with a new world record?" the woman asked.

"Yes, it is, and she is very tired. We just want to go home. Can you help us?" Miranda asked the woman at the airport counter.

"I sure can, Ma'am. Your money is no good here, your daughter just did a pretty amazing thing, and we'd like to treat her. Well, all of you. So don't delay, catch that bus. Miranda was surprised and impressed, and in a hurry to catch that bus.

They boarded, got comfortable and in no time, they were at the airport, running for their gate. They laughed and squealed. They dropped things, laughing out of breath picking the things up. At one point Lena was laughing so hard, she was crying tears of joy! "Stop, stop, my sides hurt from laughing." but they did not stop. It was the best trip ever for the four of them.

In Georgia they boarded a flight to California. When in the air they watch a movie and April penned a letter to her friend Miranka in Poland. This was a long flight, some of the people recognized April, but most did not. So, she was able to relax, sleep, and do what you can when you are in the air for four hours.

When they landed in California, April put a call in to the hanger where Mr. Stevens housed his plane for a ride home. They would be there in one hour. Then it would be a hop, skip, and a jump to get home. Mr. Stevens' word was good, in flew the D Farms Cessna. April knew that airplane the minute she saw it, and it was Scott flying, bonus!

The ladies all felt a sense of relief, they knew Scott too. "Hello, ladies. I have been waiting here to escort you girls all home, safe and sound," and he smiled from ear to ear. The women clamored to carry their luggage walking the tarmac to the Cessna. Scott ran up to them and took their baggage. He managed all three suitcases. April lugged her suitcase and Scott teased her, he said she needed to build muscle.

This was the same airplane that took Mr. Stevens and his family to check the farms to be purchase. It was the same one on which April took flying lessons. Often Scott would ask her if she wanted to take the helm. Sometimes she did, but right now April was dogged tired.

The Cessna was comfortable and roomy. There were captain chairs and two sofas. April sat on one of the sofas and looked out of the window. During takeoff with the Cessna, it never ceased to amaze her, and away they went, home, home, home.

They landed at the stables and Gordon met the women. He loaded his car with their luggage and took them all home.

Once at their own home, Gordon carried the luggage into the house and placed them near the stairway. Miranda came in looking tired and disheveled. Gordon put his arms around his wife kissing her forehead, her cheek, and then her lips. "I need a shower and some sleep," Miranda protested. Gordon laughed at her, and she went up to do what she had planned.

April was still not in the house and finally came in. I wanted to see how many ponies were out there, Dad. Not too many."

"I know, Sweetie. I did not have you here to help me." Gordon said. He pulled his daughter to him. "I am so proud of you. Do you know that?" he said to her. "I was able to watch your team swim on our TV, and, Honey, I am telling you, you had me standing and cheering for you. That surely was a house of noise," he said.

"Yes sir, it was something for sure," April replied. She too was out of synch, tired, and needing a shower and a nap.

"Well, you go on up there and take a few winks. I am going to work, and no one will be bothering you today, right Ruby?" he said. Ruby was twirling in circles at April's feet for her to pick her up. April did, and Ruby melted in her arms.

"Some watchdog," April said. Then she left to go upstairs with her little friend. April did not wake up until 2:00 p.m. that afternoon. She and her Mom sat on the porch sipping a watermelon drink that Miranda made with ice.

April sat there and said, "Mom isn't it so surreal that yesterday this time, we were still in Germany. I can't believe it all happened so fast, like it was not real."

"Oh, it's very real dear," and Miranda handed April the newspaper. On the front page was April poised to dive in her lane with the caption reading, "LEAP FOR GOLD." April still could not comprehend she was famous for anything. She just said it was one day, one thing, but this is who I really am.

Just then the telephone rang, it was Grandpa and Contessa both fighting to use the phone, talking over one another. They were trying to say they too saw April in the Olympics, but in their newspaper, it showed different photos and listed Grandpa and Contessa as April's grandparents. "We are so proud, you know. Everyone sees us and talks to us now. Reporters came out and we were overwhelmed. They do not realize all the talents April has. Yes, this is amazing, such power and speed for a small girl. They had no idea she tamed a big powerful wild animal all on her own."

That conversation went on for twenty minutes or so, and when they hung up Miranda sighed and said, "I don't want to cook dinner tonight. How about that, I feel lazy and tired. Maybe we can talk Daddy into going in for a pizza. He can bring it home or we can go out. What do you think about that?" she asked. Miranda made the call to her husband. He said he would bring pizza home. Miranda laughed at him. He was such a good man. She noticed he did the dishes, everything was put away, and he must have vacuumed the floor. There was not a speck of dirt anywhere. When he got home with the pizza, Miranda kissed her husband and said, "I love you, Gordon Di Angelo, and she kissed him again.

April made a salad to go with the pizza and some iced tea. "Okay, lovebirds, dinner is ready, come and eat," April hollered to them.

Gordon bound into the kitchen, grabbed his daughter, and hugged her so tight, rocking her.

"Dad!" April exclaimed.

"Yes, he said, "What is wanted," and they both laughed. "Man, oh man, did you fix up the pizza dinner?" he asked her.

"I sure did, Mom needed a break. I hope this is okay."

"Mumm," he said as he looked at the table. April knew it was no big deal, but when you are tired, it's nice to have a little help.

After two slices of pizza, Gordon got up and pulled down a letter from the top of the refrigerator. "Look what came while you were away," he said. It was a letter from the Farm Competition.

"Why didn't you open it, Dad?" April asked.

"Because it's your letter," he answered her.

April tore open the envelope open carefully and it read that she was to report to such and such station for public transportation that was provided on August fifth, that was the beginning. Her very first place would be in Pennsylvania, a very cold place to be in the winter.

Miranda and April had a devil of a time finding "winter clothing." They ended up shopping online and hoped the sizes fit.

April had to have an examination by her family doctor, an eye examination, and blood work. This was all done in two days, and so far as she was concerned, she was packed. If she needed anything more, she would buy it there.

Before she left April wanted to talk to the school board. It was a private meeting, and they welcomed her in. April discussed that there was gang mentality in the high school. It did not bother her, but it did others. She asked if the honor society could have a type of "court". Send the perpetrators to the honor society court and sentence them to work with the city employees. April pulled out a statistic and showed the school board that it was kids without parents or parents who were not involved in their kid's lives that caused these problems.

In this way, the child would be punished but also learning. Learning to speak with respect, ask and not lean to their own understanding. Those who worked with the kids on their jobs were heroes to April. If people's gutters needed to be cleaned, let the worker stand there holding the ladder while the kid cleaned them. Let them paint the yellow on the sidewalk while the workers supervised. Let the kids paint curve areas. Let them help, as they didn't at home. April said, the workers who worked with the kids were what the kids needed. And the School Board heartedly agreed. It took a bit to get organized but in two weeks a boy started a fight in the bathroom. He did go before the honor society, and they sentenced him to three months with the township workers. The jobs were endless, and they kept him busy learning things. April called Mr. Stevens and asked if he would authorize funds at a nice restaurant with awards for employees and kids who worked with them. It was a brief conversation and Mr. Stevens said he would be honored. He said he would be delighted to be at the meetings to ensure all was followed. April said she hoped she would be at the next one and thanked Mr. Stevens.

The Girl in the Mirror Book 4

"I sure did, Mom needed a break. I hope this is okay."

"Mumm," he said as he looked at the table. April knew it was no big deal, but when you are tired, it's nice to have a little help.

After two slices of pizza, Gordon got up and pulled down a letter from the top of the refrigerator. "Look what came while you were away," he said. It was a letter from the Farm Competition.

"Why didn't you open it, Dad?" April asked.

"Because it's your letter," he answered her.

April tore open the envelope open carefully and it read that she was to report to such and such station for public transportation that was provided on August fifth, that was the beginning. Her very first place would be in Pennsylvania, a very cold place to be in the winter.

Miranda and April had a devil of a time finding "winter clothing." They ended up shopping online and hoped the sizes fit.

April had to have an examination by her family doctor, an eye examination, and blood work. This was all done in two days, and so far as she was concerned, she was packed. If she needed anything more, she would buy it there.

Before she left April wanted to talk to the school board. It was a private meeting, and they welcomed her in. April discussed that there was gang mentality in the high school. It did not bother her, but it did others. She asked if the honor society could have a type of "court". Send the perpetrators to the honor society court and sentence them to work with the city employees. April pulled out a statistic and showed the school board that it was kids without parents or parents who were not involved in their kid's lives that caused these problems.

In this way, the child would be punished but also learning. Learning to speak with respect, ask and not lean to their own understanding. Those who worked with the kids on their jobs were heroes to April. If people's gutters needed to be cleaned, let the worker stand there holding the ladder while the kid cleaned them. Let them paint the yellow on the sidewalk while the workers supervised. Let the kids paint curve areas. Let them help, as they didn't at home. April said, the workers who worked with the kids were what the kids needed. And the School Board heartedly agreed. It took a bit to get organized but in two weeks a boy started a fight in the bathroom. He did go before the honor society, and they sentenced him to three months with the township workers. The jobs were endless, and they kept him busy learning things. April called Mr. Stevens and asked if he would authorize funds at a nice restaurant with awards for employees and kids who worked with them. It was a brief conversation and Mr. Stevens said he would be honored. He said he would be delighted to be at the meetings to ensure all was followed. April said she hoped she would be at the next one and thanked Mr. Stevens.

Going to Pennsylvania

THAT LAST SUNDAY IN CHURCH CAME FAST AND IT WAS A testimony meeting. It was a time when members could go up front if they felt prompted to. They would bear witness of spiritual things in their life, or about the Savior and his influence.

April did feel she should go up front and bare her witness about the Savior Jesus Christ. Jesus prayed and it never mattered where we went to teach and do good. He accepted all that was put on him. April did not thank anyone. These meeting were not thanks-a-monies. They were to show gratitude to our Savior for his atonements. He died on the cross for all mankind. No longer would anyone remain a slave of the grave.

That evening a few church friends stopped by to say "see you later" to April because she hated goodbyes. Some neighbors and friends also stopped over. April begged her Mom NOT to have a going away party and she did not.

Gordon and Miranda both wanted to speak to their daughter for her to understand the rules. That she could not call home, only at Christmas, but she could write whenever she wanted. They encouraged her to keep a journal to mark her progress and keep track of where she had been and what she had done. It was a quiet evening for the Di Angelos at home. In the morning her Dad would drive her to the bus station. Her ticket was already paid for. She was expected to arrive the next day.

Gordon kissed his daughter and held her close to him. Her dad was the strongest support she had ever had. She did not know what she would have done without him all these years. He was often unappreciated and got very little credit, but he never minded. He was tough as Sheriff but wrapped around her little finger if she wanted him to be. She loved him, it was evident April was proud of her Dad, and proud to love him.

This "see you later" was a difficult one for her. "Dad, I hope everything works out," she said.

"It will, Honey, just be patient. You know that things will not be like they are on D Farms, everyone does everything differently."

"Yes, I know, I will keep a detailed journal. It will keep me busy and out of trouble."

"That is what I am concerned with most, if anyone makes trouble." Her Dad looked at her, right in her eyes and said, "If anyone touches you, hurts you, or otherwise, TELL. Go and tell someone in charge, make it known. They have no right! Do you hear me, April. You tell." He hugged her and she went to board her bus.

The bus pulled out as she snuggled down into her seat. Next stop is the airport. There would be one lay over, and she had forty-five minutes on that layover to get something to eat or look around or rest. At the airport she browsed at the shops and settled down with a warm pretzel and a fruit drink.

April was hungry but did not want to spend a lot of money. So, the pretzel would do. April sat close to the gate she would be boarding at.

April flipped through some of the magazines that were lying on the seat next to her. She did not see anyone she knew and did not want to draw attention to herself, so she waited patiently and quietly. Soon one of the airport employees turned on the microphone announcing boarding at gate three for her flight number. She waited as people went before her, boarding near last. She had one small personal carry on, that she kept with her.

The flight was great, no problems, and able to see clearly. It was a clear day and as they flew north April could see white on the ground and plumes of smoke trailing up into the sky. She had not experienced cold since her Poland days. She pulled out her Winteck jacket laying it on her lap. She knew she would need it when she departed the airplane. After landing she waited for her one suitcase to come down onto the turnstile. When her suitcase was in hand, she walked along the route to go out into the main area of the airport. All the while April looked for someone to identify with the competition of farms.

She was waiting and almost gave up hope when an older women came in a hurry walking along the sidewalk with a sign hanging down in her hand that read "De Angelo". April walked up to her and said, "I am April Di Angelo."

The woman was a bit startled and said, "Oh, I thought I was picking up a boy."

"No, I am not a boy," April said to her. "Di Angelo is my name pointing out her misspelled name.

"Okay then, let's go," the woman said. With suitcase in hand, they headed out to the parking lot. April was told to put her suitcase in the back of the truck. They left for her farm destination.

The silence was deafening in the cab of the pickup truck on the way to the farm. April broke the silence with questions. "Where is your farm?"

"We are about a two-hour ride from this airport. We live in Berks County on a 485-acre farm. We have another farm run by our son in Lancaster, but we wanted someone with experience on our farm for the competition." The woman introduced herself as Helen. She was the wife who was very much involved in the daily operations of the dairy farm.

"I don't milk anymore. When we went to carousel milking, I stopped because it's too fast for me. But I tend to the calves and was hoping for some help with that. And their feeding and general help," she said.

April told her she had experience with all of that.

The woman looked relieved. They did not stop anywhere. The woman was more concerned with getting back. She never asked if April was hungry, or if she needed anything.

"How cold does it get here?" April asked.

"At night it can easily dip to eight or sometimes lower."

April told her she would need to get warmer clothing. There was nothing available in California.

"Oh, we have several places you can get coveralls, or insulated pants. Remind me and we can pick them up in a day or two."

"Wow! April thought in a day or two I could freeze my you know what's off. I will have to make the best of this."

It was obvious Helen did not think much of other's needs, mainly her own. It was not the first time April saw something like this. Many people are like that. You do a favor for them or help them, and they never think of reciprocating or paying you back. April was taught if someone helped you, you help them. "Do unto others as you would like them to do unto you." But she found that many people were self-centered. The thought of helping someone never crossed their minds, it was all about "me."

April had a feeling this was going to be a long three months, she quickly realized that she was here to work, not so much for competition or to make improvements, but only free labor. Well, it was what it was, and she would make the best of it.

They arrived at the farm, and it was a nicely laid out farm. There was the house on the upper side and the farm layout all around the acreage near the house. April grabbed her suitcase and felt a sing of wind hit her in the face. She grimaced and headed to the house behind Helen.

"Your room is upstairs on the right, go down the hall and your room is the last one past the closet doors in the hallway."

April took her suitcase and opened the door. There was a small twin bed with one dresser. The room was brightly lit with a window shade up. April pulled the shade halfway down to keep the room somewhat warm. April saw the snow swirling around on the cold hard ground outside.

April opened her suitcase and put on the insulated underwear her Mom had purchased for her. Then she put on a long-sleeved sweatshirt and her blue jeans. She carried her hat, gloves, and jacket with her downstairs. She stopped in her tracks at the top of the stairs to offer a word of prayer. It was short but she felt it was necessary.

Helen showed her a list of what she was expected to do. That did not explain where these things were to be done and April had to ask. April made notes along the side of the "to do list" for her own benefit. She did not know where anything was. Helen was obviously agitated. It was apparent she did this routinely and did not like repeating what was to be done or where. They had a lot of unrealistic expectations so far as April was concerned. This was a poor start indeed.

April thanked her and headed out the door where the wind greeted her, and she scurried as fast as she could go into the barn. There she met Grant. He was Helen's husband. April quickly introduced herself. Grant was a big man, tall with a large frame and big hands. He asked April if she was familiar with parlor milking, and she looked and saw a round merry-go-round type of milking. "No, Sir. I have never milked with that type," she said.

"It takes a little getting used to, but in time you'll get the hang of it," he said. Grant took her to all the places where April was expected to work. The calf pens were small and were built in long rows. They were built out of wood connected to each other. They had no roof and did not need one as they were in a big, covered building. Each calf was expected to have a bottle or bucket of milk. There were charts on each pen to keep records. April thought this was a waste of time. All a person needed to know was if the calf was on a bucket or bottle and when they would turn six weeks old.

Next to the feed area, she was shown where the calf feed was, and the dry milk to be mixed for the calves. They preferred to buy dry calf milk rather than give the natural cow's milk to the calves. On D Farms it was not like this, the calf had mother's milk for four weeks then transitioned to dry milk.

Grant showed April where the feed mixer was and explained the amounts from day to afternoon to evening, there was a chart to follow. This would be her job three times a day. He also showed her where the hay was for the dairy cows. They were fed every day at each mixing. He expected the trough cleaned before every feeding. This would be her job three times a day. "Okay then, you got it?" Grant asked.

"Yes, Sir. I do," April answered. Now she knew she was here to make improvements, to make suggestions. But she realized Grant wanted things just as they were, they were looking for help and that was it.

For the next two days April worked the jobs she was asked to. She also swept the floors and cleaned the pens. She cleaned in places no one had in years without being asked.

Dinner was at six promptly each evening. If you were late, you ate alone or got it out of the refrigerator yourself. On one of those days April noticed a heifer having a calf. Her backside was bloody, and she was in obvious stress. She called on the barn phone to get help. When Helen answered the phone, she said Grant was eating, and would come out when he was done. Well, obviously she did not tell Grant. April waited and waited, and then she took two strings and made a loop on each end. Put them around each leg of the calf and using a manure fork for leverage she pulled the calf out to assist the heifer. This was an unusually big calf. The heifer would never have gotten it out on her own. When finished the heifer recognized her baby by smelling it.

April went to wash her arms to get the blood and manure off. She then headed into the house to find Grant asleep on his recliner in the kitchen. There was no food. She opened a cupboard to get an oatmeal packet and warmed it in the microwave. As she was sitting to eat out came Helen to give her hell. Helen went to take the bowl away from April saying this was not dinner, she knew to come in and eat.

April told her point blank. "Listen I just helped deliver a big heifer calf that the mother never would have made it without help. If you are so unhappy with me, call the company that sent me here, and have them send me somewhere else. I did my job," and she finished her oatmeal and headed back out to the barn. April did not like Helen's attitude. Helen never came out to the barn, not ever, so she lied to April.

Soon Grant was out at the barn and found April at the heifer that just had her calf. "It's a nice calf," he said as he went into the pen.

"Yes, she is," April said. Then she decided to open her mouth to get much off her chest. "Grant I am never going to adjust to a place that keeps time. Cows do not have calves in a time frame. I am not here as a hired hand. You do not pay me. I am here to make improvements and a detailed critique on your farm. Right now, it's not looking so good," April said.

Grant was stunned and said, "First of all we requested a boy. We have been in this program for five years. All the boys worked and did their jobs, no one ever complained. I do see that you keep the barn much cleaner and do more then we ask of you but give Helen a break she has the house to take care of."

April rolled her eyes, "Big flippin' deal," she said, "My Mom does more than she does." April was ready to walk. "Do not give me excuses. I am here to make improvements, it's part of my education, if you let me. If not, I walk," she said.

Then Grant confided in April that Helen had depression and mental health issues. That is why his son would not stay and moved to Lancaster County. "She tries but some days she can't do much more than dress herself, and her temper, oh wee, does she ever have a bad temper," he said.

"She needs medical attention," April said. "Depression is a disease, and it needs management. Have you sought help?" she asked.

"Well, no. You see we do not want anyone to know. We are a big name here in this area and we . . ."

April cut him off. "You are more concerned with your big name than Helen, then her wellbeing, her happiness?" She asked.

"No, but you need to understand if any of this was to leak out . . ."

April interrupted again "Then the doctor can be sued. Helen's medical condition is not for general knowledge, it's no one's business."

Grant hung his head. He knew she was right, but for his business he was afraid. "I doubt you'd get her to a doctor. She disagrees with me," he said.

"Well, that is just plain stupid," April said. "You make the appointment and I'll get her there" she said.

Two days later April needed a ride to the school she attended three days a week. April and Helen were headed into town to buy winter clothing but stopped at the doctor's office first. Helen believed the doctor was for April and when she went in at first, she was angry. Then she realized it was for her own good.

Two hours later after tests, Helen came out of the office with scripts to be filled at the pharmacy and had feelings of hope. "This might just help," she said. She seemed a bit happier. They did stop at the Tractor Supply store where April bought a good pair of coveralls, a pair of muck boots, wool socks, and a pair of lined winter gloves.

They also stopped at Cracker Barrel and picked up dinner. "This will be a nice change, a night off from cooking," Helen said. As the days and weeks went by April did go to church, she did have prayer at the table and at night. They all read scriptures and she was able to suggest improvements on the farm and in the home. April insisted Grant take Helen out once a week on a date night, either to dinner or for a walk or even just to the store. As time went by the general atmosphere in the home became calmer, more peaceful. By the time of the last month at this farm, April had made eighteen improvements, and in the home many more. Grant noticed the difference of the spirit in their home, it was good.

Grant admitted they never went to church, but April did. They did continue what April taught them. It changed their lives for the better.

School was so, so. April did not make many friends and it is difficult when you are new. You did not grow up there and you don't know most of the kids. They were a tight group. There were gangs, girl gangs, that April avoided at all cost. If they crossed her, April would stand her ground. They disgusted her. They were not aware of the talents within them. They resorted to their fists and poor language.

Helen continued her medication and went to therapy. Her depression came about when her son left their farm angrily. He had married and his wife did not like Helen. The therapist was working with the son, by talking on the telephone. He wanted to rekindle their relationship and create one with the daughter-in-law. The therapist could understand both sides. The daughter-in-law encountered a mean, cheerless woman who was not very nice to her. And their son, well he was in the middle. He loved his Mom inwardly, but the day after day arguing, and Mom sleeping all day, took a toll on the son. He never knew what he would encounter. Many things on the farm were not done, and it was a headache for him.

There were a lot of wrong assumptions, and the therapist was able to offer an olive branch and get communications going. This was to allow for an extended family to have closer ties and good communication. April was glad, there is no reason for anyone to suffer alone. There is help out there and all they need is someone to see or recognize their failings and get them the help they need. Nope it was not immediate, but over time, therapy and counseling helped tremendously.

April was so happy she had a small part in helping Grand and Helen. Depression affects everyone in the family, not just the one who has that disease. If untreated the entire family, friends, and loved ones all suffer. No one understands depression fully, that is why counseling is necessary.

It was a lesson April never forgot, she just felt that if there was help available a person should seek it out to have a better quality of life. and for those who live with, or work with, if they are unable to get help on their own. Hopefully they will have one good friend that cares enough to get involved and get them the help that they need.

Those three months flew by, and now it was time for April to move on to the next farm. Grant offered to take her to the airport. It was a chilly ride and about to get chillier.

Wisconsin Here She Comes!

THE FLIGHT WAS INTERESTING AND THOUGHT PROVOKING. They could not take off from the airport until the wings of the airplane were de-iced.

April thought, "What if the wings would ice up in flight? She felt confident the airline knew what they were doing. It was their job, not hers.

As they landed it was pretty much the same routine. April was to look for someone with a sign with her name. As April entered the terminal there was a person with the name "De Angelo" waiting for her inside. April grabbed her suitcase and approached him.

"Hi. I am April Di Angelo."

He looked at her and his face turned white as if her were in shock. "A girl, you're a girl?" He asked.

"Last time I looked I was, and I doubt anything has changed," April joked. It was obvious he was not happy, so here was another challenge. April followed him out to a small sedan that was quite beat up, rusty with dings. She threw her suitcase in the back seat that was full of soda and beer cans and food wrappers. April got in the front seat and buckled up, not one word was said.

April broke the tension. "So, what is your name and what do you do on the farm?"

"I am Nick, and I am manager of the milking. All hell is going to break out when they see you. I can tell you that much."

April didn't care if they were so stupid, it was their own fault. On her application it was clearly marked that she was a girl.

The rest of the ride home was in silence and soon they arrived at the lane of the farm. This was a big dairy farm, similar to some of the D Farms. Nick had to gun the engine of the small sedan to push through the snow drift that blocked the lane, he drove to the barn, and parked.

He got out, went to a door, and went in letting the door slam behind him. April followed. He was looking for someone as he went through the barn. There were several other kids in the barn, April waved to them, and they waved back. Soon they were in another part of the barn, a huge built-on section where there were dry cows waiting to calve. There was a large man looking at the pen and Nick called to him, "Alan can you take a few minutes to talk to us?"

Alan came over to where Nick and April were and Allen asked, "What is going on?"

Nick stood there and pointed to April, "Here is the competitions newest candidate to work here, did you know it was a girl?"

Alan spit chew onto the straw and said, "No I didn't know., Barbara was the one who filled out the application. I can talk to her about it, but there is nothing we can do about it right now."

April held her hand out to Alan and said, "Hi. I am April Di Angelo, pleased to meet you. I am not an it. I have a lot of experience in dairy farming and in general. I can pull my own weight. Don't treat me disrespectfully, and I will not be that way to you."

Alan said, "Let's go and see Barbara. Let's see what she has to say about all of this. Nick, you stay here with this cow and wait. She is having some trouble." Alan left with April close behind.

They went into the house where Barbara was sitting in the living room on a recliner. She had a turban cover on her head, still in her pajamas. Alan came to her and bent on his one knee to speak to his wife.

"Barbara, can you hear me?" he asked her.

She opened her eyes and patted his hand, "Yes, Dear. I can hear you. What do you want or need?"

"Honey on the application for the farm competition what did you mark, for a male or female?" Alan asked.

"I made a copy of the application. It's right there in the manila envelope on top of the desk. Can you get it?

Alan stood up and went to the desk. He pulled the manila envelope out and pulled out the contents riffling through to find the application. He pulled it out and scanning it with his eyes. He came to his wife with his finger marking a spot on the paper. "Right here you marked female, Honey. Why did you do that?"

She looked at her husband and said, "Alan I did not pay attention to male or female. I chose the one with the most qualifications that matched what we did and needed on our farm. Is there a problem?" she asked.

"Well, the boys don't like it," he said.

"Well, too bad," Barbara replied. Some of them are lazy. You said so yourself. Maybe she will shame them into working."

April just stood there, and Barbara said, "Come in here, Dear. I want to see you." April took of her boots and then came forward. "You look strong and agile. Are you able to do the things you put on the application?" she asked.

"Yes, Ma'am, and more. I am capable and willing, but I am not going to be picked on, bullied or disrespected," April said.

"Good for you. Nor should you be," Barbara said to her.

Barbara looked at Alan and said, "I guess that's that. Those boys need to be taken down a peg or two. You know it too, Alan. Let her do what she knows and watch out for her."

With that, Alan turned to go out. April slipped her boots back on and quickly following him. He went into the barn and walked every area with her. This was a very big barn. There were large loafing barns where the cows were turned out to eat after milking. Then in five hours they came back in to be milked again.

They milked three times a day at this farm. April knew of other farms that did this same practice, but she did not want this at any of the D Farms. People need a life, and she knew the cows made more milk production, but she felt they needed a rest too.

There was a separate area for heifers (cows that have not yet had a calf). They did not use a bull. At this farm they only used an inseminator. The inseminator man would come often in his pickup truck, bring out the canister of frozen bull semen, some who have been dead long ago. Their semen had been collected and frozen in tubes that would produce offspring from that long-deceased bull. When the canister was opened it was steaming from the dry ice. It was incredible to realize you could produce offspring from most any line or stock, amazing!

The real trick was to catch the cow or heifer in heat. That was a very small window of opportunity. Each cow comes into heat every 21 days for one day! That happens in one day! So, you had to be watchful.

If you were not always paying attention to the cows, you could miss the heat. D Farms utilized bulls, so they rarely ever missed a heat from a cow or heifer.

That afternoon April was milking in the merry-go-round milking parlor. This farm did not clean the cows, they burned off the dirt. April did not like the smell of burned hair.

After milking was lunch for the five who worked the afternoon milking. They came into the main house and had lunch of soup and a sandwich.

April noticed Barbara had not moved and she went into see her. "Have you eaten anything?" April asked her.

"No, Dear. I have not. I had a treatment yesterday and I feel sick today," Barbara said.

"Do you have cancer?" April asked.

"Yes, I do. I had a bilateral mastectomy two weeks ago and it has been difficult," Barbara told her.

"But you do know you should eat, or you will get run down. Your blood cells need good nutrition," April said to her.

"I know. I just am not hungry for soup or a sandwich," Barbara said.

"What are you hungry for?" April asked her.

"Oh, um, peanut butter and crackers," Barbara said.

April went into the kitchen and found peanut butter and some crackers and made about a dozen sandwiches for her. She also put some clear grape juice in a glass and took it to Barbara.

"Oh, thank you so much," Barbara said.

April returned to the kitchen and one of the boys said, "Brown nose."

April took off her hat, hit him lightly, and said, "What are you, a special kind of stupid? She is hungry and can't get up to get it herself."

The boy was shocked. No one ever talked back to him.

"I don't know what is wrong with you guys. Do you think the world revolves around you?" April said and she got up and went out. What incredibly stupid, selfish boys they are she thought to herself.

April ended up at the feed area where a guy named Tim was to show her what to do. She followed him to the feed room which was a huge area connected to silos for different kinds of grain. Tim was a tall, lanky fellow with a soft voice and easy manner. He was shy when he told her his name. He was Alan's and Barbara's son. April told him she was glad to meet him and began her lesson on mixing feed for the cattle at this new farm.

These two had an immediate friendship. They laughed at each other and in time played a lot of pranks on each other. Some of the boys were jealous. Some of them threatened April saying, "You better watch yourself, accidents can happen," or "You better keep to yourself or you're going to get into trouble," and they would hit their fists.

April told them, "Bring it on cupcake," but she did not follow her father's advice.

April told Barbara one evening, who in turn told Alan. "You talk to these boys. If they lay one hand on her, they will answer to the law." she said. Barbara took it one step further. She also spoke to her son Tim who had just returned from the United States Army after eight years.

Tim had come home two months earlier. He was in and out of the barn and he was the one who would hear about trouble first. "You watch out for her. She is spry, but the boys are all bigger than her."

"They will not touch her, or they will answer to me," Tim said. "She is a likable girl. She works hard, and never says no to any job. They are jealous."

Barbara added, "Not only jealous, but they also don't have girlfriends and they may try to use her wrongly."

Tim said, "No they will not. I will choke the life out of them if they do anything like that."

Nothing was said and April was busy, school was strict and demanding. There was much for her to read on her own. On the farm she did find the slurry tank needed some improvements she also had the clean out chains upgraded and oiled. Alan was glad the amount of money he paid for those improvements saved him thousands of dollars later.

April's schedule was out early to school for a half day. Then she came home to run the skid steer to clean the loafing barn after the cows went in to be milked. It kept them cleaner when they lay down and kept them from slipping and falling. April told Grant that the chopped corn stalks were just fine and worked very well.

Then April got the milk washers ready for when the workers finished milking. All they had to do was hang up the milk machines and the rest was done for them. April then gave the cows hay every day with the help of a turn out, and she mixed feed for the evening and had lunch. After lunch it was her turn to help milk. In the evening after milking, April filled the feed bunks, took care of the calves, and each evening she made a general round to make sure everything was in its place, swept up, and clean.

On one of those rounds in the evening four of the boys thought they'd catch her off guard. There had been trouble brewing for a while now. Those boys did not like April being chummy with Barbara and that was a no brainer. Barbara was a woman as was April. April often warmed broth for Barbara, or soaked her feet, or did small errands for her.

As April walked through the loafing barn to an alley way, they stood blocking her from going forward. She stayed back to see what they would do. "Where do you think you are going little snitch." One of the boys said to her.

"Me? I am no snitch. You are stupid and lazy and can't do your own work half of the time. I cover your rear ends" she hissed.

"How about if we covered your rear end for a change," and they lunged towards her.

April was quicker and she began to run. She could leap, climb, and pull herself up and over. They could not anticipate her moves. All of this caused some calamity in the barn and the cows began to moo. Since at night cows are usually quiet, Tim heard the cows and thought something might be wrong.

Tim got up, put on his jacket, boots, and cap, and headed out to the barn. When he got there the cows had stopped mooing. But he heard some boys yelling to go this way or that way. Tim thought one of the calves had gotten out. They can be difficult to put back in a pen. Tim walked to that area of the barn where he heard their voices. Upon entering he realized what was going on. He climbed the ladder to walk the beams and was able to keep up with them easily.

April was cunning and fast, but with four boys going in different directions they would mostly likely catch her when she got to the far end.

Tim wanted them to catch her so he would know who to punish.

They did catch her, and they slapped her. She spit in their face. They pulled her hair, and she stomped on their instep or kneed their private part leaving them on their knees wincing in pain. But there were four. And four on one is no fair fight.

April handled two of them, then the biggest boy stepped up taking off his belt. He attempted to strike her when Tim who had come down without them noticing, grabbed the arm of the boy who held the belt.

"You like to play with a belt?" and he hit the boy over and over.

All four of them began to beg to let them go, some began to cry.

"What's the matter? You wanted to play, now let's play," Tim said.

Tim was tough. Never would April have guessed Tim was so strong and fierce. He was angry as he dealt the blows. He told the boys about having respect for women. If he ever so much as heard a peep from April about them acting against her, he would kill them. By the look on Tim's face the boys never doubted him.

Nothing was said to anyone. Only those six knew what had happened. The boys did come to work with black and blue eyes, or bruises on their arms, hands, and legs. One had his eye swollen shut, another limped when he walked. But they never said one word about this, even when Alan asked. They said they had quarreled with one another.

"Must have been some quarrel," Alan said.

Later two boys leaked that they were going to go after April. When of the boys who had been involved with Tim cautioned them not to. "If Tim catches you, or even hears about it, he will kill you. And believe me, he would."

So, life was good. April was able to do her jobs, but her biggest concern was Barbara. Barbara was embarrassed to go out with the loss of her hair. So, April spoke with Alan. She heard of a place nearby that would give Barbara a wig. So, Alan gave April a day off and she and Barbara had a ball together. They laughed, had lunch, and got Barbara a nice practical wig. They even bargained for the Styrofoam stand to put the wing onto. From that time forward if Barbara had to go somewhere, the wig went with her.

A few days later something had gone very wrong. Barbara was found at breakfast time unconscious on the living from floor by one of the workers who went in for breakfast. Alan was away, purchasing cows and Tim was on the farm working separating heifers when someone told him. When he got into the house, April was with Barbara supporting her head, talking to her.

"We have to get her to the hospital," April said to Tim.

"I doubt we'd get far. This snow keeps coming." He put a call in for an ambulance, but no one answered the phone.

April asked him, "Who owns that Cessna that I saw in one of the hangers?"

"That belongs to one of my Dad's friends. He is an avid pilot and keeps his airplane stored here," Tim said.

"That is out ticket out," April said. "Let's get some help moving her out. I hope you know what direction the hospital is in. We are going, now!" April said.

"April, I don't know how to fly, so we are not taking that plane anywhere," Tim said.

"Well, I do know how to fly, and we are leaving in ten minutes or less," April replied. "So, let's get some help and get her loaded," and they did.

Carefully they put her on the green Gaiter. Barbara was all covered up to keep warm and drove her to the airplane hangar. There they inched her little by little up the steps all the while talking to her. Barbara was somewhat aware of what was going one. The Gaiter pulled the Cessna out onto the ground and April started it up, its engine whirring. She knew the field was their airstrip, there was no other. April headed that way, bouncing on the bumps in the field.

Once in a clear open space they radioed the tower, and they gave her coordinates to where she was heading. April explained she had an emergency case of an unconscious patient would need an ambulance as soon as she could reach the hospital. The radio dispatcher knew the family well, and she knew of Barbara's condition. Her Mother also had chemo when Barbara was in for hers. This town was not that big. She hoped the pilot knew what she was doing, the wind speeds were strong, and another storm was impending.

April looked at Tim and said, "Before we go anywhere, I am saying a prayer." April bowed her head and began to pray for a safe journey, no accident or mechanical error. This was to save a wife, a mother, and a friend. "Please, please watch over us and keep us all in your care," she said. And with the "Amen" she pushed the throttle forward and began their fast pace down the runway to lift off. Once in the air April checked the instruments and kept on the coordinates given to her. Tim was amazed at her skill. She was not nervous. It was obvious April knew what to do.

April radioed to the tower when she was two miles from her landing destination. She wanted to make sure she had a place to land near the hospital. The radio tower assured her that there was, and if the storm blocked her views to let them know, they would talk her in.

On they went, April felt the Cessna being bucked to and fro, and she wrestled with the steering to stabilize the little airplane. She kept praying all the while she was at the helm.

The tower contacted her saying she was spotted one half mile from the hospital, to bring the plane in a little lower and keep to the right. There was an old corn field to the right of the hospital and a dirt road lightly covered with snow, if she had visibility to try and land on it. The little plane bucked and coughed but kept on the coordinates she had.

Then she saw the corn field mixed in with the snow squall that had settled in. She wanted to wipe the window clear, but the snow was in the wind, and she could not see very well.

"Father, I cannot see. I need to see to land, or we will all be hurt or killed. Father, please help us," she prayed out loud. And just like that, in seconds, as if a hand wiped a slate clean. The wind blew the snow from her views, away from the plane and surrounding area, allowing her to see the cornfield and the little dirt road.

April made sure the wheels were down and she began to pull the handles forward and felt the plane buck. Slowly they came down, then a big bump when the wheels hit the road and a couple of other bumps. April cut the power all together and then they were down, safe.

No sooner than they landed, and an ambulance came blazing towards them. The ambulance crew had Barbara off the plane and in the ambulance in precision work. Tim went with his Mother and April sat there as if in a daze. She bowed her head to pray. "Thank you, Father in heaven, for your much needed help. I could not have done this without you. I am so grateful, so humbled, and know that I endeavor to serve you as I serve others. May this glory be for you. I pray in Jesus' Holy name. Amen."

April got out of the airplane and was met by a blast of snow and wind. It almost buckled her. She walked as best as she could down the dirt road when a pickup truck tooted and came towards her. "Hey, I am from the tower and wanted to know if you needed a lift."

"I sure do." April said climbing in his truck. She turned to shake his hand.

"I am Jake and I own that Cessna you just flew."

"I sure hope it's all right. I mean Barbara was unconscious and we had to get her here. No ambulance could get out or make it to the farm."

Jake said "Absolutely. I understand. I have been friends with Alan and this family for over twenty years. I would have done the very same thing. What confounds me is I never fueled that Cessna when I put it in the hanger last fall. At most it may have had a half quart of fuel, and in this wind, I don't know how you got it here."

Jake drove his pickup right to the Cessna and unscrewed the fuel cap. He banged on the side and put his fingers inside the fuel lodge. He came back and said, "You must have angels on your side, girl, because that fuel lodge is empty, pure bone dry."

April did not say a word, inside her heart was bursting full of love for God. She wiped her tears from her eyes. She said a silent prayer of gratitude to a kind loving Father in heaven who never left her. He always helped her in time of need. How would she ever repay him, it was impossible. April realized long ago every breath she took in she was further in debt.

He had given his only son to die on the cross for her, even in her rebellious nature. He loved her, just as he loved all his children on earth. Those that have lived and who had died, those who are living and those who have not yet been born. What a wonderful thing this to know. To feel it and know it is real. To have miracles happen. There is no such thing as coincidence, everything happens for a reason.

It was now December and April was looking forward to her call to home.

It never seemed so sweet to call home before as it was now. She did not care about Christmas, a tree, or gifts, she wanted to hear her Mom's and Dad's voices and receive messages of what was happening in her hometown.

She wondered if they had heard from Hugh. Gosh it seemed like so long ago since she was home, and it was only five months. She had seven more months to go. It was not like she had nothing to do, she was busy and that was good. Just entertaining the thoughts of home make her homesick. She did the only thing she knew to do. She prayed and threw herself into work and keeping tabs on Barbara.

Yes, Christmas was a great year that year for the Smiths, they all had much to be grateful for, their Mother was alive and doing better, yes it was all good.

At their age Christmas was not so much about gifts but about health, happiness, and wellbeing. There is no amount of money to make any of those things happen. They never said much to April, they knew better. April was not one to seek praise, she said she had to get Barbara out and she did. They were so grateful April had the knowledge and experience to get Barbara to the hospital. If not, Barbara would have surely died, and December would always have a much darker feeling to it.

There was a tree, but the challenge was for the workers to decorate it with things from their past, maybe from their home, what they remembered. It had a myriad of things on the tree and that was fine. They had a nice, cooked meal, a warm place to stay, good company.

The attitude of the boys changed. They not only gave respect, but they changed to know they deserved respect. At first April was made fun of for praying at mealtime and at night. But since that hospital flight, if she missed or did not, they reminded her to. April encouraged them to pray, and some said they did not know how to. April offered to teach them. She showed them in the bible what the Savior said as an example, and they did. Some said it helped them a lot, they felt at peace in their life. Others said it opened their eyes to a lot more in life.

And now it was Aprils turn to call home. She could hardly wait. She wanted privacy of course and that was difficult in a house with sixteen others. April asked Barbara if she was allowed to take the phone into the basement to talk to her parents. Barba said "Of course, it was fine."

April dialed the number, and the phone rang twice when she heard her Mother say "Hello."

April almost broke down and cried and said, "Hello, Mom. Merry Christmas," and then she heard screaming.

"Gordon. Gordon, come here. It's our daughter." Tears fell down April's cheeks. Oh, how she missed her family, and she could not help but smile.

"Hello, Sweetie, how are you? This is Dad," and April cried silently.

"Hello, Dad. Merry Christmas. I am fine, going to school three days a week. I work here on this farm. It's very cold here, but all is good," she said.

She knew her parents were on two telephones in different areas. If they got too close to one another the phones would squeal.

Mom was the chatterbox, and Dad usually listened. They talked about fifteen minutes about town, and how everyone was. That is when Dad asked, "Are you playing your guitar for Christmas?" April laughed, cried, and said, "I didn't think about it, Dad. I guess I could," and she cried some more silently. April was glad she was on the telephone, and they could not see her crying. They talked for about another hour about people she knew. She asked about Nora and Lena. And they were doing really well. They had come over for the Thanksgiving meal and it was a nice dinner. April was glad.

April asked about Manny and Contessa, Gordon laughed and told her what Manny said about the last race. They were famous now too! He told her the animals were growing and there was a new girl working with the ponies. She was a good rider, but they had to remind her to be patient with the little kids. "She is not like you were, Sweetie."

"Have you heard from Hugh" April asked.

"No, but you know he is busy, and boys do not write. You know that," Mom said.

As the time slipped away it was Mom who said, "Sweetie, we love you so much, but we know that you must go soon, and rest for tomorrow. This time will pass, and you will be home before you know it. Then we will talk and talk and talk. Miranda made April cry and laugh at the same time. April could hear her Mother's voice change and April knew she was crying too.

April said, "Mom wait. I want to tell you and Dad something I realized being out here. I want you both to know I love you so much. I took a lot for granted at home. I realize how much you did and still do for me. I could not have picked better parents. I am so grateful. This has been a good experience for me, but too often I have been missing you both and home. My mind wanders on jobs here, and there I am at home. I can almost smell Mom's cooking, Ruby dancing around me, Dad reading the newspaper or going out for ice-cream together. Those simple things mean the most to me. Just to know you were there was a big safety net for me, and I thank you." There was silence on the other end. "Hello, are you both still there?" April asked.

"Yes, we are. We are still here," they said in strained voices. "Okay now, we better hang up now. You need your rest and so does your Daddy. Goodbye for now, take care and be safe," they both said in unison. And then they were gone. April dried her eyes and looked at the clock it was 7:00 p.m.

April came out of the cellarway and hung up the phone. She looked at Barbara and said, "I'll be right back. April came downstairs with her guitar and asked if it was all right if they wanted to hear her play Christmas songs. They all did. So, she began with "The First Noel", then "Silent Night", and other favorites. They all sang along. Barbara loved it, praising her. "Oh, this is so lovely isn't it Alan," and Alan agreed.

For almost an hour she played and then she decided it was time to go to bed. She said, "Good night," and headed up to her room to rest, ponder, and sleep. On her mind was her home, the little things she missed: her bed, Ruby, Nora and Lena's laughter, making dinner with Mom, and hearing her sing in Spanish. These were her thoughts as she slipped into sleep.

Oh, Tim

SHE STILL HAD JANUARY TO MARCH IN WISCONSIN, AND everything was looking up. School was good, not nearly as much reading as the last round. Her grades were all A's and B's. April continued to do all that she was asked of and she developed a close relationship with Barbara. Alan and Tim were very grateful for her help. In time Tim became fond of April, spending as much time in the house with her as he could. This came under the scrutiny of Barbara. "Now Tim, she is leaving in March!" Tim would answer his Mother, "Yeah, I know."

"But, Mom, she is such a nice girl, and our age difference is not that much. You and Dad have nine years difference. April and I have seven," he said. Barbara was concerned they knew so little about April's home life. The program was designed this way, no favorites. One day when April had made dinner for the crew, working in the kitchen, Barbara asked her to come into the living room and talk with her.

"April, do you have a boyfriend at home?" she asked.

"Yes, I do have someone, but he is not a home, he is in the military. When I graduate, we will make our plans," April said. She showed her the ring on a silver necklace around her neck. Barbara reiterated this information to her husband and son.

"So please, Tim, let her alone. She already has someone she cares for and someone who loves her."

Tim was disappointed but not giving up. April was here and her intended was far, far away. He made opportunities to help her when he could. On occasions the group would go to the movies or go out and get a bite to eat. Tim never missed the chance to sit by her, buy her popcorn or soda. April was not aware of Tim's feelings. She thought he was just a nice guy to everyone. Tim tried to be reserved, keep his feelings in check, but April frustrated him. One evening as they drove home together, just the two of them from a grocery pick up he out right asked her.

April, I don't want to frighten you, but you do know I care for you a lot. I would like you to know that I wish you would stay here with us. I would love to date you and get to know you much better. There is a seven-year age difference between us, but I enjoy your company. You are funny and full of antics. I would love to settle down with you and have a family of our own. Dad said long ago I could have a house on the other end of our farm, and I can see you as a Mother with five or nine kids running around the farm." Then he laughed.

April sat there stunned! She quickly gathered her wits and answered him as tactfully as she could.

"Tim I am flattered, but I have no intention on cheating on my boyfriend. I am not like that. I made a commitment with him before I left, and I will not break it. Our age difference is something you should consider. I am sure there are woman here in your town who would love to meet and marry you. Wisconsin is not home to me. I have parents that I am very close to back in California and I don't see me leaving them any more than you would leave yours and the farm here."

Tim did not expect his, because he did not know her or anything about her. He began to back pedal, "I did not mean it like that. I would love to meet your parents and get to know you better. I think in time you would see that we would make a great couple."

"Look Tim," she said. "I like you. We get alone well, but we would not make a good couple. You see I believe in God. I go to church every Sunday. Not because I am good or perfect, but because I am a sinner and I need help. You do not go to church at all. You are comfortable staying at home, shopping, or working. Over time, I would follow you, not go to church and die inside." April said.

Tim rubbed his chin as he often did when he was perplexed. "I would go to church with you, I'd do anything you asked me to," he said to her.

"Yes, I know you would, but I want to be with a man who knows me well enough that I don't have to ask," she said.

The remainder of the ride home was silent other than the radio playing a country song. Neither one of them was angry nor upset. To April this was unexpected, it came out of nowhere. She wanted no part of this and due to this she began to avoid Tim at every turn. He on the other hand tried to find her and be with her when she was working on the farm, sitting at the table, or in the living room on a couch.

Barbara noticed something was wrong one day after April was cleaning in the house. Barbara spoke to her again. April got it off her chest. She explained what Tim had said to her and she flat out was not interested. April was not angry, she did not want to hurt Tim's feelings, but that is how she felt. Barbara understood and between her and Alan they spoke with Tim to let April alone.

"Already she was shirking jobs because she knew you would be there," Alan said. "She has come to me several times, Tim, wanting to do her job, but she would not go to do it knowing you would be there. This has got to stop."

Tim was disappointed, hurt, and he scowled. He felt this was such a great idea. Heck, April already liked his Mother and Dad. He went out and walked around the farm to cool off. His Dad was worried about him. Tim did not fall easily for girls. He just never did. So, Alan thought it was time for Tim to go out with some of the local boys dancing or do whatever they do to meet girls his age.

Meanwhile back in California, Miranda and Gordon were having Family Home Evening on Monday night when they both felt strongly that something was not right. They felt so strongly they wanted to call the Smith farm in Wisconsin, and they did.

"Hello," a deep voice was on the other end of the telephone. "Hello. This is Mr. Di Angelo. I would like to speak to Alan or Barbara please."

"This is Alan. How may I help you?"

"Well, Sir, my wife and I are concerned for our daughter. We get the impression or feeling that something is not quite right, it is unsettling, and we felt we should call. Is our daughter April all right and doing well?" Gordon asked.

"She is. She is a great asset to our farm. In the beginning we were disappointed she was not a he. We did not want any problems since most of our workers are boys, and then a girl showed up.

We straightened things out pretty much and since that time she has been such a blessing to our home. My wife had a very bad episode in the middle of December and if your daughter had not been here, I shudder to think what might have happened. She is not one much for praise though, so we did not make a big fuss over her. But the way she took over the care of my wife, keeping the house clean, and making good nutritious meals for all of us. She goes to school, works on the farm, and has made several improvements that have been extremely helpful. To be truthful we will be sorry to see her go."

Gordon felt better, but he asked, "Do not tell our daughter we called. Keep this conversation between us. Just watch out for her. We have trusted that each home would look out for her, just as you would for your own child. That is all we ask." They spoke a little longer and then hung up.

Alan knew April did not call home. She was obedient to the farm rules. How her parents got an inkling as to the turmoil that was going on here, he did not know. But he did know he owed her parents this much, to keep her safe and sound. Alan strode out to the barn and found his son. He looked at him, they were face to face and then he reached out for him and embraced his son in a bear hug for several minutes. It was something neither of them had done since Tim was a little boy.

"Son, I love you. I am so proud of your service in the military, and it's so great to have you home safe on our farm. You cannot keep your mind on this girl. She does not belong here. That has been made clear to me and you must understand this. Get her out of your mind and system. She has a home with parents that have intuition of her wellbeing. I cannot, I will not let their daughter be in any trouble, turmoil, or otherwise. No more than I would want you to go through that somewhere else, like she is. Do you understand me?" he asked his son. Tearfully, emotionally torn, Tim agreed, this had to stop. He knew April did not want him.

So that Saturday as everyone gathered around the television in the living room to watch the newest released movie on video. Tim was driving into town to a restaurant that also had line dancing in the back of their eatery, all on hard wood floors. It felt like a punishment, like pulling teeth. He would much rather have been in that living room with his head on a pillow beside April.

He promised his Dad, and he would follow through. There were a lot of women at the line dance. Most had a guy but there were a lot of single women too. Some came up to Tim and he did not like that, so he shied away. He had danced in the line dance and winked to a girl. In no time her guy was pushing him to the sidelines. Tim explained he did not mean it, and it turned out peaceful, but Tim had enough of this. He went to the local downtown diner and got something to munch on. No one there was single, except for the waitresses, and he knew all of them pretty well. Tim paid his bill and left for home.

As he walked into his home it was dark, there was an eerie light coming from the Television room and he saw bodies everywhere, on the couch, on the recliners, on the floor. There was April leaning her back against the couch as she sat on the floor. She liked a blanket to hide under when the movie was scary. He would have liked nothing better than to grab a pillow and sit beside her, but he knew better.

Tim headed upstairs to go to bed.

Barbara was improving daily. April had Alan pick up a walker and in time Barbara was walking all around the downstairs of the house. Often, she would sit on a stool and watch April make dinner, sometimes she helped. So slowly Barbara was coming back. Alan was grateful he had so much to do outside. He did help with Barbara when he could but most of her care fell to April. Alan did not know what he was going to do when April moved on to the next farm in March.

That too was on April mind a lot. She checked with agencies, made calls to volunteer lists. But for now, in the winter, not one wanted to travel more than they had to. April pushed for someone to make a commitment for spring. Four women said they would call her in early March, and April told them if they did not call her, she would call them. And she meant it.

March rolled around so fast they all had been busy during February with their regular work, tearing down equipment, replacing parts, painting what needed a coat of paint, and greasing parts. It was important to be ready for spring planting season now. Before long spring would be here and they would not be ready.

School finals were looming, and Aril had to study but the crazy part was she would study here but test out at her next place as testing was in April or May and she would not be here. She would move on to another farm.

As she studied, she had Barbara do rounds in the house. Barbara was doing much better. She could walk on her own if she held on to furniture, sometimes she could make two steps without holding one, but for now, that was her maximum.

The best news was Tim had a girlfriend. Her name was Jenna. And April liked her a lot. She was funny and liked Barbara, and she was a spark for this family. Barbara liked Jenna and encouraged Tim to hug her or "give her a kiss, Tim." April thought it would be best to let thing happen on their own, not push them. April was too busy studying, reading, and testing herself. She was helping

Barbara one hour in the mornings and one hour in the evenings. And she kept up with all her barn jobs, mixing feed, moving hay, and taking care of the calves. To put it lightly, April was busy.

March came around, April had penciled in her notebook to make calls to the volunteer list, so she did. She was relentless to find someone to help with Barbara. When planting season came Barbara would be alone. One woman came out, her name was Ona. Ona had taken care of an elderly man until he passed away in early October. She wanted to take some time off for herself. She was not a fan of driving in the snow either. When she drove out, she was happy to see it was a farm. She had grown up on her grandfather's farm when she was a little girl. Ona came, knocked on the door, and never left. When April came home, she found Ona in the parlor room with Barbara having tea, they became fast friends. Ona said to April, "I had her walk around the kitchen three times and back."

As it turned out, Ona rented a fully furnished, small apartment in town. But his was too far for her to travel back and forth, so, Barbara said Ona could live with them. Can you guess whose room Ona was to use? You guessed it, April's.

April didn't mind, not really. She slept on the sofa in the parlor room. She was leaving in three weeks, and it was best for Barbara to have someone here she trusted and felt safe with. Someone who encouraged her to do more, that was Ona!

Later, after April had left, she penned a letter to Barbara who did write back. Barbara wrote in her letter she and Ona walked around the entire farm every day. She and Ona were able to give the calves bottles of milk and she hoped to be able to do more by fall. It made April's heart happy to receive this news.

The eighth of March Tim broke up with Jenna and had the saddest eyes ever.

Barbara and Ona had a small going away cake made for April one evening and they all said nice things to April. April felt humbled. Tim did not come for supper that evening and avoided the little get together.

The boys told funny stories about April. Alan gave a small but very heart felt speech about her. Alan said April was the best guy that came and worked on his farm. It was meant in fun, but his eyes told April what his lips could not. It was hard to see Alan tear up. Barbara came to his rescue, she patted his hand and said, "It's all right."

That night April went out again to do her rounds and Tim found her. "Hey, may I talk to you for a minute or two? He asked her. They stepped into the birthing room where it was warm and quiet. "Look, I just wanted to add to what may already have been said. I think you're great. You are a good sport and a darn hard worker. I don't want to make you mad at me, but I can't help myself. If it doesn't work out with your boyfriend, keep me in mind. I am here. I would follow you to the end of the earth. I love my parents, but I know that when I find someone to love and spend my life with, my life is with her, no matter where that may be. So that said . . ." and he leaned forward and kissed her on her forehead. "I wish you the best that life has to offer, stay well, be safe, and I hope you never forget us here in Wisconsin. It's cold here but we have warm hearts, and mine beats for you."

April felt sorry for Tim, there were times she wanted to hit him, but she just sighed, she shook her head and kept on with her jobs. As April walked away waving her arms over her head, as in "whatever" she admired his tenacity, but her mind was firm, she would never ever cheat on Hugh.

Back home Miranda and Gordon were marking off their calendar each day to the day circled in red when their daughter was expected home in September. That was going to be a happy day for them and many of April's friends. They planned to have a fall picnic on their farm by the pond. They already spoke to Ava, her parents owned the company, Action Party Rental.

April walked toward the terminal at the airport. She hugged Alan before she left. Her heart was happy she had left on good terms with everyone. Wisconsin had been a good place now she was looking forward to spring in Ohio.

Oh Ohio

While flying above Ohio April could tell they were still having cold weather because she saw smoke rising from the chimneys. She was not too concerned, she still had warm clothing with her. However, she would love to wear shorts and short sleeved clothes again.

As the flight continued, April took out a pen and wrote a letter to her parents. Not a long letter as this flight was going to be much shorter than the previous two flights. All April knew was that she would be on another farm. There were no other details whatsoever.

Touch down in Ohio was sooner than April could finish her letter. She quickly put the letter in her bag and waited to hear the captain's orders. She unfastened her seat belt and waited. Before too long the lights were green and the stewardess was on the mic saying they could depart from the airplane. This was not a large plane. It was a small commuter. The seats were very close together. There were three in a row, and there were seats on both sides. The word "cramped" came to April's mind!

As she walked to get her baggage, she looked around for someone with a sign containing her name. She wished they would be more careful to spell her name right. De Angelo is similar to Di Angelo, but she wanted it right. She knew beyond a doubt that her name was spelled correctly when her application was sent in. Perhaps someone "typed" her name wrong, since it happens a lot. Truthfully it was not a big deal, but she just wished someone would get it right. So far two had it wrong.

April stood there waiting, and before long she saw a man in full uniform complete with a cap. Not a hat, but a cap like what a service man would wear. He was in a dark suit with brass buttons. "Holy smokes!" April thought to herself. What did I get myself into this time?

She walked up to the man and introduced herself. The man was very quick to take her suitcase, but no handshake. He was wearing white gloves and did not say much. April got in the car, it was a limousine - black and very shiny. April sat in the back, and it was a slippery seat. Again she thought, "Oh dear, please don't send me to a place that plants fancy flowers. I will give it my best, but I know I am not as good as my Mom is.

The driver was British, at least that's what April thought. He did not say "Ma'am", he said "Mum".

"Well, it is what it is," April said to herself.

They drove along at a slow speed, and she was able to take in the sights. Ohio is fairly flat. There were railed fences that housed either cattle or horses. The greenery was delightful, what a relief after coming from Wisconsin. The air was chilly, it was the month of April. She decided to clear her mind. There is no sense trying to figure anything out when you don't know anything.

They arrived at their destination and April wanted to whistle. It was a castle of sorts. Now what type of farm is this, she wondered. She got out at an overhang of the house. As she stepped out, she saw mosaic tiling on the floor and the pillars were very tall holding up the terra cotta roof of the carport. The house itself was truly a castle with turrets. The windows in them were very small. April could not get over that here in Ohio was a modern-day castle.

April went to the door, and she was greeted by a young girl dressed in servant's clothes, complete with a cap, apron, and wooden shoes. April stood awhile, then was going to set down her suitcase and guitar, but the young girl took them from her to some place in the house.

Before too long a man came into the kitchen in his wheelchair. He looked quite young as well. He had a beard and scruffy mustache. He was a bit overweight, but April assumed it must be because he was disabled and in a wheelchair. He said to April "Welcome to Countryside Manor."

April thanked him and asked him if he knew where the girl took her suitcase. "Oh, no worries. Ann put them in your bedroom upstairs, as I am not able."

April asked him what was it he wanted her to do there on the farm. They talked for a while. At first, she could barely believe what she heard, but had to be true. This man could not make up what he was telling her. He said he needed help to reconfigure his horse barn and a few other things.

That is when April said, "Do you ride?"

"Oh, yes. Yes, I do, with some help," he said. "My father is an English Lord. Well, he was, and he finances everything on this manor. I raise horses for equitation for English show riding and they are very fine, well-bred horses."

April was astounded! She saw the man and his condition and wondered if he did the work or did the others here do it all.

"We will go out to the stables in a little while. It will be lunch time soon and we can have a nice lunch," he said to April. He wheeled his motorized chair into a very large sitting room.

He looked at April and said, "Go ahead and make yourself comfortable."

April sat down and looked around when he started the conversation. He began to talk about some of the changes he wanted. Then April said, "Excuse me. I must have missed your name."

"I apologize. We don't get many visitors or company here and I forget. For that I am sorry. My name is Earl Rodney Stewart, but please do call me Rodney. To let you know a little about myself, I was born in England as were all my ancestors. My father is the one who is a stickler and still calls me Earl Rodney." And he laughed.

Just then a small bell tinkled and in came lunch which seemed like a feast to April. There was vegetable soup, homemade biscuits, slabs of ham, and meat with cranberries around the side of the plate. There was also a plate of all different varieties of cheese along with mustards. Yes, mustards of all types as well. The beverages included buttermilk, whole milk, and tea. The sugar cubes were in a jar with tongs at the top. They also brought out a cart with sweet biscuits and cookies of all different kinds.

Rodney maneuvered his wheelchair out of this room into a long hallway. At the end he turned right into the dining room. This room was filled with light. The windows extended from the top of the frame to the very bottom. There were pots filled with ferns around the room and ornate furniture. This was not a farm, it was an estate. From this room you could see the vast property and creeks, it truly was a beautiful place.

Rodney moved his motorized chair to the head of the table, there was no chair there. April waited to be seated. "You may as well sit down, there is no one else," he said.

April did. She put her linen napkin on her lap and waited. April was so glad Nora and Lena had taught her the manners of a lady!

Just then Rodney lifted a bell, and an older woman came in. She recited what was on the table and asked if anything else would be needed. Then she excused herself, and a man came in to assist Rodney.

April was confused did he like being waited on, but could manage the horses? Humm. This conversation would come before too long.

As she ladled some soup into the bowl in front of her along with a biscuit, April began the conversation. "How long have you lived here?"

He answered her, "I was born here, right here in this very house."

"Are your parents still alive? And why don't they live here with you?"

"I was born in this condition and my Mother was not pleased. From that time forward I had a Nanny. Unfortunately, she passed away when I as a baby. My father wanted me to grow up, be independent. He felt if I was on my own, I would do much better than being coddled."

April then asked him, "Do you go away from here from time to time?"

"Not typically. The servants pick up my groceries, cook, and clean for me. Of course I do pay them, and truthfully, I don't like going out that much. I don't like the stares or comments," he said.

April understood, but part of her felt he was missing out on much in life. Granted, he could not walk, but many people can't, and they go out and live their lives.

After lunch, they left the dining room and headed outdoors. Not before Charles, the man who drove April here, put a Jacket and hat on Rodney. Then he handed the man gloves, and covered him with a wool blanket, securing it with pins so the blanket would not fall off.

They were heading to a large stone barn. The wind was nasty, and it blew the hat off the man. April caught his hat in the air and gave it to him. He smiled at her. As they reached the barn the man opened the large doors, and they went inside.

April was impressed, there was not one blade of hay or straw on the floor, the isles were swept clean and dry. The horses were finely bred. Their stalls were unlike anything April had ever seen before. They had brick walls and at one area near the front the brick was shorter and in a "U" shape. She guessed it was to allow the visitors to see and pet them easier.

This was an amazing barn, but April bet this was an England style, and she asked Rodney. "Is this the type of barns they have in England? I have never seen one like this before."

"Oh, yes, it is," he said. "You see this was my father's vision, not mine." And he seemed to hang his head.

April said, "They are different but also beautiful."

"Do you really mean that?" Rodney asked.

"Of course I do. Look Rodney, I know we don't know one another at all, but I want you to know I don't lie and, I am a horse nut too. I have a stable of racing horses myself."

The Girl in the Mirror Book 4

"Then what are you doing on a farm competition?" He asked her.

April kind of dug her toe as she usually did when she felt uncomfortable. "Well, this was my idea and my parents supported me. I wanted to contribute to my Dad's business, and if I win, it will give me my education and help him in his business." April hated to say it like that, but in the farm competition you were never to reveal much about yourself.

April was drawn to a thoroughbred that was black as oil. She walked up to the mare and Rodney cautioned her that mare liked to bite. April stood there looking at the mare, and the mare at her. As they stood there, April slowly reached her hand to the mare's forehead. Speaking so quietly and softly the mare closed her eyes and allowed April to scratch and pet her head. April reached a bit further and touched her forelock and then her neck. The mare stood there enjoying the gentle touch of this girl.

Rodney was watching all of this and said nothing. He was amazed since this mare was usually so prudish and rude. Not many could work with her. April looked at him as she stepped away and said, "She's a sweetheart." The mare's head was going up and down wanting more attention from April.

Already Rodney was maneuvering his wheelchair to show April the other horses. They finished their tour and went back into the house. April asked Rodney if he had a list of chores for her.

"Well," he said. "The horses will need to be fed, and I will come out with you. I wanted to change the barn a bit. You know, make it bigger. I also wanted to make sure the fences in the pasture were good, no weeds, and no missing wire – that sort of thing."

April thought to herself this must be a blessing from God in Heaven above. She knew she would not only enjoy this third farm, but she was going to love it. Rodney handed her a typed list.

The next morning, early before the sun was up, April was outside working on the fences. She had a bucket of staples, a hammer, double rounds of wire, a crowbar, and insulators. Some of the insulators were cracked and April used the crowbar to remove the nail. Then she picked up a new insulator and a nail, and put it in its place, reattaching the wire. The fence on the roadside was not too bad, but in the woods, however, it was nasty.

The bugs were flying around her head, so she stopped working. When she was in the shed earlier, she noticed an old bee-keeper's head covering. She took that and headed back to the wooded area. April took limbs out of the creek and moved stones that were quite heavy. She repaired all the wires in the woods and up through the hillside. By nightfall she was finished, both with the work and herself. She was that tired.

At the house Ann greeted her and April asked if she could have a towel or a bed sheet. She would not wear her clothing inside the house. Ann came back in a few minutes with a huge towel. April undressed down to her underwear and went upstairs for a bath.

Ann apologized profusely saying she would have drawn a bath for April.

April hugged her and said it was fine. She soaked in the tub. She had really overworked her muscles, and that hot water felt good. She would drain some water out then add more hot water for over an hour. Finally, she got up, dried herself off, and wondered where her clothing was.

When she opened the door, there on a nearby chair was April's suitcase. "Oh, that An. She sure is on the ball." April got dressed in a plain pullover blue dress that came to her shin. She put on a white belt and went downstairs.

She was a little confused in this big house. She did not have time to explore, and she was unsure where the dining room was. She knew where the kitchen was because she could smell the food and it was tantalizing. April knocked on the kitchen door and the woman that appeared at the table yesterday was there. She took her hand and asked what her name was. She felt it rude to say, "Hey you."

The woman said her name was Becca, but Rodney never asked her what her name was. He simply rang a bell, and she did her job.

April felt bad, these were not servants. They were people. Human beings who all had needs and wants, the same as Rodney had. April reassured her she treasured her delectable delights and asked where the dining room was. Becca smiled and showed her where to go. When April came into the dining room, Rodney was already there. He was about to ring that damn bell when she interrupted him. "I wanted to talk to you a little bit if that's all right. I did the entire fence line from the house side, along the pasture, and into the woods. It went beyond over the hill and back around. The wooded area had a lot of wood in the stream. I pulled the wood up on the other side of the fence and into the woods. I did use one entire roll of wire in that area. I guess some of the fallen wood did damage to some of the wire. I used most of the insulators as well. Many of the ones on the posts were cracked and broken. I did not trust them."

April had more to say when Rodney interrupted her, "You did the entire fence line in one day"?

"Yes, I did. I have pastures at home too. I am quite used to this type of work."

"You will finish my list in 2 or 3 days," he said.

"Well then, we will have to find something more to do," April answered him.

Becca came out without Rodney ringing that bell. She announced what was for dinner. "Turkey and filling, mashed potatoes and gravy with green beans, and the dessert is apple cobbler," she said.

April asked Rodney "Do you always have such big meals? I know others here need to eat, but it's an awful lot. Don't you think so?"

Rodney said, "I don't really care what is for dinner. I eat what they bring me. My dad hired the servants to come here for a job, and this is how it is."

April asked him, "If you had a choice, what would you chose to eat? I mean sky's the limit."

He sat there for a minute and said, "I have never had a taco and wonder what they are like. I have wondered what many other foods are like, but this is how it is."

"You know Rodney, I can cook. Why not give these good folks a day or two off every week. They can still live and sleep here, but a day off is like a refresh to the soul. I will cook for you, and we can go some places too. What do you think about that?"

"I told you. I don't like to go out in public. People stare and make fun of me," he said.

"No, they won't. Not when I am around. You need to take care of yourself. You order around the people here, it's no different out there," April said. "Let's give it a try. Let's say, Saturday. You can show me around this area since I am a stranger here."

As they ate their dinner, every now and then Rodney would look up at April and sort of laugh. Soon April was laughing too, and she asked what was so funny.

Now April was confused, she ate very little and gathered her and Rodney's dishes taking them into the kitchen. Becca and Ann helped her wash them. She asked them to sit down, she wanted to talk to them. They did. Then April asked what was bothering Rodney.

Both women looked at one another not wanting to say. April pressed. "Mum, you see when Rodney was born, he was not wanted by his Mother. She threw him down the stairs as a baby, breaking his bones, his back, and legs. He never was right after that." And she pointed to her head.

April looked at them and said, "Breaking your back and legs has nothing to do with your head, unless he had head damage too. When has the last time Rodney was seen by a doctor?"

Both looked at one another and they shrugged their shoulders. "I have been here twelve years," Ann said. She was she was now twenty-two, so she came here when she was ten years old. Becca first stayed with Rodney's father and then came her. She was fifty-four years old. Neither of these girls knew of a time that Rodney saw a doctor.

April did not know what to do. It was obvious Rodney needed help, physically and maybe psychologically as well. What to do and how to do it was April's dilemma. She excused herself and asked where her room was. Ann took her to her room.

It was a very big room, a private bathroom, with a king-sized bed. There were ornate paintings, and dressers with horse statues on them. April was too tired to look. She undressed, put on her nightgown, said her prayers, especially about Rodney, asked for a tactful way to discuss this with him, blessed the others here, and went to bed.

April awoke at 4 a.m. as usual. She went outside on the back porch and sat there listening to the morning sounds. Soon she heard Rodney's wheelchair coming. He did not see her, and he came out and sat there as well. April got up, sat beside him, and asked if he slept well. He said he did, he liked mornings best and usually came out here. April agreed with him. She held his hand and asked, "What happened, how did he get like this?"

"I don't like to talk about it. It's not a pleasant story," he said.

April said, "It's just once. I won't ask you again. I want to help you."

"I am sure anyone here would tell you." he said.

"I don't want to hear it from others, I want to hear your own story, not theirs."

He sat there and matter-of-factly told April his Mother did not want them and kicked him down the stairs. She did not want him. And a few hours later jumped out of the attic window killing herself.

April felt sick to her stomach. She urged him on.

"When I was little, I was in and out of hospitals to reset my legs that hurt like hell. I went through resets four times in my life, and it sucked! I am angry inside. If she hated life so much, why didn't she leave me in the bassinette and then jump out of the window. I was a baby and did nothing to her." He sat there and cried.

April knelt near him and hugged him. "Of course, this was not your fault. She must have had demons that drove her crazy," April said. "I have known a lot of people who have had not-so-good babies, they endured it, and loved them. This is not normal." April was crying too.

"You do know there are counselors out there that can help you."

"I have been that route and they did nothing for me," Rodney said.

"Would you be willing to see my doctor. I trust him with my life," April said.

"Is he a miracle worker?" Rodney sarcastically said.

"No, but he is a very caring doctor and if he can't find the answer, he knows others who will," April said.

"I don't know. I hate being like this. I want to live. I'm twenty-six years old and live like a seventy-year-old.

April said, "I will call my doctor. You can talk to him. He is a good, smart man and very caring. I believe you went to doctors who thought they knew it all and didn't. Never give up hope."

Rodney said he was hungry and wanted breakfast. "That's another thing," April said. "You need to eat better, make smarter choices. The more weight you put on, the harder it will be for you to walk."

"Yeah, yeah, tell me that again and again, just like others did," he said.

April got in front of his wheelchair, and he had to stop. "Look I am willing to help you. Will you help me or are you so jaded you give up? Seriously, you have someone here who is willing to help you."

Rodney just sat there looking at her and said, "Why? What's in this for you?"

"I will know I did the best that I can for one of God's children," she answered him.

Rodney was not prepared for that. He asked her, "Do you mean that?"

"Absolutely I do. Look, Rodney, medicine and practices have changed in 27 years. Granted you may not be able to walk anymore, but for heaven's sake it's worth looking into."

Rodney said, "You make the call, and I'll talk to him."

"Nicely," April said as she showed him her fist.

The day passed by and at precisely 10:00 a.m. April called her doctor. The phone rang twice, and the doctor answered. Rodney was tapping his fingers on the table.

"Hello. Is this Rodney I am speaking to?"

"Yes, Sir. It is," Rodney answered.

They both spoke about Rodney's condition and the doctor thought it would be good to have him looked at. He had a friend that he graduated with who was also in sports medicine. He was astounding when it came to putting bones back in place. He also said, "Rodney you are older now. Your bones are mature, not like when you were little, and your bones were like greensticks. I will speak to my friend who lives in here in California about you. Now I know it's a trip, but I have a feeling it might well be worth it." That was it.

An appointment was set, and airline tickets purchased for three: Rodney, Ann, and April. They left in two days with Rodney sweating profusely. April knew he was afraid. Who wouldn't be after all he had been through.

April also arranged for him to have a good therapist to come to the manor and treat him. If you have money and sit there in misery, what good does it do you!

The exam went well. The doctor wanted Rodney to have an MRI as soon as possible. It was done at noon and Rodney was to come back to the office at 3:00 p.m. for the results. This doctor understood Rodney was far from home.

When Rodney came into the room, the doctor explained it was possible for Rodney to have his condition changed. "Now this is not going to happen overnight. I can do the surgery, and you can go home via a commuter. Your recovery will be slow. The first three days you will be down. After that I want you up, and taking physical therapy, ah, every other day including weekends. I believe if you put forth a good effort within six weeks you should be walking.

Rodney was speechless and had tears in his eyes, both April and Ann did too. What a wonderful thing!

The appointment for surgery was scheduled for April 15th. April asked Scott to fly them to the hospital in Ohio. He did own the airplane. They arrived and the hospital, and Rodney had his surgery. Later he went home in the commuter, in mild pain. At home he lay for two days, and then physical therapy began. Yes, it was painful at first. He yelled, he swore, and he grimaced. In a month Rodney was walking with crutches. It was amazing.

During his recovery time, April set to work enlarging the barn. She had the bricks taken out of the stalls, since the horses were in the pasture.

April found a crew of construction guys who were looking for work and she hired them. When they saw Rodney, they decided to cut their price in half. The barn was revamped and when it was finished, April had Rodney come out on crutches to see it. He was overjoyed. Now he would be able to do much of the work himself when he was up and about. And Rodney lost forty-two pounds. He was now trim and fit.

The three of them did many things together. They went to the zoo, and to a theme park. And for the first time in his life, Rodney rode on the skyline drive ride. The more he did the better he walked. April liked to take Rodney for a buggy ride. They rode to get ice cream and to the grocery store. Granted it took longer, but on those rides, he saw more than speeding by in a car.

Often April cooked healthy meals and indeed Rodney loved tacos. He learned to love salads. He started to lift weights and swim. One routine they had was to sit outside by the back porch and have tea.

April said to him, "You are not the person I first met when I came here. You are happy and moving around on your own. It's such a joy to see you like this.

He said, "I have a confession to make. I don't know how I got the farm competition papers, since I do not have a working farm per se. I laid it on my desk and day after day I wheeled in to look at it. That was my routine. I knew it was wrong and I felt guilty, but I said a prayer and sent it in. Never did he expect this outcome. Never did I think someone would come out here and turn my life around by pushing me to get better. I want to thank you but don't know how."

That night everyone was sleeping, all was quiet until morning. A knock came on the door of the Manor, a very loud persistent knock. Ann ran to answer the door.

Ann opened it and there stood Rodney's father. "WHERE IS MY SON?" he demanded.

"In bed, Sir. It is very early."

"Well, EVERYONE UP. EVERYONE GET UP!" he shouted.

Rodney came down the stairs in his pajamas and robe.

His father did not notice that his son was walking. His anger was so intense.

"Who authorized you to run up medical bills for me to pay?" he asked his son.

"Dad, I didn't! Dad, can you see me? I am no longer in a wheelchair. Dad, I can walk!" he said.

"You can walk? Now what? Now you will go out and spend my money, run around with woman, and make a mockery of yourself. I liked you better in the wheelchair, you were controllable. I knew you would not go off wandering. Who in the hell gave you this idea?" he demanded.

By this time April was downstairs standing at the bottom step when she said loudly, "I did!"

"And who are you, his harlot?"

Now April was getting angry. "No, I am not his harlot. I am here on a farm competition. You are a nasty, dirty-minded old man to say that about me. You don't even know me. You came into this house. You are not happy your son can finally walk after twenty-seven years? You criticize him of things he did not do. For heaven's sake you can't be happy your son is walking?"

The Father came to April and went to strike her. "You better not, or I will lay you out. You are picking on the wrong girl here."

As the old man turned around, April knocked him down and yelled for Rodney to help her. They put the man in a chair and tied him there. "Now you will sit there and listen," April said to him. They left him sit there until 10:00 a.m. when they called the doctor that had done Rodney's surgery. The old man did not want to listen, but April held the receiver to his ear.

He heard all about how painful the surgery was and the recovery time. The doctor was pleased and said there were no bills to the Father since everything was paid by Rodney's insurance. The statements were routinely sent out by insurance companies, but the deductible was met, and no payment was required.

"GET ME OUT OF THIS DAMN CHAIR!" the old man said.

April wanted to laugh at him and asked Rodney what did he want to do?

"Dad, we are going to let you free. If you want to stay, be nice. If you can't be nice, leave! I won't tolerate you picking on anyone here. They were all kind to me and helped me when I was at my worst. I will not allow you to yell at them. Got it?"

The old man nodded his head. He admitted that the insurance bills are what set him off. He didn't know what happened.

"I didn't tell you," his son said to him. "I wanted it to be a surprise, Dad!"

"Surprise me you did. Son, you know I have a bad temper. I am sorry though. I did not know if you were in an accident," he said. Indeed, he was untied, and he hugged his son crying on his shoulder saying, "I'm sorry. I am so, so sorry."

It all worked out in two or three days. Rodney's father saw the new stables and he had to admit they were more suited for horses. Rodney made a decision of his own. He wanted April to have the mare.

April cooked the meals for the next two days and the old man asked where Becca was. "I gave her two days off, everyone deserves a day or two off," April said.

The old man sat there smiling and began to laugh, "She's a spit fire, eh, Son?"

"Dad, she is much more than that."

April was happy for this rekindling of son and father. So far as she was concerned, she was a bystander as she was not staying, in less than six weeks she would be leaving.

One evening as everyone retired and went to bed, April did not. She sat out on the back veranda looking at the moon and stars. It was a lovely night. April reflected on how happy she was at first coming here. She never thought there would be such a calamity. I guess that's family dynamics. April was so glad her family was not one to accuse and then apologize. They were not like that at all. She was a bit ashamed of herself at how angry she had gotten, but no one has the right to behave like that, it's stupid and childish. April sat there outside for almost an hour when Rodney came out to join her. He asked her if he could get something off his mind.

April was curious and clueless when Rodney said what he wanted.

"Look I know we don't know each other, and I may never run or do a lot of physical things . . . ."

April stopped him. "Rodney, you are a nice guy, really you are. I am promised to someone else," as she showed him the ring around her neck. "Do you know Ann has feelings for you? She cried so often wanting to help when you were angry, and . . . ."

"April, hear me out. I am not poor. I am rich beyond rich, and I could buy you anything."

April said, "I don't know where this came from. You don't know me at all, but there is someone here that has been here for twelve years. You know her and she knows you. She lives here and knows you. Wouldn't you rather choose her? "I am not staying here. I am moving to the last competition.

Rodney looked at her and said, "I can pay that entire amount. I wish you'd stay."

April felt sorry for him. He did not know her, money meant little to April. She loved the simple things in life.

"Rodney you can't change who you are, you can try, but you will go back to your old ways. I love simple things. Seeing a waterfall and walking beside it. I like to have my dog in my arms and her sleeping beside me. I love nights with fireflies shining their beams of light. I love children, their laughter, and when they want to learn. I love old people who appreciate life and all they did. But most of all I love my Father in Heaven. I have felt him in my life. I owe the Savior so much. He died for me, to show us the way. This is who I am. I will never be royal, not in this lifetime. I leave in four days, and I want to leave under good terms. I hope you understand. I wish you only the best in life." She got up, kissed his cheek, and went to bed, happy!

Rodney thought about what April said, and she was right. Never in his lifetime had he bailed hay and cleaned pens. April liked the simple things in life, and he did not believe that would content him. He took April's advice and began to spend time with Ann.

April had less than a week left here at Countryside Manor, and she would be glad to go. There was not enough to content her. The only one who did was that black mare. Oh, well she said to herself, it's not like I don't have other horses to ride. I just hate to have anyone say she is nasty because she is not.

Without April knowing, Rodney called the farm competition. They did relent and give them the number of the Di Angelos.

But God is so good. It did not ring the Di Angelo's phone. It rang at Marty's desk. Marty answered and he listened. He nodded his head and gave the caller the address of the stables, nothing more. The mare would be trailed from Ohio to the airport and from there flown to California by a professional company whose only job was transporting equine animals.

When Marty saw the mare, he knew what April saw. She was not nasty. She simply wanted attention and she would surely get it here.

In a small space of time that mare would walk right up to you in a pasture and let you pet her, and you could lead her out by her following you. Yes, April knew horses and this one was a gem. Marty decided to name her Gem although that was not the name on her papers.

Of course, the mare would be ridden, mainly by him or someone he trusted. He wanted her ready for April when she came home. The more she was ridden the calmer she would become.

That was something Marty could not get over, why people get so many horses and do not use them. They could either cart, ride, or work them. The uses for horses are endless. It was a darn shame he thought. So often as he drove to town and back, he saw that many were thrown away. They wanted a huge sum of money just to move them out. What a darn shame that this was happening all over the world. Horses were for sale online, in ads, everywhere and in every state. It was always for profit, not for the love of the animal.

Maine Here I Come

ON THE AIRPLANE FROM WISCONSIN TO MAINE, APRIL REFLECTED on all three places she had worked so far. She had made some notes on how to improve D farms. They were not big improvements, but time savers, and everyone liked saving time. April nestled into her seat to rest and had another passenger sitting beside her.

Now April was not one to watch television, the only movies she had seen in the past year were on videos. But she thought to herself she had seen this person before. Either he was a singer or a movie person, or maybe both. She was curious so she extended her hand and said, "Hi. I am April D. May I ask what your name is?"

The man was not very tall but seems anxious. He had thick black hair and deep dark eyes. Then he reached out his hand and said, "Who me? My name is Eddie Van Halen."

April just stared at him and said, "I think I know you. I mean you did a video with me riding on a horse named Rodger in the Olympics a few years back."

"Oh yeah, Rodger Dodger, and are you the itty-bitty girl that rode him over those big jumps? I mean you look a lot like her, only you got taller," he said to her.

"Yes, I am, and I love that video with the song "JUMP" that accompanied it. I must have watched that video one hundred times or more," she said. "How ever did you time your song with the jumps?"

"First of all, we are professionals," and they both laughed. "Secondly, you know, that video went over the top. I mean there were more hits on that video than any other we put our music to," he said.

"Wow! Who would have guessed I'd be flying to Boston and get a seat with an Olympic superstar," he said.

"And I was thinking, Wow! Who would have thought I'd be flying to Boston beside Eddie Van Halen," she said, and they both laughed and laughed. That sure broke the tension!

"Where are you heading?" she asked him.

"Well, I am joining up with the band. We are playing a venue in Boston with a number of other bands."

"Oh wow! I am headed to Maine," she said, and she filled him in on what she did.

"A farm competition?" he asked. "I never pictured a pretty girl like you on a farm."

"Well, there are a lot of beautiful girls who grow up on farms, and we know how to have fun," April said.

"What kind of fun?" he asked winking at her.

"I can't speak for all of the girls, but for me it's clean fun," she told him.

"What kind of clean fun?" he asked.

"I could take you swimming, boating, or horseback riding. Maybe you'd like hiking, picking berries, or riding on top of a hay wagon. Would you prefer milking cows or giving a baby calf a bottle of milk larger than a two-liter soda bottle? How about four-wheeling around the fields? You'd see deer or a bear, and we can go through water. We also build bon fires in the winter and summer. It's a good time to kick back and enjoy the company of friends," she said.

"Oh, wow. I would never have guessed girls did all that. I thought they baked and cooked all day," he said. And April laughed at him.

"Hey if you can get away, we will be playing at the amphitheater in Boston this week. There will be several bands there: Styx, the Eagles, Kenny Logins, Tina Turner, and more. I can't remember them all. You could come down for one of our concerts. Here, wait a minute," he said. Eddie scribbled down on a note pad and handed it to her. "That will get you into any concert where I am," Eddie told her.

She thanked him and said, "I wish you could come to our farm and see the beauty there."

"I see it already," and he winked at her again.

April blushed. "Well, maybe someday we will," he said.

"All right, you try and get some sleep," she said to him. "I will be quiet."

He looked at her and said, "I was hoping you would talk to me about all the things you do and teach me something." So, all during that flight, these two talked like magpies. She told him many things and explained them clearly to him.

"I don't think I'd like to be a farmer," he said. "I'd hire someone to do the work."

April told him that was part of the fun, to see the changes that came about by your own two hands. Soon these two were thirsty and sleepy. They both put their heads back and began to doze off. One of them snored, so the other made the best of it.

Touch down and the two new friends shook hands, and then she hugged him outright. They came down the alley, each looking for someone to pick them up. April found her ride quickly. Once she had her suitcase and guitar in hand, she followed him to the parking lot.

April's ride was from a man named Tom. Tom was a tall, thin man, about forty, who was the brother of the sister who owned the farm where April was to make improvements. He was chatty, much more than Helen or Nick were. April liked Tom a lot. He told her that the farm was a hobby farm. His sister was a famous movie star, and she did not live on the farm all the time. But when she was there, she always wanted certain things to be done.

Her husband was a practical man who wanted to live on the farm full time. He wanted to make improvements and make some money of his own. Since her job was in the movies, they lived in Los Angeles.

As they pulled into the driveway, April gasped. It was like a picturesque home, like an English Tudor with flowers, and tall ornamental grass. And, well, it was like a photograph.

Tom helped April get her things into the sprawling house. When April came downstairs Tom tried to explain to April what his sister wanted done on the farm. 1. There were no animals, just an empty small stone barn. Fix that! 2. She wanted a small gazing pond, maybe to put two ducks on it, some frogs and lily pads, and maybe a swing. That was it.

Holy Molly this was going to be easy. April set about looking around to make improvements. Tom followed her all around like a puppy dog. It was imperative that at each farm April kept detailed notes, describing what was there when she arrived and how she improved it.

April also had to register at the local school, but there wasn't one. The closest school was run by the Catholic Church. So, April made an appointment and went there the next day with her last transcripts and her last report card. April met with the Mother Superior and April just loved the sister immediately. She was an older woman, older than the other sisters. She also wore a habit, veil, and gown. The veiled hat framed her lovely face and April thought she almost radiated. "Where are your parents?" the Mother Superior asked.

"They are in California while I complete in this farm competition," April said.

"I have never heard of anything so lame and preposterous. A child needs her parents," the Nun said.

April said, "Well, Ma'am, here are all of my transcripts from Wisconsin, and . . . ."

Mother Superior interrupted her. "Wisconsin! I thought you were from California?"

"I am, Ma'am. I am in a competition that takes me every three months to another farm. I have been to Pennsylvania, Wisconsin, Ohio, and now I am here in Maine. This is my last area. In September, I will be leaving to go home," April said.

This did not sit well with Mother Superior, but she took April's grades and scrutinized them.

"Your religion is not marked on this form. Are you Catholic?" she asked.

"No, Ma'am. I am Mormon. Do you know about Mormons? Would you like me to teach you? There are no local schools here, and with me working on the farm, I cannot travel far. Surely you can find in your big heart a place for a little Mormon girl. I won't be any trouble," April said.

"Well, that's a relief. We have enough trouble as it is," she said.

Mother Superior took the papers and laid them on her desk. She rang a bell that brought two nuns into the room. "This is Sister Mary Margret and Sister Louise, please follow them to show you around, in particular the school."

April got up to leave, turned around, and thanked the Mother Superior who got flushed in her face. She used her hands to motion for all of them to go.

Sister Mary Margaret was tall and skinny and very young. Sister Louise was quite the opposite, but both were funny and loved children, that was evident. April followed them and listened where things were. As it turned out, during her three days of school, she would eat lunch here saving her a lot of time.

After the tour April took each of the nun's hands and in turn kissed the back, saying thank you to them. Both nuns were embarrassed and taken aback as this was not expected or necessary. They stood in the doorway waving goodbye to April as she walked home.

The next morning after breakfast, April looked over an area behind the house. About twenty-five feet from the back of the house was a small swell or depression in the ground covered by grass. It was quite large, and April asked Tom why that was there.

Tom said there had been a fuel oil tank buried there, but it was taken out when his sister bought the property. They had everything changed over to propane and electric. April measured the area and thought it would work quite nicely for this project.

She then asked Tom if there was a place in town that had old tires, possibly tractor tires. Or if there was a tractor place that serviced tractors, they might have tires too. Tom said there was, it was quite a little trip but this coming Saturday he was willing to drive out and they could check what they had there. "May as well take the tractor and brush mower, they have not been worked on in years. I can easily load them on the trailer they came on," he said.

That Saturday, Tom had the ford tractor mounted on the trailer it had arrived on with the mower attachment in place as well. They pulled out around 8 a.m. The drive was about an hour, all on winding roads. They pulled onto the stony driveway and pulled to the side of the building. Tom got out and he and April went inside. An order was filled out to service the tractor and make sure the brush mower was worked on as well. Then April asked if they had any tractor tires, or tubs they wanted to get rid of.

The servicemen at the counter looked at each other and they called the manager to come to the desk. The manager came and introduced himself as Mike. April asked him the same question. He said, "Come out with me," and April followed Mike into the boneyard as they called it.

There in the back beyond the driveway in a field were tires and pieces of tractors all over. April spied what she wanted and asked. "How about that tire over there? What do you want for it?" she asked.

"Let me put it to you this way, what do you want with it?"

"I want to make a small pool with lily pads and that looks big enough to me," she said.

"Well, I have to agree with you," he said. "That's a Euclid tire."

April knew right away what that tire was. They are huge trucks, ten times bigger than a regular dump truck. "Well, I have use for it if you don't want too much for it," April said.

"I don't want anything for it. In fact, I'd be happy if it was gone. But how are you going to move it? That's the problem," Mike said.

April thought for a minute and asked, "Do you think it would fit on our trailer, I mean standing up and fastened with ratchet straps?"

"Yes, that can be done if Tom doesn't drive too fast. Keep in mind when you unload it. Be sure where you want to unload it, because moving it can be difficult. It's heavy," Mike said. So, the guys in the shop all got together using a skid steer and loaded the tire onto Tom's trailer and strapped it down.

"Now, if you are not in a hurry, Bob, I, and a few others live out near where Tom lives. We can help unload it for you and then take our straps with the trailer. We will need to load the trailer when we finish with the tractor and mower. It should be sometime in the next two weeks," Mike said.

April's eyes lit up, "That would be awesome. Thanks so much." And with that, she and Tom were headed for home going under the speed limit. At home April quickly whipped up an apple pie. She felt the guys should have some kind of treat for doing this favor for them.

Tom was a good man. He pulled out his camera to document everything that happened so his sister could see the before and after pictures. He took some shots of the depressed ground, which was about five feet deep, the dirt that April had dug out, and the huge tire that was on the trailer. When the men stopped by, he snapped photos of the entire procedure of putting the tire around that hole so it would fit just right.

The next day was Sunday, and April really wanted to go to that concert. She asked Tom if he would mind if she went. He said it was fine with him and he looked a bit forlorn.

April asked, "Do you want to come along with me?"

He said, "Sure."

The day of the concert, the two of them dressed, had money in their pockets, and left at 10 a.m. They arrived in Boston three hours later, had a nice lunch, and walked all around Boston. Finally, around three in the afternoon, April said they should try to see if they could get in and so they walked to the venue. Sure enough the door was unlocked. They pushed the door open and walked inside. They heard noises. It was the stage crew setting up and then April saw one of her favorite bands.

It was the Gibb Brothers, all three of them, on the stage doing their sound check. April half ran, half skipped down the steps to the floor when someone noticed her. "Hey, you can't come in here," they said.

"Well, I did. I have a pass and the door was not locked," she answered back.

"Let me see your pass," the man said to her.

April was not stupid. She did not want the man to take her pass and destroy it, so she said, "Who are you? Are you security?"

"No, I am not security, but . . . ."

"Then you are not getting my pass," she said defiantly.

Just then April caught a glimpse of Eddie Van Halen, and she yelled his name as loud as she could. "Hey, Eddie!" He looked around and came up the steps to the stage. When he saw April, he waved for her to come up on stage. Tom just sat down in one of the seats.

"Is that your daughter, Eddie?" someone asked.

"Absolutely. Can't you see the striking resemblance?" and everyone laughed. Eddie said, "Look at her. Don't any of you know who she is?"

"Robin Gibb came over as did some of the band's crew and a few of the stage crew members. Someone began to snap their fingers saying, "Oh, I know. She is, ah, ah. Oh, I can't say it, but I know."

Eddie said to her, "Tell them how many medals you have."

April just stood there. "Go on and tell them" as he tapped her on her shoulder.

"Eight. I have eight Olympic Medals," April said.

"Oh, yeah," one said. Another said, "I know now. She rode that jumping horse to your video. Yeah, yeah. I know now."

"I remember her skiing and saving the Chinese girl. That was awesome, it made me Mum and me cry," he said. And everyone laughed again.

"How did you meet her?" they asked Eddie.

"We met on the airplane. Our seats were beside each other. Let me tell you guys this, I learned a lot." Eddie said. I gave her a pass to come tonight."

"Well, that was right nice of you Eddie," someone said.

"She did not tell me, but I learned she can sing too."

April's face blushed.

"Did you see that, guys. She blushed, an honest to God blush," someone said.

"Don't give her a hard time," another said. "I'd like to hear her sing."

That is when Eddie asked April, "How about coming up on stage and sing with us?"

"I don't' know, April said. I like to play my guitar, but I don't think I'd like to sing in front with the seats all full of people," she said waving her arms wide from one side to the other.

Someone walked over to April and handed her an electric guitar. "You like to play guitar, well then, here you go."

"Oh, no. I don't play electric guitar. I play acoustic guitar," she said to them.

"Oh, a purest," someone said. Soon someone was handing her a really nice acoustic guitar. April put the strap over her head and adjusted it to fit. Then she stepped to the front of the stage and began to play. Eddie nudged someone, and they did not move. They wanted to hear her play and sing. April broke into a love song, an old one, but a classic.

The guys all stood there nodding their heads and tapping their feet to the beat of the song. Someone got up on a drum set and accompanied her. Some began to sing along with her, and soon all of them were singing along.

April kept playing, looking from side to side smiling until the song ended.

"Wow, wow, wow! What do we have here? A singer, a player. Wow!" said Eddie.

Then someone suggested she sing on stage with one of the groups. "The crowd will love her. She is famous and . . . ."

April shook her head. "No, the people have paid their hard-earned money to come here and see you play and sing. They would not want to hear me. I would not feel comfortable up here. Besides, I really wanted to hear all of you sing and play," she said.

The concert was amazing. There were many bands playing that evening. They all sang their most popular hits, and the crowd whistled and cheered. There were many lighters lit, it looked like candles. All of them were fantastic: the Bee Gees, the Eagles, Sting, Fleetwood Mac, Van Halen, and there were so many big names. The music was catching and to April uplifting. Who could sit in their seat with them playing. It was so wonderful. April laughed and sang as did Tom.

After an intermission, someone summoned a security person to bring April up on stage. April protested lightly but did not want to make a scene. She followed the woman until she got to where she was to be. Some of the guys wanted her to sing with them. April pursed her lips and reluctantly agreed, "I am not that good. I warned you."

The Eagles agreed she could sing and play with them. They showed her the song they were going to play. As she strummed, she was thinking, "Thank God Mom encouraged me to learn how to read music and not just play by ear." After playing one set they called for her to come out. They introduced her to the crowd. "Do you know who this girl is? She is an American Hero. She represented the U.S.A. in the Olympics several times. Who remembers her?" he asked. The crowd whistled, shouted, and cheered. April began to strum her guitar to the beginning of the song.

The crowd began to whistle, light lighters, and cheer. Then April sang together with the band. After she was done, she was soon forgotten. That was just as she had hoped. April kept her part of the bargain, and to be truthful, it was an amazing night. April was delighted she was able to go. She would remember this night for the rest of her life. She lived, and it was great.

But she was not forgotten, her picture on stage circulated all throughout Boston. "Olympian Can Sing" was the headline. Sheesh, April thought, "I can't go anywhere without being known. That is except at home. They don't care, and I am glad. They like me for who I am.

The next day April worked putting a thick line around the tire. She put it into the hole with some extra liner. Using a lever, Tom had to hold the leaver down so the tire would lift. Then she could tuck the plastic underneath the tire, all the way around. When they were done, it looked like a huge tire going for surgery. That entailed another trip to the nursery where they bought ornamental flowers and shrubs, especially Water Lilies.

The ground pump, to pump water, was slowly added. Then a chemical for algae to grow and make it more natural for plant life and fish was emptied into the "pond". That took almost an entire day. Then by evening they added the plants around the tire and put the Water Lilies on the water. Truthfully, it looked very nice.

The next day April chose a site and dug it out level. She found an old swing in the garage. She also bought two extra strong springs, and had Tom hang the swing up on each end. They found that swing in the garage that was surprisingly in good condition. April then asked Tom to take it off again so she could paint the swing bright yellow with blue trim. When it was dry, they both put the swing on the coil springs. Both of them sat down, and it held them quite well and it looked nice. The swing was at least five feet from the pond. A good distance away, but close enough to see.

The following week the tractor was ready to come home. They rode out in Tom's truck to bring it back. April had spent the entire week mowing grass everywhere. April found there had been a pasture here, but the grass was so high it hid the fences. She mowed and fixed the fence lines and posts. After a week of mowing, it looked so different, and Tom had it all in pictures.

At the school, April was having trouble with some of the history. She was not stupid, but what they were teaching was not right. She went to the public library on a trip to town and brought back the book that she knew had the correct information.

The Nuns took this book to the Mother Superior, and she was not happy at all. She brought the book back to April slamming it down on the table in front of her, making her jump!

"Remember you said you would not make trouble, but here you are," she said.

April looked at her and said, "Mother Superior, in the Bible it says, 'The truth will set you free.' Does it not?"

Mother Superior nodded her head.

"Well, this book has authentic documentation of this incident, so how can it be wrong. Since this is the truth, I wanted to share it with you all, so you would know."

Mother Superior was flabbergasted. She knew quite well that this girl was acting innocently as if she did not know.

"Did you do this deliberately?" She asked April.

"No, Ma'am. I did not. I just felt in my heart that what was being taught was not quite right, so I wanted to bring the truth to you. That's all."

"All right then. From this time forward, we will teach the truth. But since it is truth you seek, I insist you join the sisters in vespers," she said.

"Ma'am, I don't want to be ignorant, but what are vespers?" April asked.

"They are prayers. After school you will join the sisters from 3:00 p.m. to 7:00 p.m., and then you are fee to go.

April knew that Tom would be worried, so she asked Mother Superior a question. "I will gladly, if you would be so kind as to let Tom know where I am, or he will be concerned."

"Is Tom your relative?" she asked April.

"No, Ma'am. He is the man I am staying with for the next four months."

"A stranger, a man?" she was defiant.

"Yes, Ma'am. Tom is a good man, a kind man and for now he is to watch over me and my care."

"How absolutely ridiculous," Mother Superior said. She walked away saying, "Unacceptable, absolutely unacceptable. Like a wild animal."

April looked at Louse who just shrugged her shoulders. As April joined the sisters in vespers, she was unsure what to do, but she was sure they did. She sang when they sang and at the end, each sister was to say their own heartfelt prayer out loud. So she did. When April knelt and prayed it was so innocent, honest, and humble.

The nuns began to weep.

She prayed for her Mom and Dad, and Nora and Lena. She prayed for the animals like Ruby and the horses, and for good friends. For Helen who was battling depression, and for Barbara to have full recovery from cancer. For Barbara's family to be patient with her while recovering. She prayed asking God to watch over Tim, that he might find happiness within himself, and not in others. For Rodney, so that he and his father could rekindle their family relationship. And that he would see the goodness in Ann to cherish her. They all needed to understand they are of great worth. She prayed for all those here to do what they needed. None of us are stars, but we all shine brightly in God's eyes.

April's prayer was long, and tears rolled down her cheeks. The spirit was felt, and it was strong. She ended with "In Jesus Christ's Holy name, Amen."

All the sisters then said, "Amen," and came forward to hug her. As they headed out, there was a nun scurrying towards them. A man had called for April.

April continued to follow that nun and picked up the receiver. "Hello. Is this Tom? Yes, I am still here. I had to pay penance for revealing the truth in class. Yes, I know. Will you pick me up? I would be so grateful since it is dark outside now. All right. I will see you soon and thank you.

Word went quickly to Mother Superior, and she hurried from her changer downstairs to meet the man who had this unacceptable arrangement. When Tom arrived, he did not come inside, he waited outside in his pickup truck.

Mother Superior insisted no men could come inside, so she put on a cloak and told April to follow her. Outside, Mother

Superior knocked on the driver's side window for Tom to roll the window down. He did not. He sat there staring straight ahead. So, she knocked again, this time much harder. Still, he sat there unflinching as if he did not notice. April got in on the passenger side and Tom waited until she had her seatbelt on and then he put the truck in drive and took off.

April looked at him asking, "Did you know Mother Superior wanted to talk with you?"

"Yes, I know. She always wants to talk with me, and I avoid her like the plague," he said.

"Why is that?" April asked.

Tom told her that this place and his family had a very hard time a while back when his sister's son committed suicide. They would not help unless a large amount of money was given to them. His sister had no problem with money, but Tom felt it was not right.

April sat there stunned. "So, they did know one another," she thought to herself. Then why was Mother Superior so nasty about men, and especially this family who has gone through a difficult time that would last a lifetime. April could not come up with any answers. She was determined to find out. They got back home, and Tom had a stew on the stove for her still warm.

"Oh, my goodness, that smells so good," she said to him. Tom said it was late and he was going to bed. April took a small bowl of stew and ate it slowly mulling over the events of the day. She was glad the weekend was here.

Tomorrow she wanted to go to a cattle sale. Tom had told her he would like some cattle to keep the pasture grass down, and the only way that would happen was to make it happen.

The next morning, they drove to the cattle sale which was a two-hour drive away. Tom did have a trailer to transport the cattle. It was not currently inspected, and he hoped no one would notice.

At the cattle barn there were all breeds of cattle. Tom did not even know the difference between a cow and a bull. April had to give Tom a quick education. They bought six crossbred steers. There were four Angus and two Angus crossbred with white-faced Hereford. Each was no less than four hundred pounds. They would look nice on pasture. It was fairly early when they left the auction.

By the time they got home it was still light. April made sure there was electric in the fencing. She knew to be careful opening the gate.

Tom was not so good at backing up with his trailer. He had to make several attempts before he got close enough and in line with the gate. The steers were unloaded and began to run around and play in the high grass. They were happy and it was nice to see.

Tom put the trailer away, but April followed and cleaned it off first. Then they went inside, and April made supper of soup and a sandwich. She also wanted to talk to Tom about planting crops on the farm. Tom said they used to plant crops the first two years, but all that stopped when his nephew died. April asked how the planting was done and he told her that a neighbor had a no-till planter and did that for them.

So, Tom put in a call to the neighbor, who said he would put the corn in that same week. He also asked Tom if he was interested in making hay. April shook her head "Yes", and Tom told the farmer, "Yes, he was, and they would check the hayfield for him. Sure enough, on Monday the planter came and planted about sixty acres of corn, leaving thirty acres for hay. That would easily take care of the small number of steers if they decided to keep them until fall to finish them. Tom made sure all of this was documented in pictures which he kept packed in a box in chronological order.

April had school on Tuesdays, Wednesdays, and Thursdays, sometimes she could change them around and go on a Monday or Friday. But she had to tell the nuns so they could plan accordingly. April preferred consistency, and if she could go in the middle of the week, those three days helped her be organized and keep a schedule.

The small farm was growing and beginning to look more like a farm, and it was lovely. The cattle were a mix of colors, and they made a pretty sight on the hillside. While at that steer auction, April talked to several women farmers and one had sheep that she wanted to sell. It was a small flock of Dorper sheep, six ewes and one ram. April wanted to go and see them. That farm was only about twenty-five minutes away, and Tom was excited to see the sheep too. He liked sheep more than cattle.

When they arrived, they spotted the sheep right away. The woman was outside and saw them as they pulled in. A border collie was by her side, and he barked when Tom and April walked up to greet her. "Zip, stop that. These people are here to see the sheep," she said. The dog walked to April without hesitation and licked her hand. "That's unusual," she said. "She does not like most people."

The woman took them down to the meadow and told them about the sheep. Most of the sheep were three years old and bred to the ram that was also three. They were registered and purebred animals. She got them when her aunt passed away, but now she decided she wanted to travel. She spoke to Tom about a price, and it was very reasonable. In fact, April thought it was cheap. Tom was happy as a lark. The Border collie did his job, even though a bit stiff and not able to keep up with the sheep all of the time, still, he did an amazing job. He did much better than she would have done running all around in circles with the sheep going in all directions.

When the sheep were loaded on the trailer, and they were on their way home, April spoke to Tom about possibly getting a dog to help move the sheep or cattle. Tom said he loved dogs, and he would talk to his sister when she called again about that commitment.

Cattle and sheep are different, they both are for human consumption. They feed the world. But a dog is a lifetime companion, a commitment. Tom did not want to get a dog and then be told to take him to a shelter. Dogs have feeling and a brain to think, and it grieved him to know so many dogs are thrown away just because someone got tired of them, they moved, or the dog got old. He said, "It's inhumane how people treat pets."

April agreed with Tom.

Tom said many times that he had visited shelters where there were so many dogs and cats for adoption, and he just couldn't handle it. It broke his heart. So, if he ever had another chance to own a dog, it would be for its lifetime.

At school April learned from a novice nun that the Mother Superior never intended to take money from the family. The school kept falling behind on money coming in to feed all the poor, hungry children they fed at school. April was unaware they did this, and she was impressed.

She asked them, "Do you have any help with donations of food or money?"

"No, we do not. Everything we feed to the children, we grow here, or we purchase at discount grocery stores," the novice said.

The truth was, the Archdiocese was contemplating shutting down the school and the church. Both were in dire need of repair. There was no money for them. The roofs leaked and buckets sat out to catch the dripping rainwater. There were holes in the walls, cleverly covered with tapestries. The drainpipes were full of mice or the larger variety that come up for regular meals. They did set out traps, but it was a constantly repeating process.

The nuns did not want this place to close because they did not want to be separated. They were a family. Mother Superior was their mother. All the young novices were fearful. April once unintentionally watched Mother Superior berate a novice. She also saw Mother Superior hold her close in a hug, stroking her back to encourage her.

For now, all April could do is focus on school and pay attention to what was going on.

On her days away from school, she and Tom were busy building a farm that had been long neglected. They had to mow every weekend, all the summer long. They planted more ornamental flowers than April had ever seen in her lifetime. The problem with flowers was, they often died, and the only local place to buy them was the hardware store.

One day on one of their drives, April saw a huge brick building about three blocks from where she went to school. There was a for sale sign hanging on the wall. It must have been there a very long time since one side hung down, and the sign was full of vines growing over it.

April jotted down the number and one evening she called it.

The person who answered the telephone on the other end was retired from real estate, but she said that indeed the building was still for sale.

April asked if she could look at it sometime, and the woman said she would get back to her in a day or two.

The woman did not know who to call, so she called the original people who wanted to list the property for sale. Eunice drove to the seller's house and explained that someone wanted to see the property. The sellers were the Bonds. They had this property listed for sale fifteen years ago and no one ever wanted it. So indeed, they were interested and asked if they could come along as well with Eunice. Eunice explained she had surrendered her real estate license a few years ago so she would not be able to represent them in any way. But, sure, she would go along.

The appointment was made for the end of June. April decided that she would have to ride a bicycle to the meeting. She did not explain anything to Tom, not yet! You can only imagine the questions the sellers had to see a young girl riding a bicycle to view the property. Was she qualified? They doubted it. It was probably another waste of their time.

April introduced herself, and Mr. Bond caught her name right away. "Are you D as in D farms and the one who races the great Native Son?

"Yes, Sir. That is me," April said.

Mr. Bond asked what April was doing here in Maine. April explained about the farm competition and how the last draw for her was here in Maine.

"Why a farm competition if you race horses? He asked her.

"Well, you see, Sir. I also own D Farm. Are you familiar with them?

"Oh, yes. Yes, we are. We go there ourselves sometimes for less expensive meat at their meat stores. Meat is so costly you know. How did you become involved with D Farms?" he asked.

"You don't understand, Sir. I am not involved. I am D farms! It was my idea from the beginning to end hunger in America and help those who were willing to work to go to college and graduate with no debt." April talked about how the program worked in D Farms. Mr. Bond was impressed this young thing had a heart of gold.

"That's a mighty fine thing you are doing there, and I hope you know it?" he said. "Let me get my keys and I can show you the place." On the outside of the building was a big hulking brick wall. On the inside was an oasis of peace and beauty, and April liked it immediately.

As you walked inside you were met by a tiled courtyard. It could be used for almost anything, for play, for eating, it was awesome! To the right was another huge room, it had been used for painting classes. The long wooden tables were still there, only chairs would be needed. Upstairs were twenty-two bedrooms and four bathrooms. They were all plain, white with brown baseboards and wooden floors.

Back downstairs they went from the courtyard back to an open terrace that had been used for gardening. Beyond that inside was a huge, and I do mean huge, kitchen. Then they left the kitchen by the back door to the outside. There at one time were raised beds for planting. One hundred feet further there was another building. It was very big and had been used for potting plants and storing soil.

April's mind was racing. She knew exactly what she would do with this if it was up to her, but it was not up to her. The Bonds looked at her and asked what her intentions were. April looked at them and said, "This is not a waste of your time. I am interested in your building depending on the price and condition of the utilities. I need to speak to someone before I can make this decision," she said.

"Well, we originally had this listed for $1.3 million, but that was fifteen years ago. It is in need of repairs, but it's not too bad. If you wanted, you could change it around," he said.

"And that would be very costly," April said.

"Yes, no doubt about that. At present labor is more expensive than materials," Mr. Bond said. "Here is our number a home, all right. I also know of an abstracting company we can use, so we will not need a realtor," he said.

"Yes, Sir. Thank you, Sir. I need to speak to someone before I make a decision. I don't know how much of a hurry you are in to sell, but I will not be home until September, and this is July.

That night April broke the farm competition rules. She used Tom's telephone in the kitchen and called Mr. Stevens. "Hey, April. My goodness, how are you?" He asked her.

"I am okay. I have a bit of a dilemma and needed to speak with you," she said.

"Okay, go! I am listening," Mr. Stevens said to her.

"I found a building I would like to buy, not for us or D Farms. I want to give it outright to a group of people who truly need it," she said.

"I see," Mr. Stevens said to her. "I don't know if I can help you with this. You see, April, as a business, you can't take money for personal reasons, and we don't loan money like a bank. I am sure if you wanted money from the bank, they would loan it to you with the signature of your parents since you are still a minor."

"No, I don't want my parent to know, not yet" she said, and she poured out her heart to him explaining who it was for and why.

"Sigh. That's an amazingly generous thing you want to do. Unfortunately, D Farms can't buy it for the business. But I think there are other avenues for you. Did you think about a business in flowers, selling online or retail. You know similar to the catalog your Mother gets?"

"No, I have not, but I am not sure that would work, but hold on, I am not sure that they want this building for any of that.

"I have asked if someone would want to donate a business of flowers, for them to sustain themselves. The building was in good shape not needing major repairs should this be approved. The person said yes, providing it was inspected."

"So go and get the building inspected, that will buy you some time. The seller must pay for the inspection, but you will have to earn this one kid. There is a big race starting to bloom, I hear there are two maybe four horses from the United Kingdom and two from Dubai. I don't know all the details, but from what I hear this is just starting. The race will not be until sometime in September. This might be your ticket, April. It's already the end of July. When are you to come home?" He asked.

"September, I think. I am not sure though, but a purse of two point eight million would sure come in handy," April said. April thought for a moment. She could not remember when exactly the farm competition ended, so she said, "Hold on a minute. I need to see when the farm competition ends," she said to him.

"No need, kid. I have it right here. You are free on August 31st, and you are in the clear after that. Like I said, I am hearing the race will be in September, usually the second week."

April felt some relief. Then she said, "I am not sure who Manny will select, but no matter who he picks, I am fine with it. Please explain all of this to him so he understands what I am doing and tell him to not say anything to anyone. I do trust him. Okay then, I am going to get an inspection and then make an offer," she said.

"Good for you, April. Your heart is in the right place. I will talk to you again soon." And he hung up.

April called the owners and explained that she needed an inspection. They agreed with her that due to the long period of time that the building has been empty, it should be inspected. They asked April if they could call Eunice. They felt confident she would know of a reliable inspector. So, the next day the Bonds did just that, and Eunice said she would contact one she had in mind. He was very thorough. He would check pipes, the heating system, and everything in between. It will be well worth it."

As she waited, April began to work tirelessly, trying to rebuild her muscle tone again. She had not run in a while, so she no longer rode the gaiter, but walked or sprinted. She ate less and better. April tied Velcro weights on her ankles and wrist for a better work out.

Each night she prayed, not for herself, but for the Mother Superior not to reject this offer. She knew this was risky, but she felt she had to try. All the children they fed would go hungry. Her prayers were sincere and long. April prayed as she worked, and as she ate. In all she did, she had one thought, one direction to ask God for mercy and his grace. This was not for her, but for the good of others, especially for the children.

One night as April walked down to that building, it began to rain. It poured and she made her way to the school. April stood there on the small overhang getting soaked when a car pulled up. Out stepped Mother Superior, she was shocked to see April standing there all soaking wet.

"Come in child. You will catch your death of cold in those wet clothing. Louise, take her to the laundry area and give her clean, dry clothing to wear, and dry hers.

April followed Louise dutifully. Louise pealed April's wet clothing off and put a long white nightgown on her. The nightgown was high at the neck, with long sleeves and all the way to the floor.

After she was dressed, it was made known to Louise that April was to go to the kitchen. April followed Louise to the kitchen holding up the bottom of the nightgown so she would not trip and fall. In the kitchen was Mother Superior dishing out a warm bowl of pea soup and she had some biscuits laid out for April. "Sit down and put something warm in your belly," she said.

April was grateful. She was cold to the bone. After she ate, Mother Superior was sitting on a rocking recliner that was made like a love seat. Mother Superior's eyes were closed. April sat down beside her and laid her head on Mother Superior's lap.

"What is wrong?" she asked April.

"I am homesick. I get like this sometimes. Is it okay if I hug you for a while?" April asked her.

Never having had a child, Mother Superior was taken aback. She was not shocked, but she never was in this situation before. Her needy children were eighteen years old or more and she never bothered much with the school children. They were loud and unruly. She liked order. April began to cry and held on to Mother Superior like a life vest on a boat sinking. Mother Superior stroked her head and her hair until she felt April relax a bit. She realized that although this girl was a teenager, teenagers need their Mothers from time to time, and since hers was not here, she was glad April turned to her. She was a good child, really she was. She learned from the nuns about her deep fervent prayers, how sincere they were.

She knew April was on a competition and really that was a lot, leaving her family for a year, not having contact with them, and working when she was not in school. Then Mother Superior laughed a bit at what a stickler she was about truth in history class. If she had the chance to do it all over again, she would not have been so harsh with April. But children have always been such a nuisance. That was one big reason she chose to join the rank of sisters and become a nun.

That punishment is what brought out the truth to be known about this girl, or they never would have heard her prayers. As she stroked her hair her crying stopped, and April was almost asleep. "Poor little drowned rat. You are dry now and your tummy is full. Now you want comfort." She said this very quietly, but out loud. And it hit her like no force had in a long, long time, the feelings of internal Motherhood. She caught herself as tears began to well in her eyes.

"Someone has done well with you. You are not like many other children I have seen. You love openly, you care about everything. You are obedient and love God." She wiped tears away. If I ever had a chance to be a Mother, I would have wanted a daughter to be like you, fearless and full of love. She was trapped, but in such a loving way. She just wanted to sit here for a while and feel what it was like to be a Mother, just once, for a short while.

The two of them slept right there until 5 a.m. vespers. Mother Superior awoke to music. At first, she was confused, she was not in her bed, and she was dressed. Then as she was fully awake, she remembered the night before. She stirred April who was still on her lap, "Wake up, April, wake up."

Slowly coming to her senses, April sat up. She yawned and stretched as Mother Superior straightened out her wrinkled clothing "You have some breakfast. The girls will be in soon," she said and left.

April did not know what day it was and felt confused when she saw a calendar above the cupboard. It was Friday. No school for her, so she ate a bit in the kitchen and slipped out to sprint home. Tim had been away to pick up a pair of ducks that a friend of his kept on his farm. He had over one hundred ducks and he was glad to see his old friend again. Tim was not expected home until Sunday. It was a long trip and April did not want to go. She wanted to see the building again, that's when the deluge of rain met her.

So here she was, what to do, what to do, and the telephone rang. "Hi, April. Mr. Stevens here. I spoke with Marty, and he too wanted to enter the filly in the race we spoke about. So, if you are in shape to ride and can be there on the 13th of September, that would work out for everyone. I did tell him to be discreet, and he gave me his word."

April danced in the kitchen. It was all coming together. Then she decided to kneel and pray. She poured out her heart to her Father in heaven for his mercy and to give her strength. She then got up, dialed the number of the Bonds, and made them an offer of $800,000. Mr. Bond was surprised and happy. April told them she would pay them the entire amount in cash on the 15th of October. The Bonds had no problem with the time of payment. They were happy the building would be gone.

Now how would she tell Mother Superior and all the sisters.

She wondered about that and as it turned out she did not have to. The Diocese sent a letter to Mother Superior and the nuns. The letter read that someone was interested in donating a building that was in much better condition than the one they had. Of course, nothing was final, but if they came through on their end, they would approve it. Keeping the church open and allowing them to stay together and continue the good work they were doing in the community especially for all the young children.

This was an answer to prayer and all the nuns were to pray for this generous person. That is how April found out, she too was to pray for this person, and she felt awful. She could not pray for herself. So, she asked God to help her ride well and for the filly to be blessed for the good that was here to continue on and on for those living here.

Meanwhile she spruced up the new place as much as she could. Tom helped her. They put in new mushroom soil in the raised bedding and brought in dump truck loads for the flower business. All the wood was cleaned and polished, and the cobwebs were all gone. The floors were scrubbed and gleaming. The gymnasium floor shined, and new string was added to the basketball hoops. Tom made sure the hoops electrically folded up and down. He also made sure the scoreboard worked. These two worked frantically to get it done before the end of August.

Now April had one thing left to do, and that was to rename this building. April confided to Tom that she wanted his nephew's name in brass over the doorway. This would be Peter's legacy of good, healing many wounds and hopefully bring them back around to loving each other again.

The Tyler building was the talk of the town. Everyone wanted to know who bought it and they all wanted to see it. But the big brick wall did not talk.

April needed to talk to Tom, she needed him to keep this secret. April told Tom what her plans were to pay for the building.

"What if you lose." he said, and April hit him.

"How about thinking positively, okay," she said. "Here are two envelopes, one is marked with "win", the other is marked "lose". Give them the one that is appropriate. Even if we don't come in first, we should make enough money in second place, but I am not entering to lose," she said. On the afternoon of September 15[th,] I need you to bring Mother Superior, and whoever is with her to the gym at 1:00 there will be a television there. It is black and white but works well. It's set on the channel that carries the race and when it is over hand them whichever envelope it is, win or lose. That's the HUGE favor I am asking of you, Tom. I hope you are okay with this. I am depending on you."

Tom looked at April and said, "You want me to bring the battle axe here and entertain her?" "No, I never said that. You are being difficult, Thomas! But Tom, I want you to know if you ever decide you want more for yourself, call me and I will put you in touch with a dear good friend of mine, Mr. Stevens. He will set you up on a D farm and have you working. And when you are finished, you can find a companion for yourself." Tom was silent, his chin quivered, and he could not talk.

"It's all right. I know that you have a good heart, and you should have a companion," April said.

"No one would want me. My sister said so," Tom tearfully said.

"Oh, that is hogwash and not true at all. You are a hard worker. You are funny and you have the patience of Job. I am telling you the truth. When you are ready, 'if' you are ever ready for a change, to leave here, and make a life of your own, it will be there waiting for you," she said to Tom.

"Now, I need to get a bus ticket for me to be at that racetrack on time," April said aloud.

"How about I buy you a ticket to fly," Tom said.

"I can't let you do that," April told him.

"Oh, it's okay when you help others, but no one can help you?" Tom said to her.

April understood, and he was right. "I am indebted to you, Tom," and she kissed his cheek.

That night to celebrate they went to town for pizza and soda April had to be careful, so she wolfed down the salad with water. When they returned home there was a big surprise. His sister had come home a few minutes before they did. When April saw who Tom's sister was, she recognized her right away. She WAS a famous actress, she looked older but beautiful. She was a delight to be around and had energy and then some.

She walked into her home and then clapped her hands together wanting to see everything. April asked her husband Dom to cover his wife's eyes so she would not see until it was time, and he did. As they stood beside the yellow swing, he could not help but say, "Beautiful, just beautiful," and then he took his hand away from his wife's eyes and she was thrilled.

"This is so wonderful, and look at those ducks, Honey. Aren't they so cute?" she said.

They told her to sit down on the swing and she did, then April told Dom to sit with her. He was afraid the swing would not hold them both. April assured him it would.

He sat down beside his wife, "Hey this is nice," he said. "We could sit out here almost year-round." He snuggled his wife to him, and she giggled.

She turned to April and said, "I love it. I absolutely love it."

April said, "Okay, let's move along on this tour."

They climbed into the gator and April had Tom drive the four of them around. "Wow, it looks so much nicer all mowed. What a nice job." Then they went to the pastures and Dom was thrilled. "I just knew these would make nice pastures. Don't you agree, Tom,"

Tom just nodded his head.

Then the steers came toward the gator. They wanted grain and Dom's eyes got big. "Oh, wow. I love this," he said.

Then the sheep heard humans and came, curious to see what was happening. Dom's wife said, "Awe, they are so cute,"

April told her in the fall there would be little lambs on the ground.

"Oh, my goodness, how awesome. I can't wait. They will be amazing," she said.

Tom drove them all around the property and Dom said, "It's like seeing this place in a whole new light. I love it, April. What a great job you did."

April said, "I did not do this all myself. I had a great helper," as she patted Tom on his shoulder.

"Tommy did you this with her?" she questioned him.

"I did a little," he said.

April let it go. Obviously, his sister either did not know what Tom was capable of or just didn't care. They completed their ride and got back to the house.

April told them, "Please excuse me I need to pack so I can catch my flight."

"Are you leaving soon?" she asked.

"Well, yes. I have to. I have another commitment, but I do hope you give me a good review."

That is when Tom said, "I have it all documented in pictures. I was not sure who would show or what would get done, but you did way more than what was asked of you. I have the pictures to prove it."

April just smiled and nodded her head.

April bound up to her room at the back of the house and began to fold her clothing. She looked around the room so she would not forget anything. It took her all of fifteen minutes and when she came down Tom's sister and Dom had headed into their bedroom. They were tired from their long flight from Los Angeles. Tom was still up, and he thanked April again. He said he would be up by five a.m. and would take her to the airport himself. April was grateful and told him so. April asked him if they could make one stop in the morning, and she promised to make it quick. Tom guessed where she wanted to go, and he said it was all right.

The next morning April was up at 4 a.m. just like old times, dressed, and ready by 4:15 a.m. Tom was up and dressed, and he took her suitcase as April carried her guitar. He carefully placed them in his pickup truck, and they drove off in silence and dark.

It took Tom ten minutes to reach the Catholic school. There April knocked on the door and a novice answered it. "May I please see the sisters?" April asked.

The novice opened the doors and told April to follow her. They were all in the hallway on their way to enter the chapel.

April rushed to them and hugged all of them. Mother Superior clapped her hands wanting to know what the calamity was. "It's just me, Mother superior. I wanted to say, "Goodbye."

By now all the nuns were circled around April and listened to a tearful goodbye. "I want all of you to know I love you. I am so grateful for the time we have had together in school, on walks, and eating ice cream (some of them giggled). I loved praying with you, and I hope you found a small space in your hearts for this Mormon girl." They all hugged her with tears.

Mother Superior was no different. She was not ashamed to miss this one. She was a rebel and an angel all in one. She was a delight to her soul.

"Now where are you going?" she asked of April.

"I am going to take the biggest risk of my life for those that I love," she said. "I am going to humbly ask you to pray for me. I will need all the help I can get."

"Is it dangerous?" Mother Superior asked.

"Yes, it is dangerous, physically and emotionally," April answered her.

"Then absolutely don't do it. Walk away, and keep walking," she told April.

April looked at her and said, "I can no more than I can stop breathing, because Jesus Christ said, 'If you love me, then follow me, when ye have done for another, then ye have also done for me.' You will all know soon enough. Just know that I love you all and am so grateful for the good work you do here."

Mother Superior felt a pang in her heart, "For how long? Soon these doors would be boarded shut. You do know we will want to hear from you. How you are doing," she said.

"Oh, you will. This I promise. Okay, I must go," she said. Then she hugged them all and was gone.

April went out quickly and hopped into Tom's truck.

"Thanks, I just could not leave without saying goodbye to them."

Strangers at Home

BACK HOME, THERE WERE TWO STRANGERS THAT APPEARED AT THE Di Angelo home. The people taking care of the farm for Gordon were confused. They did not know who these people were. As instructed, they called Mr. Stevens who drove out promptly to deal with this situation.

As he drove into the driveway, he knew right away who these people were. It was April's grandfather John and his wife. Grandpa John wanted his wife to meet April and see her accomplishments. But since April was still on the farm competition, it was not possible, not yet. So, Mr. Steven made than an offer.

Your granddaughter is not back yet. She has been away on a farm competition, but if you let your luggage here and come with me, I can show you some things she has not. They looked at one another and agreed to go with Mr. Stevens. They got into his car, and he headed to the airport. On route he called Scott, their pilot, and made the arrangements. He also called a place he had in mind where they could go to in Nebraska. It was spring there, some light snow and a little cold, but very beautiful.

Grandpa told his wife Percy about things as they drove along. She listened but wanted to see it all for herself. As they reached the airport, Grandpa was excited, but his wife was hesitant. That airplane looked too small to her. With some encouragement and physical help, she boarded, and soon they were taking off. Scott smiled as he watched Grandpa with his face almost pressed against the glass to see everything. The flight was not long, and the weather was so clear. It was a smooth ride.

At touch down in Nebraska, Scott was told he could stay or leave but return in two days. Scott helped the grandparents to the small milk house that was used for guests. It had been converted to a comfortable little cottage for this purpose.

Grandpa was overwhelmed at the size of this farm and had many questions. Scott knocked on the door and asked them to come with him. The wind was blustery, and they all held onto their jackets pulling them closed. They headed to the barn which to Grandpa looked like an airplane hangar. It was round and huge. A man came out and introduced himself as the barn manager and said, "At this farm we are milking 1,500 cows. It is not unusual to see a calf delivered from their side near her ribs. The reason we do it this way is that it is an easier birth for the cow. I don't want to frighten you. Grandpa was shocked when he saw what the farm manager told them. That was crazy to him. That tour took a good two hours and Scott realized he had not made arrangements for where they would stay. He asked the barn manager to continue while he went and spoke to the house parents.

Scott went to the big house and met with Judy. She was about thirty. He told her the plan just as Judy's husband Bart walked in, so the two men shook hands. He and his wife were glad to see visitors. Judy quickly decided to make a good sit-down, home-cooked meal for their visitors and the workers. Scott told them he took the liberty of putting April's grandparents in the guest home. Judy said she would make sure the heat was turned up and the bedding freshened.

Scott thanked them and went back to join the elderly couple. He found them at the calf pens. Grandpa was overwhelmed at the number of calves. There were easily 60 or more calves running in a very large pen. Scott explained that the heifers were kept and raised here on the farm, but the bulls were sent to another farm to be raised for meat. That was all part of D Farms.

They soon went inside to escape the fall winds, and Judy gave them warm cocoa to drink. She told them dinner was promptly at 6 p.m., and they were welcome to stay in the big house or retreat to their small cottage.

Grandma wanted her time alone, so they left to go to the cottage. They rested until dinner time, Grandpa slept, but Grandma had brought along some needlework for her to work on. At 5:00 p.m. she spoke to her husband, who was awake, and told him they needed to get ready for supper. They both washed up and combed their hair to be presentable.

In the big house there were twenty-two chairs at a large, long table to accommodate the house parents and workers. This evening there were two additional chairs, added for their guests. Scott knew he had to have the grandparents back in time for the race that April entered. It was agreed they should see what April was able to build, and how generous she was.

Two days of cows, good food, and lots of company. As they lay in bed, Grandma asked her husband, "Is April rich?"

Grandpa did not answer right away. He had to answer truthfully, but in a tactful way. "She is, but not because of this. All the money made here buys more farms, pays salaries, and is for the education of the kids who work here. You heard at the dinner table all the different choices each kid wanted to do. So understand, she is rich, but she never takes from any of the farms."

Grandpa did not want his wife to get any funny notions. They were not poor. They had a modest lifestyle that suited them, and they were comfortable. They had no need to travel to see the world or have a fancy car. He did not want his wife to think since April was rich, they could help themselves to whatever they wanted. No, this all belonged to D Farms, and they had enough. They were especially blessed to see their granddaughter, her vision, and her accomplishments.

After the second day, they all said their goodbyes and boarded the Cessna. Scott then flew them to the racetrack where April was scheduled to race. Grandpa loved horses and this place had some of the finest horses he had ever seen. It excited him in a way his wife did not understand. He was determined to see them, touch them, and ask about them.

It was a wonderful day for him. He never would regret this trip. It opened his wife's eyes and helped her get over the harsh feelings she had for April and her Mother. There was no need to hate. It only makes the hater feel worse. Besides it was ridiculous to have bad feelings when they were unfounded. Yes, this was a trip that was needed and proved to his wife what was true. He was grateful for all that had happened.

Meanwhile back in Maine, prior to the race Tom understood and said, "When you win," and he winked at April. "Don't you think they will want to see you again, after all you did for them?"

"Yes, they probably will, but I just can do it, not right away. I have not seen my family in a year, or my sweetheart. I will be a senior this year in school, and I need to work on a few things. I will be in touch with them. I am old school, I write letters," she said.

They drove for a long time, "Do you want to eat before we reach the airport? We do have time," Tom said to April.

"Okay, that's fine. I just don't want to miss my flight," she told him.

They ate at a nice family style place, and Tom was so kind to her.

"One day you can treat me," he said.

"I surely will," April told him.

At the airport the traffic was ridiculous. The cars went fast, too fast. Tom decided to drop April at the front of the airport. As April got out of the truck, Tom handed her the suitcase and guitar and said, "I am going to park and then come in."

April grabbed his hand and said, "This is hard for me, worse than saying goodbye to the nuns. I thank you Thomas for all your willingness to help me. You didn't have to. I think we are alike in many ways, old school, and treating others as you would like them to treat you. And you certainly live up to that. Look me up when you come to California, Okay?"

"Let me park and I'll come in." Tom never did. April thought he might not. She knew he did not like saying goodbye.

April had forty-five minutes to board and there was no sign of Tom. She didn't blame him, not at all. April knew that he would miss her. From the beginning they were like old friends. A person can get used to that when they are lonely. So, she sat there waiting for her plane to take her home, what a lovely sound that had.

April arrived at the Los Angeles International Airport at 12:00 p.m. She exited from the airplane not knowing if anyone would be there. April looked around and there stood her Mom, her first Mom and Lena. They were all there waiting to greet her. They hugged her, they kissed her, and they all laughed over and over. They had so much to talk about. April was relieved. Right now, April had what she needed most, to bask in the love of these women who did dearly love her. How lucky she truly was, it was like having three Mothers. They talked as they walked and one or another would hug her again.

"Who drove to this crazy place?" April asked.

"Lena did. She has nerves of steel driving in heavy traffic," Nora said.

Miranda piped up, "I was so glad Lena offered to drive. I don't like busy road with cars flying by."

"That is my talent then," Lena said laughing. "It really doesn't bother me at all."

It was a good two-hour ride home with Lena gripping the steering wheel of the car. She navigated them out of the airport onto the freeway like a pro.

Before too long the city faded away and they were in smaller towns. As they drove along someone's belly growled. "Who did not eat their breakfast?" Miranda asked.

Both women in the front seat laughed, "Neither one of us. We were too excited."

"Okay then. We stop some place to eat, so driver be aware we have hungry people aboard," Miranda teased. They stopped at a buffet. April loved shrimp and that is what she had. The ladies had all sorts of thing on their plates.

"Is that all you are eating, shrimp?" Miranda asked her.

"No Ma'am, I am going to have a corn muffin too," April said.

Soon they were all back in the car, and on they went. Before too long, Lena was pulling the car into the Di Angelo's driveway. It was 2:30 in the afternoon. Miranda pulled April's guitar and suitcase out. She waited as April hugged and kissed her family. Then Lena and Nora left to go home, they beeped their car horn as they left the driveway.

"So, race day is on the 15th that gives you about a week and a half to be ready," Miranda said.

"No that gives me about seven days, and I want to be there five days before to breeze her. I have two days to prepare and then I must leave."

Miranda was tired and she hoped that Gordon would see April to the race. If he had to work, she knew her father would love the opportunity to take April. Miranda hoped to get into the doctor's office to get some blood work done. She had been so tired lately, without any reason. Oh, she could reason it away, but the truth is she was tired and had less going on.

Miranda called the airline and lined up the flight for April to arrive on the 8th. Now she had more than enough time. As she hung up the phone, she began rubbing her temples, it was another headache. So, she picked up the telephone and dialed her doctor's number, requesting an appointment. They found a spot for her for the very next day.

When April came into the house Miranda touched her daughter's hand and asked if she would mind driving her to the doctor the next day.

"Mom, what's the matter? Sure, I will gladly drive you. Why didn't you say something, Mom?

"So many questions. You are giving me a headache," Miranda said to April.

April was worried, her Mother was like the Tasmanian devil. She used to whirl around cleaning, calling, and helping others. To see her down with headaches concerned April greatly. She went upstairs and called her Dad.

"Dad, did you know Mom has been having headaches and is tired all the time?" April said. "She called the doctor and has an appointment for tomorrow."

"No, I did not," Dad said. If I drove her to the hospital, she would be upset with me. You know that."

"Okay, when you come home you ask her. I am going to make dinner tonight. Boy, Dad, I hate leaving for the race, but I have to. I am committed to that race for a good reason. Trust me, Dad. Unless you have a mere $800,000 dollars laying around for me to use! Okay, see you in a bit," April said.

When Gordon came home, he went to his wife who was sleeping in her recliner. He touched her arm, and she woke up. "Hi sweetie," he said. "What's wrong?"

"Oh, nothing. I have been tired lately and having headaches, one after another," Miranda said.

"How about you and I go to the hospital together so they can check your blood pressure and maybe give you something tonight, so you can rest comfortably."

"No, no I am not making any fuss. I will be fine."

Gordon got firmer, "Honey, I am taking you. I would die if anything happened to you, so I will get a change of clothing for you, but we are going," he said.

Miranda stared at her husband in surprise, but she did not protest.

April helped where she could. She packed her Mom's nightgown, her slippers, her reading glasses, and medication list. Some books, crosswords, and search and finds. And last she slipped in a framed picture of her parents on their wedding day. As they headed out the door April asked if they wanted her to go with them.

"No, you stay here. I can take care of my Sweetie. I always have, and I always will," her dad said as he slipped his arm around his wife's waist and they left straight away for the hospital.

April took a shower to relax and some Aleve, but nothing helped. She finally fell asleep in her clothing on her bed with her buddy beside her. Ruby lay on her right side and would not leave or move, not unless April got up. Ruby was a source of comfort to April, like an old friend who was always glad to greet you and be with them.

April felt awful. She knew it was because of her Mom. Last night was the worst and longest night of April's life. April could not sleep. She was up, then she was down. She looked at the telephone by her bedside to make sure it had a dial tone. It did. There were no other problems except Dad had not called her yet. And her Mom - how was her Mom? She went downstairs and sat in her Mom's recliner, it smelled like her perfume. April fell asleep there in that recliner with Ruby lying on the footrest, half under the blanket April had over her.

At 3 a.m. Dad came in, and Ruby barked like Dad was a burglar. "Ruby, shhh," April said to the dog. She ruffled the hair on her head. "You dumb dog that is who pays for your food. She loved Ruby she knew Ruby's heart belonged to her.

Dad came in and sat in his recliner, blowing out air in a big whoosh. "Dad, are you alright?" she asked him softly.

"Yes, I am. I am a bit tired though. Mom is sleeping overnight for observation. They upped her blood pressure pill to 20 mg, instead of the 10 mg she had been taking. When I left her, she was sleeping. I wanted to wait until she dosed off, so she did not know I left her." he said.

"Dad, you are such a good man. Don't go to work tomorrow. You'd have to get up in two hours if you did go," April said to him.

"No, I am not going in. I would be useless. Besides, I must pick Mommy up tomorrow when the hospital calls." He got up and went upstairs to shower and go to bed. April followed going into her room with her companion jumping up and down beside her.

Just having her Dad home, put April at ease and she soon slept. Sometimes she felt Ruby growl, as if it had been a storm, to Ruby everything was a monster. She was always protecting April, or so she thought. For that reason, she loved her. She gave her everything she had. Yes, a goofy little dog, but her heart was honest, innocent, and all April's.

April's last day before leaving for the race was the day her Mom came home from the hospital. April got up, had all the chores done, and picked flowers on her way. The flowers included daisies, tiger lilies, teeny tiny daisies that looked like baby's breath, corn flowers and thistles. The purple on a thistle is the most beautiful purple ever. April made a nice bouquet for her Mom, and put them in a glass vase from the top cupboard. April cleaned the table off and the living room was as neat as a pin.

Mom came in, saw the flowers, and remarked how lovely they were. Dad told Miranda to come in, sit down, and talk to April for a bit. So, she did.

April came to her Mother and hugged her. Then she stepped back and said, "Mom, I love you so much. Don't scare me that way."

"I didn't mean to. I did not know what was wrong with me either," her Mom said. "But now I am on double what I was on, and the doctor told me to lose ten pounds. I could cut off my head. What do you think?" She asked her daughter.

"I don't think so, but I can make meals for you that will help, and we can walk together when I come back," April said.

"Oh, I would like that because it can be scary walking alone," her Mother said.

Just then Dad came in carrying Mom's bags and suitcase. April took them from him and put them away upstairs. When she came down Dad was sitting in his recliner less than five inches from where her Mom sat.

April saw them and as she looked, they both reached out their arms to hold hands. "Yep, I want a marriage just like that someday," she said to herself. Then Hugh came to mind, and she wondered why no one had heard from him. But right now, she said nothing. Mom needed to be stress free for a bit, so far now, Hugh could wait.

April went upstairs to pack her suitcase for the morning departure. She was excited thinking about what she was doing for someone else. She snapped the locks on her suitcase and came downstairs quietly. She suspected both of her parents were napping. She was right so she went into the kitchen, closed the door to not wake them, and began to plan a good meal. All she needed was in the refrigerator and in the cupboards. She mixed up what she felt was a good supper and then went into the parlor to put her feet up and rest. Ruby was close at her heels. She put Ruby up on her chair and she perched on the arm rest like a lookout. April looked at her saying, "Crazy dog." Then she ruffled the fur on her back as Ruby turned to lick her hand.

April nodded off to sleep in less than ten minutes. Next thing she knew, someone was banging on their kitchen door. She jumped up with Ruby barking and walked to the door. It was Dad. He wanted her to come out and sit on the swing with them. It was almost 4 p.m., so April popped their supper into the oven.

"This is good." April thought to herself, sitting on the swing with her parents. This was great. To April great things were never big things. They were the little things in life. Making muffins with her Mom, or helping Dad bleed the brakes on the old truck. Yes, those memories were so sweet to her. She could recall them when she needed them in times of stress.

They sat together and April said, "I leave tomorrow for the race. I will be down there on the 10th and the race is on the 15th. I would love if Manny and Contessa would come along.

"I'd love it if the both of you could be there, but I understand if you can't." she said.

"What do you mean?" her Dad said. "We were planning on being there. Weren't we, Momma?" and he kissed his wife.

"Absolutely, don't rule me out. I am not dead yet," her Mom said. "Besides Nora and Lena wanted to come and we would not want to disappoint them. We all want to know what this secret is all about."

April was shocked and said, "Mom, don't ever say that. Please, Mom," and April had tears in her eyes.

"Come here. I did not mean to frighten you, but it is a fact of life. I do not have any paper that says when I am leaving this place. When I go, I go." Then she hugged her daughter. Dying was not something she wanted to do, but Miranda knew one day she would surely die. We will all cross over, it is best to realize that and prepare yourself. Know the Savior really know him, that is the only way.

Early the next morning Manny and Contessa pulled into the driveway. Dad already had his truck running.

"We will follow you?" Manny asked.

"You can. We are only going as far as the bus station in town," Dad said.

Away they went out of the driveway like on a criminal pursuit. Dad flew with Manny behind him. They parked at the station pulling out what they needed. Dad went into the bus office for their tickets. Nora and Lena were already there, they boarded, and sat together. April sat by her Grandpa, he put his arm around her and asked, "What is this race for?"

"I would love to tell you, but I can't. That is why I asked you to come along. We will all find out then," she told him.

At the racetrack Marty had a new filly. She was sleek, long legged, very tall, and built like a brick house, solid. She had not a hair of white on her. She was black as night. Her name was

"Bituminous" - Bitty for short. For those of you who do not know, Bituminous is a type of coal.

April and her family arrived later in the day, including her grandparents on her father's side. April was relived, she had ample time to breeze Bitty. Golly Goodness this girl had power and could run. Every time April showed up at a racetrack, reporters soon followed. It was a fact, and she did not like it at all. She wished she was unknown, but it was way too late for that.

"What cha' got there April D?" they hollered at her.

She answered back "Just a Bitty of a horse. Nothing to see here." They all laughed. They all knew when April was being evasive there was something big looming. They snapped their photos and wrote on their tablets. April just walked Bitty around the track.

At night when the lights were up, Marty wanted April to open Bitty up. No one was at the track and if it rained, like it so often does, it's dark and ominous. April did as Marty asked. It was like riding a whirlwind. Bitty was faster than Native Son, or so it seemed. She certainly inherited some of his genes. Twice around, and that was it. Then Bitty got a good washing from Byron and was fed.

Marty told April the United Kingdom horses and those from Dubai were fast, but Bitty could hold her own. If she was bumped, she would not care. Bitty was not fragile. He also told her he would walk the track as he always did, and he would see her in the morning.

Race Day

RACE DAY WAS EXCITING. THERE ARE NO ADEQUATE WORDS TO describe it. Everyone is dressed up to the max. Some were wearing hats, and there was music and banners. The announcers dressed in uniforms. And the silks were so colorful. To hear the horn blow for the start of the race always gave April goose bumps.

April was dressed and weighed out before most went in. She was wearing purple that really stood out on Bitty's coal black color. Manny and Contessa, John and Percy, Nora and Lena, Mom and Dad were to go to the stands in a special seating section for racers and their families. That is when April's Dad asked her, "How much should I place on her?"

April made a face and said, "Dad, I am not a betting girl, but she is going to win. That is all I can tell you."

So, Manny, Gordon, and John went to the track office while the women secured seats halfway up in the Di Angelo box. They were smack in the middle, which gave a good, clear view of the track. That is unless someone with a tall hat would sit in front of them.

Marty was with Bitty. He and Byron helped April mount since Bitty was so tall. There was an escort for April and away they went. Bitty was a tad nervous. So, April stroked her neck, patted it, and talked to her, which helped.

Bitty loaded nicely and was nowhere near the United Kingdom or Dubai horses. It was a field of fifteen today. The purse was not $1.8 million, it was $2.8 million. The Dubai people really wanted to up the stakes, which was great for April, should they win.

The gates opened and away they went, down the stretch, and right in the middle. Biddy was not like Native Son. She did not need encouragement. She plowed through like she was on a mission. She knew what to do. She kept her pace to the half mile turn and then she opened up. April felt like she was a passenger as she did not have to encourage Bitty. When they reached the quarter pole Bitty was out ahead by four lengths. She did it, this girl beat out the boys, and April could not help but feel elated. April could not stop smiling. Her heart was beating very fast.

Back in Maine Tom had his sister and husband come along to the Catholic School, where Tom had made an appointment for two hours with the boss, Mother Superior. They were escorted into the hallway and Tom told the novice that he preferred to sit in the foyer and wait. And he did while the novice retrieved Mother Superior. Now Tom hoped he could get her to the building without a fight, so when they met, he told her a little white lie. Tom told her there was a needy family that required assistance, but she had to come with several nuns that she trusted. She could follow them or come with them. It would only take about an hour.

Mother Superior was eager to help but did not understand the secrecy. Tom helped some of the nuns into his truck, while his sister and her husband put Mother Superior, Louise, and two other nuns into their car. They all drove to the brick building that had "The Tyler Building" on a gold plate on the door frame header. His sister paused and almost choked up.

But that can't be our Tyler. That plate must have been here a long time. Although it did look shiny and new, there was no tarnish on the plate. In the past, she had seen how they turned a greenish color. Oh well, she thought and went in.

When they were all in, Tom asked them to follow him. As they did, they could not help but notice the solid beauty of the inside of this brick place. Who would have guessed behind those red walls was such grandeur and beauty? The route was designed for them to see as much of the building as possible. At last, they wound around to the gymnasium with its gleaming floors and shiny bleachers that were open for them to sit on.

"Okay, now I need you to sit down and make yourselves comfortable," Tom said.

"What is the meaning of this? Sit down? Where is this family?" Mother Superior asked in a harsh tone.

Tom explained, "Do you remember April D, the girl in your school?"

"Of course we do. So, now you tell me, what does April have to do with any of this?" Mother Superior demanded. Her face was getting red.

"Well, if you just sit down, you will find out in about ten minutes or so," Tom said.

He turned on the black and white television, it was already set to the channel April instructed. There was a program airing and all the nuns watched it intently. Then it was over, and a horse race was coming on.

"What's going on?" the sisters asked.

Tom's sister and her husband were sitting on the second step of the bleachers, right in front of the nuns. His sister turned around to them saying, "Just be a little patient. I believe Tom was to show you something. You did agree to give up an hour."

They sat there while the announcers reported that the race had a big purse of 2.8 million dollars. The betting had been opened up to the United Kingdom and Dubai which made it the largest prize they had ever seen. Then they ran down the list of horses, which had little meaning to the audience, but they kept watching. As the riders came out, they mentioned each horse, the horse's number, and who the rider was.

When the announcer came to number 7, the horse's name was Bituminous, a filly owned and ridden by April D of D farms. This is when the sisters heard and all of them began to talk with a flurry.

"Shhhh," Mother Superior said loudly. The rundown of the riders and horses finished, and they loaded into the gates and soon, "They were off!"

The sisters watched for #7, and they kept saying, "Come on Bituminous. Go, April. Go." Some cried, and there were four who prayed the entire time. When they saw the pair at the half pole, some stood and screamed. At the quarter pole they knew she was going to win, they jumped up and down, and hugged each other. Mother Superior wiped her glasses and her eyes and admonished the sisters to sit down.

As they watched, they saw their little girl in the winner's circle. A huge wreath was around that big black horse's neck.

The reporters were asking many questions when one asked, "What do you plan to do with all that money?"

April sat with dust on her face and goggles, and she said, "I am counting on a dear friend to handle something close to my heart. If he followed through, and I hope he did. I hope he hears me – now is the time."

With that Tom turned down the volume on the television, much to the protests of the audience. He pulled out an envelope from his jacket and handed it to Mother Superior. On the envelope was marked "win".

She opened the envelope and pulled out a paper. It was a letter. As she read, many of the sisters wanted her to read it out loud. So, she started over and read the letter out loud for all to hear.

Dearest Sisters,

If you are reading this letter, then we have won. I could not let you know who I was and for that I am sorry. I never lied to you. I know that you are losing your beloved school and that grieved me too. So much that I took on this venture.

The building you are sitting in is now yours, all of it including the kitchen and the gymnasium. Out back there is a huge area with built up raised beds for gardening. Beyond that is a place you will have to sustain yourselves so long as you are willing to learn and work. I want you all to know how much I love you and appreciated you putting up with a little Mormon girl who sometimes made trouble. I will forever treasure the time I had with you, and now I hope you will never forget me. The Diocese knows, they approved this gift two weeks ago. Now no one will have to leave. You can continue your mission of helping the poor and needy, and take care of the children, feed those hungry bellies.

> *My understanding is that the school and annex building will be torn down, but the Church (which is three blocks away) will be restored.*
>
> *Today we won. We won our freedom to do good. The check for 2.8 million dollars I am forwarding to a representative who will pay off the owners of the building. Whatever is left will cover your cost for all you will need and help with the repairs of the church. No one will have to dig deep into their pockets, instead they must search their hearts to know that the truth shall set them free. Be happy and live well. Always a servant of God, April D.*

Everyone was crying, no one could say a thing. Tom collected himself long enough to tell his sister she was wrong, the Tyler building does bear her son's name, and it was April's hope there would be healing between the family and the church.

His sister began to weep, as did her husband. "What a wonderful thing," she said. She turned to hug one of the nuns and it was Mother Superior right behind her. Mother Superior did hug her, and they held on to one another for quite some time.

"Do come back," Mother Superior urged the woman. "You do know that she did all of this for all of us, to heal and to bond again. Tom, when will we see April again. I mean is she planning on coming back to see what good she did?"

Tom answered her, "I asked April about that. And she said that as much as she wanted to, she could not come, not right away. Her Mother is ill, and she wanted to spent time with her family. But she will be back."

At the racetrack, Manny and all the rest wanted to know what April meant and she told them. She told them the entire story and Contessa began to cry and kiss April.

"Bless you. Bless you for helping them out. This means so much," she said.

April felt humbled and happy. There were no words from her. She was satisfied, tired, and hungry, but most of all satisfied. What she did was for God.

They left to go back when April sought out Marty. She thanked him and told him to do what he felt was best. It was her senior year, and she had some things to do yet. Marty told her he was going to run the filly with another rider and to April it felt good. She hugged Marty and Byron and ran to join up with her parents and family.

Grandpa John nudged his wife and asked her if she understood what their granddaughter had done. She nodded her head and sniffled. She too was overcome with pride. Helping so many, the needy, and the poor, and her heart suddenly softened toward the one she had hated for so long. As she walked along, she had a prayer in her to ask forgiveness. It seemed as if a voice came to her saying, "When you give forgiveness, know ye are forgiven."

As they walked along, she wept. No one knew why, but it was so obvious by her newfound kindness and words of praise to and about her granddaughter. Grandpa could not have wished for anything more, it was a healing of his family. Something he wished for, prayed for all his life. The little one was never accepted by his wife, now no one would ever say one word against her. In time her graduation picture would stand proudly on top of their television set in their living room. From this time forward she never missed an opportunity to tell anyone who came to visit about the remarkable, wonderful things her granddaughter did for everyone. She would haul out the book of farms to prove it all to them.

My Senior Year of High School

"My last year in school," she said aloud in her room. It was the first day of her last year of school. Her Mom had taken her shopping, but there was little that April needed. She liked her older clothing, they were soft and had a good feel to them. She had breakfast after chores with her Dad who gave her a blessing for comfort before he left for work.

As she stood outside waiting for her bus, she felt oddly calm. There was nothing on her plate for this coming year, except for being Mayor. Thankfully they knew she had been away, and April left two in charge covering for her. There were no problems that arose, nothing happened, and the town seemed to take care of itself, while each one took care of another. Other than Mayor she had no races, no traveling, no Olympics, and no competitions. She felt that she would apply herself 100% to her studies and elevate her grades to straight A's.

School, it was sort of bittersweet knowing in less than a year she would no longer be here ever again. She knew most of the kids, even many of the freshmen, having taken them on pony rides. April settled down and dug right in from the first day and paid strict attention. When December report cards come out, she indeed was a straight A student.

Some of the senior boys asked her out on dates. If it was to the movies with others along, she would go, but she did not go out with any boy one on one. She did write to Hugh often, giving him updates about life at home and what she was doing, but she never got a reply letter back.

In December the Captain's children came to visit him and his sweet wife Adelle. They stopped at the Di Angelo's home to speak to Gordon and April one evening. They were curious if the community center would be available for their parent's 50th wedding anniversary. April pulled out the calendar for the town and flipped to the month of April.

"What week were you thinking of? She asked.

The date was set for the middle of the month. They wanted to extend an invitation to the Di Angelos as they knew their Dad enjoyed running with April. They wrote down their address and left. April thought about a gift for the Captain and Adelle, but nothing she saw, or her Mother mentioned, seemed right.

One evening April put a call into Tom up in Maine. "Hello," Tom said.

"Hi, Tom. This is April Di Angelo calling you from California. How are you?"

"Oh, April, good to hear from you, really it is. I am doing well. My sister came home from L.A. to visit and caught the flu. She has been here for quite some time recovering. Sure hope I don't get it," he said.

"Is there any way I could speak to her or to her husband, just for a minute or two?" April asked. "Just a minute, I will get Dom." Tom said.

"Hello,"

"Hi, Dom, this is April D. I was there last spring on the farm competition. Do you remember me?" April asked.

"I sure do. Of course I remember you," he said.

Then April asked him, "I am looking for someone who has the experience and know how to make a hologram of a couple dancing for a good friend of ours, for their 50th wedding anniversary."

"Okay, I do know of someone who might be able to help you. He is always busy, but his daughter is just as capable as he is. Let me give them your number and he will get back to you. He does travel a lot, but eventually he will call you. I am sure about that. You need this in April you say?"

"Yes, his children want to have a party for them on the 15th of April at the Community Center."

"Hang in there and you should get a call this week or next, depending if he is traveling for his job or not," he said.

"Awesome," April said. She thanked him and wished for his wife to recover quickly and ended their call.

By the end of that week a call came, and the people left a message on the Di Angelo's answering machine. "Hi, this is Rosa. I am looking for April about her request for a hologram," and she left her number.

April wrote the number down and erased the message, she did not want her parent to know. April wanted this to be a surprise to everyone. When Miranda went to take care of someone from the church that afternoon, and her Dad was out helping someone with their car, April picked up the telephone and prayed Rosa was in. She was. "Hi Rosa, my name is April. I am looking for someone to make a 50th wedding anniversary very special," April said.

"Ah, yes. I think I already know. I spoke with Dominick, and he explained it all to me. Yes, I can help you. All I need is a photograph of the people when they were young, and a brief history of the couple.

April was a bit skeptical, "I would like to see your work if you are not offended."

"Oh, no. Many people are not familiar with holograms, so by all means come and see," Rosa said. She than gave April their address. They were two towns over, not too far.

April called her Dad on his cell phone and asked him if she could borrow his old truck for an errand. She might be gone three or four hours.

"Go ahead. Just leave a message for your Mom, so she doesn't worry." April did and she also took along her checkbook to put down a deposit.

When April got to the town, she had to ask several people where this address was. They were located in a remote area. When she pulled up, a Pitbull was lunging at the end of his line to get at her. April got out and said, "What's your problem? What did I ever do to you?" in a soft tone and the dog sat down and began to paw in the air at her.

Soon a man and a woman came out, "Hi, I am Rosa, and this is my brother Ramone," she said. "Don't mind Petie, he is a lover not a fighter. As April approached them, Petie licked her leg and April bent down to scratch behind his ears. "Oh, now you've made a friend. He loves scratching," and they all laughed. "Come in", Rosa said. April followed them into the house that was small but comfortable. They walked through a small kitchen and living room to a back room that was bigger than the two rooms combined.

"This is our graphics room, where we create." and she put on a disc of music and before April's eyes a couple appeared and they began to dance.

"Go ahead, touch it," Rosa said.

April put her hand into the hologram and felt nothing.

"A projection is beamed through light to create this image. It is not difficult really," Rosa said.

Then April asked, "What is the typical cost of something like this?"

Rosa said, "Anywhere from a few hundred dollars to thousands, depending on the graphics, how complicated they can be, or how long."

April whistled and said, "Whoa, I didn't know that, I . . . ."

Rosa interrupted her "I got word from Dominick that you are not to pay a penny. He was so impressed with all the work you did on their farm that cost them nothing. He guaranteed that he would find us work in a film that Disney would be starting soon. So, we appreciate recommendations like that.

April looked at her and said, "This would be for two very dear friends. He served in Germany during World War II. He met his sweet wife in a canteen. She hums a tune all the time, it was from that time era, and the place where she worked. I just want to surprise them and make them happy.

"And you will. All I need are two photographs of when they were young, one of him in uniform would help and maybe some as the years went by. Try to get them to me as soon as you can. Oh, yes. When is the party?" Rosa asked.

"It is on April 15th in the Community Center and it's in the park of our town, weather permitting," April said.

They got up and talked a little more and April had to go. "Sweet" she said out loud. Yes, doing your best in all things matter. She started the truck and headed back home. She got home and looked at the clock. She was not gone for more than two hours. Her mom was home and asked how her visit went. April knew her Mom would not stop trying, "It was good Mom, thanks for asking."

April found the number of the Captain's son and she explained to him that she needed photos of their Dad and Mom when they were in Germany, of his Dad while in the service, and a few of them throughout the years. He said his wife would help with that. She gave him her address and that following week a package arrived for April. She bound up to her room and carefully cut open the brown paper envelope and the pictures of the Captain and his wife spilled out. There were about two dozen of them. In one of the photos was the Captain in full uniform, and another had Adelle in her apron with her hair up in pins wearing a cap. These pictures were great, just what Rosa was hoping for.

She called Rosa's number, and they were home. They were excited to get the pictures.

April asked again to borrow the truck, "Where to this time?" her Mom asked.

"To the same place I was last week. And no, you may not go along. It's top secret," she told her Mom.

April got into the pickup truck and headed out. She thought she would be home even sooner this time. Now she knew where she was going.

She arrived in half an hour and again Petie the dog was growling at her. This time April brought along a big biscuit for him. "Uh, oh. Now you did it. He will follow you anywhere for food," Rosa said. Petie was enjoying the big biscuit and looking at April as if in disbelief that she bought him this delicious biscuit. They went in, April handed Rosa the package of pictures.

"Oh, these are great," Rosa said scrutinizing the photos. "I want to assure you this will be awesome. Let me get started on this right away and I will be there at the Community Center early to set up, about 5:00 p.m. It is best if there is darkness, cause the hologram will show up much better. Set up takes about an hour," Rosa said.

April said, "Come and eat. There will be tons of food." April drove home with a happy heart. She imagined how much fun the hologram would be for the Captain and Adele.

To be truthful, April was so grateful there was now a milking schedule. She had a chance to get out and milk. Not having anything to do but write letters to Hugh which he never wrote back, and attending the town council meetings once a month, April was bored out of her mind.

April checked the days off on her calendar, and soon it was April 1st. She called Rosa again and asked how it was going.

"It's going to be awesome," Rosa said. "You wait and see. This is one of the best we have worked on so far. I do want to tell you, Dominick set us up with a project so the timing of this has been perfect."

April went to the Community Center, unlocked the doors, and began to clean up. She wiped down cobwebs and swept the floors. Her Dad stopped by to see who was there. He said the family had hired a crew to clean up, cook, and clean up again afterwards as he took the broom away from April.

April was on pins and needles. She was so bored, so she joined the committee in school for a school play. They were up in the air on which theme to choose. April suggested they do a comedy, many agreed. They were all tired of movie themes. The band also wanted to do something, so they offered if anyone wanted to play a character in a song and sing it. April liked this idea and signed up. They had practice two times a week.

Before April knew it, she was marking an X on April 15th. Tomorrow was the 50th wedding anniversary party for the beloved couple. Her parent got an invitation in the mail and penned on the bottom Adele wrote, "Please be sure to bring April."

April and her Mother went shopping for a dress for the event. Her Mom chose a pretty dress that was black with sequins on the left shoulder and a small slit up the left side. April chose a light blue dress that caught her eye. They had a devil of a time to find her size, but they did, as there were others in the back of the store. April was glad her Mother had asked.

They arrived at 1:30 p.m. Dad was able to get off work at noon. He was dressed in a light blue suit and looked so handsome. When they pulled into the Center's driveway, there was a valet that took their vehicle to the parking area. Dad was a little nervous and he told the valet to be careful with his baby. That made the boy nervous. After all her Dad was the Sheriff of their county. They walked through and the smell of food would make anyone hungry. April was searching for Mexican food and behold, they had it, lots of it. Yum, yum!

Mom and Dad got a plate of food. April saw Trevor and waved to him. He came over and hugged her. "So, how's it going," he asked her.

"Good, did you sign up for the play or the band to sing a song?" April asked.

"I signed up for the play, whatever it is. I like humor too," and he laughed.

"Go find a seat and save one for me beside you," she told him as he began to walk away. Trevor put his thumb up to signal, Okay!

April felt alone, there were many people she knew here but she wanted to be with Hugh. She sighed and said to herself, "Wish in one hand, fill the other with stones, see which one fills up first." She got a plate of food and found her parents. The Marshalls were sitting with her parent and Trevor did save a seat for her.

At 5:30 April was looking for Rosa and their family van, nothing yet. At 5:55 she noticed a white van coming up the driveway. April saw her in the passenger seat and waved to her. They came and parked near the stage. The van's front was facing the stage and Rosa's Dad was there helping. They were completely set up in an hour and April told them to go get something to eat and drink. Relax and enjoy the evening too.

They did, and as it began to get dark, they approached April. They whispered to her, "It's time. Do your announcement and then put the couple near the hologram more towards the center of the stage if you can. We will run the hologram four feet from the center of the stage. As the hologram is lifelike in size."

April was so happy. She went to the Captain's son and asked if they would help her. She said she had a little gift for their parents. Then April handed the bundle of pictures back to his wife. April explained when she got up to announce, to put their parents near the center by the stage.

The Captain's table was almost at the spot. The son just moved their parents table over a bit, more to the center. Then the

Captain and his wife Adele sat down again near the side where the holograms would appear.

April stood up with a microphone in hand and said, "I have a gift for you and your wife, Captain, and a brief history to share. For a long time, I have wondered where Adele picked up that tune that she hums all the time." And suddenly the hologram appeared. It showed a beautiful young woman with an apron and cap. It was Adele in the canteen bar. She was cleaning glasses and humming that tune. The entire bar scene was showing, men at tables, noisy talking, smoke in the air, and then the door opened and in walked a very young handsome Captain. It showed him taking his gloves off, stamping snow from his boots. He then took off his coat to reveal his uniform and he looked and saw Adele.

Adele brought him a beer and he said he did not want it. He wanted to dance with the prettiest Fraulein in the canteen. He got up and began to dance with Adele. People were astounded. It all was so real. The Captain and Adele pointed to the young couple on the ground dancing and having the time of their lives, and it was them.

April continued, "The United Stated captured Germany, but Adele captured the Captain's heart. Now you all know where this tune comes from." At that moment the young Captain and Adele in the hologram held out their arms to ask the now older couple of the Captain and Adele to get up and dance with them. The arms and hands of the hologram motioned for them to come, and they called to them too. The Captain took his sweet Adele by her hand and led her out to the dance floor.

They danced alongside of the young couple with both couples staring at each other. They could not get over this, it looked so real. There were cell phone videos and pictures taken, but April had asked Rosa to record the entire dance for the Captain and Adele to keep.

As they danced April looked out at the crowd. No one was sitting down. They all stood up to watch. They could not get over how realistic this was. The hologram couple began to blow kisses and wave goodbye and then they vanished in the air. It was over. There was a groan of disappointment, but all things come to an end. April thanked Rosa and hugged her. She pushed two one-hundred-dollar bills into Rosa's hand. "Take it, please, even if to cover your gas expenses," April said.

"Okay. then were you happy with this?"

"Happy does not come close. I was elated," April said. They hugged again and soon Rosa was helping to tear down the equipment, and they left within a half hour.

April went to the Captain and gave him a CD of the hologram dance. "This is for you and Adele. You can watch it anytime you chose."

"Thank you, April," the Captain said. It was really something. I never saw anything like it before," and then he hugged April as did Adele.

April headed to the tables where her parents were sitting with the Marshalls. "That was amazing, Sweetie. How did you ever come up with that?" her Mother asked.

April told her about the last place she worked. The owner was a movie star and she and her husband knew of this place. It was fairly close by. "Rosa and her brother live a mere two towns over from us," April said.

Mrs. Marshall and her husband were full of praise at how

wonderful the hologram was. "No one was sitting. You had to stand to see what was happening," he said.

April was content, she wanted to do something special for the Captain and she did

All the kids in town heard about a strange play April had suggested. The storyline was about the three bears, but in a whole different light. This was a bit crazy as it was a comedy. The cast was huge to cover all the characters and it was no problem filling the characters. Everyone wanted to be in the play. The school decided to have three showings, one on Friday night, and two on Saturday – one at noon the other at 7 p.m. This way everyone could see the play once, or more if they liked.

The play was a hit, everyone laughed, and the parents pointed out their son or daughter. The best part about the play was the original director came to the school and gave of his time. It was truly a professional production. Everyone said it was their favorite play ever. Mainly because they did not know what to expect. This was brand new. April did not have a part. She was content to sing. Her parents, Nora and Lena, and Manny and Contessa all came and had a wonderful time.

The other commitment April had made was to help the band by singing a movie or hit song. April chose two songs. For one of the songs, April was Diana Ross. She wore a wig and wore the exact replica of clothing Diana Ross wore as she sang, "Someday, We Will Be Together." April mimicked her hand motions and body language. Her Mother was in awe and loved it. She got a standing ovation for that performance.

The other song was one of her favorites from the movie

"Fievel". When a little mouse and his family travel on a boat and get separated in the new world. *"I pray we'll be all right, until the morning light, lead us to a place, bless us with your grace, to a place where we'll be safe."* This song brought many to tears, especially April's Mothers and Aunt.

They all had a wonderful time. Nora was in awe how talented her daughter truly was. She could sing and mimic. She was so proud of her. It seemed that April's happiness radiated. Nora was so unbelievably happy for her daughter.

She hoped that April would continue to sing, if not in public, then to her children. It was not going to happen soon, but she was sure that it would happen. April was a good girl, kind, loving, talented, a darn hard worker, and very smart. Nora had no doubt that someone would find her and love every bit of her daughter. She was precious.

After the event, the ladies wanted to treat Miranda and April. They ended up in a very nice place near the ocean in Fresno. The restaurant was beautiful. Its décor had a Mexican theme with huge pillars and was very tastefully decorated inside. They scoured the menus, neither of them was very hunger, so they opted for dessert. They all decided on fried ice cream. The owner of the establishment came out and asked how the play turned out. Her daughter was in it as well. Her Dad was to bring her home later. April said she knew her daughter and enjoyed her company. "Yes," she said. "She has mentioned your name more than once in our home."

April asked, "Didn't you go to any of the showings?"

"Oh, yes. I did. I enjoy it very much. I laughed until my stomach hurt. But we do take turns here in our restaurant." she said. April was glad, and especially glad she met Maria's mother.

Graduation

THE TOWN HAD BEEN BUZZING FOR MONTHS NOW. MANY FELT that now was the time for awarding the special community award at graduation. It was for Outstanding Community Service. They kept it quiet though, knowing who to talk to and who to avoid.

One of them contacted the Superintendent of the school to ask if there was a petition to sign and they were told all that was required was a letter explaining why that person should be nominated. From that moment on it was like a crusade. Word of mouth spread like wildfire, no public announcement or ad in the newspaper was needed. They reached so many, so very quickly, and so selectively.

From the onset they thought the letters should go to the office of the Judge. He was honest, trustworthy, and they knew he could keep a confidence.

One day a very large box arrived at the Judge's chambers via one of the security men.

It sat on the floor by his desk one morning, and he asked Missy, "What are all these letters and where did they come from?"

"I don't know, Sir. I just came in and I am not sure what the letters are for," she said.

For curiosity's sake the Judge opened one up and said, "Oh, I know," and he handed Missy the letter.

"Oh, my goodness this is so sweet," she choked up with a lump in her throat.

"Wow, by the looks of this box, I am no longer King," he said.

Missy punched him lightly on his arm.

"You could be sued for assault for that. All kidding aside, you know I adore that girl." he said.

The weather had been crazy. It rained for two days, then there was a day of sun and a breeze. The superintendent did not know if the graduation should be indoors or outside. Finally, after being drenched coming into work, he decided that graduation would be held in the auditorium.

When the kids heard this, many were upset. No more than April was. Because of the size of the auditorium, only four tickets were issued per family. That meant only parents, no siblings, and 1 set of grandparents. That was not fair. So, she took her concerns with fifty or so other students to the High School Superintendent's office. The superintendent said he would listen to three of them, not all fifty.

April went first. "For instance, I have two parents, two sets of grandparents and two others I would want to invite. That is just six for one student and that is not excessive. What if I would have had four siblings?" she asked him.

The other two also expressed their concerns and the Superintendent agreed they were right. It was two months until graduation and there was not enough room in the auditorium.

"What about opening the doors from the auditorium to the gymnasium. Microphones can be used and a screen on the wall to show the podium would work," one of the students said.

Another said, "Yeah let the doors open and use streamers to make it seem like a continuation of the room."

This sounded possible, so the Superintendent decided he would investigate this as soon as possible. Before he left another student made a suggestion.

"My parents have the best sound system, large televisions, and big screens. I am sure they will help. Some of the screens are even too big to display in our showroom," said a boy from April's class.

"Okay, I appreciate that information. I will make some phone calls, send memos out, and all of you will know within a few days. And that is exactly what happened.

The auditorium doors were held open. The hallway had streamers to mark "a hallway" for their parents and family to go through to find seats. On the wall was a giant screen as big as concert arenas use, and it was able to show the bottom of the stage as well as all the students up on the bleachers. There was also a small screen in the corner to show a closeup when a student was up at the podium to graduate.

April was so ready to graduate. She had grown tired of school. As much as she liked all her classmates, and would miss them, she was done! Many of her classmates were not staying in town. Some of them were heading to college, some to the military, some were going to trade schools, and some were heading off to their mission. Only a small handful of kids were staying behind to work in jobs here at home or get married and settling down.

April was ready to move on. There was no doubt about it, for all of them life was about the change.

The afternoon of her graduation ceremonies, April received a call. "Hello," she said answering the phone.

"Hey, how are you?" the voice said to her.

"Hugh! Is this Hugh?" she was so excited.

"Who else would it be?" he said laughing.

"When did you get into town?" She asked.

"I came in two days ago. I was just beat," he answered her.

"Gosh, you could have slept on our living room couch. I am so excited to see you. It has been a year since we have been together," she said.

"I will be at graduation and see you there. Okay? Hugh said to her.

"Uh, okay I guess, but" and the line went dead, he had hung up.

April hung up the telephone receiver and stood there confused. She knew that the minute she came into town if Hugh were home, she would have gone straight to his house. It was obvious he did not feel the same way and she wondered why? Did he change his mind in this past year? April pushed those thoughts out of her mind, if he was ending it with her, he would have to say he wanted his ring back. But here it was still hanging around her neck on that silver necklace.

Their meal was simple soup and salad. Her grandparents from Mexico had come and were staying with them. April got dressed in a simple white dress with eyelets on the hem. She also wore a pair of white sandals that had a small heel. April came downstairs, and her Dad was standing there with tears in his eyes.

"Oh, Dad. Don't do that, or you will make me cry," she said.

Her Dad put a strand of pearls around her neck. They were short and could easily been seen. Then he kissed her cheek. "You know we are very proud of you, Sweetie," he said.

The Girl in the Mirror Book 4

"I know, Dad, and I am just as proud of you two," she answered back.

"Time to go," her dad said. They all climbed into the car. April did not want to drive herself. She wanted her family close to her. They arrived at the school, and the parking lot was already half full. They got out, and April left to join her classmates while her family went in to get a seat, hopefully all together!

Just then April saw Nora and Lena, and she went to hug them. "I am so thrilled you are both here," she said to them."

As she went to the auditorium, she was both happy and sad. Still, she had not seen either Hugh or Trevor, his brother, who was also in her graduating class. She spoke to many of her classmates, and one pulled her along for her to get their caps and gowns.

The girls wore white gowns with gold lettering of their school's insignia and a white cap. The boys wore a deep blue gown with a blue cap. "I like the blue better," April said. "White gets dirty so much easier."

"Well, you are not riding a horse or tending calves in here girl," one of the boys teased her. That made April laugh.

Soon they were told to line up, just as they had practiced the day before. They wanted them up on the stage and bleachers before the ceremonies began. The school nurse warned that for those on the upper bleachers, if they felt lightheaded, they should get down. She did not want anyone to faint because of the heat. April was on the fourth row from the bottom, to the left of the stage. She was sandwiched between three of her best friends. One of them had tears in her eyes. "Don't cry or you will ruin your eye makeup," April joked with her.

The girl laughed and said, "You always make me feel better." April squeezed her hand.

Just then Trevor walked by her and tugged on her sleeve. "Hey, you, come here a minute," she told him. He stopped and she asked him, "Are you ready for today?"

"Yeah, I guess, I still am not sure what I want to do. I am not like Hugh. He knew what he wanted. I am not sure what I want to do," he said.

"Well, it's not easy to make a decision that you will want to do for the rest of your life" she said to him. "You will do alright no matter what you chose, you're a good egg" and they laughed. "So is Hugh alright, he called me earlier today and said he came in two days ago, I was shocked he had not come to see me" she said to Trevor.

"Well, he did come in two days ago. He will see you after words. Okay?" they hugged, and Trevor was gone.

Soon the auditorium was full, it was 7:15 p.m. and they were to start at 7 p.m. April knew it is not as easy for some to leave home as it is for others. April also knew what it was like if they had animals to take care of or chores to do before leaving, in order to get somewhere. Dairy makes it hard to get away, so she completely understood.

The music started to notify the principal to come out on the stage and for the various dignitaries to sit in their designated chairs. The graduation was a success, no one fainted. All the diplomas were received, and everyone was relaxed and began to lose interest on stage. Some were talking and April could not hear what they were saying. She was holding onto five awards she had won and wanted to read them but being here on the stage made it difficult. Her BFFs took her hand and said for her to go ahead, read, and ignore what they were saying on the stage. April could not hear them anyway!

Then the Judge came out on stage, and he had something important to say.

"When I graduated about a million years ago," and everyone laughed. "I received a Community Service Award, and it was quite something. This year we have another person that has been nominated and has won this prestigious award. Some of you know who this person is. But this person, because of who they are and what their standard is, does not allow themselves to think they could be the winner. You see, this person is humble and puts themselves last. In fact, they would not even pay attention to this because they do not consider themselves worthy, and that my friends are qualities of a good leader."

"Look at that stage, some of their classmates already can guess who this person is, but not them. And as the parents looked at the stage many of the boys and girls were looking towards the left side of the stage.

"Now the qualifications for this award are specific. The candidate must have gone beyond their normal circumstances to alleviate another's burden or a burden of their townspeople. There are boxes here on the stage that hold over 778 letters of testimony of the dedication, sacrifice, and service this person has done for members of our community. 778 letters, that's astounding."

"If you don't know who this person is, I am going to solve that mystery for you right now. April Di Angelo will you please come forward to the podium," the Judge called out! April was not paying attention. She did not qualify for that award. Besides she and her BFFs were talking, when one of them nudged to her move. On the second call to come down, April heard the Judge call her name and she walked down the steps of the bleachers to the podium. The entire audience was standing and clapping. April was in shocked and in disbelief.

The Judge said, "How does that feel, Kiddo?"

April looked at him and said, "This must be a mistake." The crowd in the audience laughed. "I never did anything to receive an award like this," she said.

"So, you are telling me all these letters are lying about you?" the Judge asked her.

"No, I am not saying that, but it can't be me."

The Judge was prepared and pulled out one specific letter, "Let me read this to you," he said.

> *When I received the horrible frightening news that I had breast cancer and had to have a bilateral mastectomy, I did not know how we would make ends meet. And just then the washer and dryer quit working. I broke down and cried.*
>
> *That very afternoon an appliance man came and brought a new washer and drier, I knew we did not order it, and could not pay for it.*
>
> *He said it was all taken care of. We both stood there wondering who in the world would help us. Then biweekly checks came in the mail from the diner. I was not working. Where was this money coming from?*
>
> *My husband called Flo at the diner, and she said she did not know anything. The very next day neighbors*

and others came, made meals, and washed clothing and bedding. They took me to my doctor appointments. We were taken care of. We had food, our home and clothing were clean, and all our bills were taken care of because, somehow, I had a biweekly check. Often there would also be a lot of cash.

It was later we discovered that it was April who had heard I had cancer and impending surgery, and she asked Flo if she could take my place. We were floored. You know no one would have changed their life so much to do such a kind thing.

Later I asked April about this, and she said quote, "I had such a wonderful time, I met so many people, and I want to thank you for allowing me to have this opportunity. I only wish it had not been stupid cancer." Imagine that!

Well, that changed us both. Now we volunteer where we can, even when it pinches. She is gracious and kind beyond words. To her this was the right thing to do when to so many it would be a terrible imposition. This is why we feel compelled to write and nominate April Di Angelo for the community award.

The entire audience was quiet and had tears in their eyes. Some were using tissues to dab at their eyes, and some people were blowing their noses. April too had tears running down her cheeks.

"Now do you believe me?" the Judge asked her.

April just stood there nodding her head "Yes".

"Now, will you accept the Community Award April?" he asked her with a big grin on his face.

She stood there for a while before answering and finally, she looked at him and said, "I can't because, sure I did those things, but it was not like you think. If you want to thank someone, it must be those who are responsible for my actions. It's not only me. I will only accept this award if I can share it with my Mothers."

April said in the microphone, "Miranda Di Angelo, come forward and Nora, you too."

Nora waved her hand as if to say, "No, not me". Miranda got up and took Nora by her hand and the two of them headed to the stage. The entire audience applauded and whistled.

On stage the three of them embraced and kissed. Then Miranda took the microphone. "Some of you know, but many of you do not. April is our adopted daughter. This beautiful woman standing beside me is the one who is responsible for the creation of this beautiful young woman." Miranda had to stop because of the strong emotions taking over. "I want to thank her from my heart to hers, for giving us the greatest gift ever.

Nora than spoke and said, "And I want to thank you for allowing me to be a part of all your lives, to watch April grow and achieve. April is a blessing to all of us." And then Nora sat down.

Miranda was still at the microphone. "All of you here with a child graduating tonight, our daughter is just like your child. She leaves her socks and sneakers in the middle of the living room, and glasses of juice on her bedroom dresser."

The crowd laughed at the same antics of their own children. "She makes mistakes, and we have to fix them or bail her out," more laughter. "She has this affinity with all animals. We never know what she will drag home next," many laughed again.

"She is always on the go. Sometimes we don't know where. You can always count on her saying, 'I need money,' and when she does bring the car home, it always needs gas." The audience erupted in shouts and laughter. "But I also want you to know this, when she was a little girl she had the habit of going out the front door and touching the glass, leaving her hand and finger prints. I would stand there grumbling and washing that window on the door every day. Then one day I told my husband to get another glass. Take that glass with handprints and fingerprints out. I took that to the framing shop, and it hangs on our bedroom wall. I will always treasure the little girl that was a gift to us."

"Yeah, they are not perfect, but they are a reflection of you, the better part. It has been eighteen years of education in school and at home, and hopefully you were not too busy, and hopefully they listened. No more will you hear, 'Mom, are you here? I need, I want,' they will be off on their own. Those days are gone. So maybe when you get home, have a heart to heart with your child. If you were never a hugger, be a hugger today. If you never kissed your child, start today."

"You do not need to give them all you have but do give them all you have within you. Give them your love, your support, and patience. They deserve that much from us. They are so wonderful and are struggling with life, love, and all the ills that come with youth. Be there for them, make a way for them to call, or have that contact. You are their lifeline, literally. And one more thing, and this has changed our life and our home, pray with your child, even if it's just once. I promise you, you will never be sorry." And then she stepped back from the podium.

The audience gave them a standing ovation, and April found her Mother's arms. They cried and laughed, and Nora joined them. What a wonderful night it was for them, their emotions hung right out there for the world to see, and they did not care.

Afterwards, everyone met in the cafeteria or outdoors near the kitchen. As April and her family approached, she was sure she saw Hugh, but he was with someone, another girl. April did not jump to conclusions it might be a relative there for the graduation. She saw Mr. O'Toole, who hugged her close and kissed her cheek. "You will always be my darling, so very pour of ye," he told her.

April went outside with her family, and Trevor found her. He put his hands around her eyes, covering them. "Guess who?" he said.

April began to laugh and said, "You are the tallest person I know who likes to pull the eye covering trick." He just laughed and she did too.

Just then the Marshalls came over to congratulate April and tell Miranda she gave an awesome speech. "I did not know. I did not prepare" she said laughing.

April noticed Hugh standing in the background. He was with a girl, so April asked, "Isn't Hugh here? I mean I haven't seen him yet."

"Oh, he is here if you look over to your right, he is standing right there." Mrs. Marshall said.

"Oh, yes. I see him now. Who is the girl he has with him? Is she a relative?" she asked.

"We don't know her. She was introduced to us as a friend of his." Mrs. Marshall said.

April felt her blood boil, "Oh really," she said to herself. "Let's see how much of a man Hugh really is, and if he has the guts to tell me."

April said to her parents, "Let's go to Flo's diner for old time's sake," and they all said it was a great idea, and they left.

April sat beside her Dad, while her Mom was in the ladies' room. She was irritated and moody.

"What's wrong, Sweetie?" he asked her.

"Dad, can I talk to you for a minute without Mom hearing us?" she asked him.

"Sure. Let's go outside for a bit," and they did. They walked to the creek beyond the diner and back. April opened her heart to her Dad about what she saw.

"Sweetie, we heard for a while now that Hugh was dating other girls. We did not want to say anything to upset you. You had so much going on, the farm competition, riding to help that Catholic school, and all. We figured you'd deal with it when the time was right," he said.

April did not cry she was angry.

"Now, Sweetie, time can change things, and I think the two of you need to hear each other out," her Dad said. "Just take it slow."

"Oh, I think so too," she said angrily. "I doubt he is man enough to tell me."

They ate and soon all was forgotten, they joked and laughed, and before you knew it the clock on the wall said 10:00 p.m.

"Oh my we need to get going," Miranda said. So, the little family left and went home. When they got home there was a message on their answering machine from Hugh.

"April, when you get this message would you please call me," and he left a cell phone number.

"Are you going to call him back?" Miranda asked her.

"Nope it's late for me and for him too. Most likely, it will wait until tomorrow," April said.

The next morning the newspaper had their photo on the front page. Word for word they printed Miranda's unwritten, unrehearsed speech. Gordon was so surprised he had to run into the house with the paper to show his two girls. April was sitting in the kitchen feeling sick to her stomach. Miranda handed her two Pepto Bismol tablets. As they sat there reading, a car drove into their lane and Hugh got out of the passenger side.

Gordon went out and said, "Hello," and asked the driver if she wanted to come in.

She got out and followed them into the kitchen. April's jaw almost dropped. It was that witch Sandra Fetterman who had been at Hugh's going away party last year.

April wanted to try and be civil for her parent's sake. She sat there and said nothing as Hugh and her Dad talked. Miranda asked April to come into the sewing room for a minute. She needed help changing the spool underneath her sewing machine. April got up and followed her Mom.

Miranda closed the door, "Here put these on," and she handed April a nice outfit to show off her figure.

"Mom, don't," April said.

Miranda said, "Do as I tell you. That girl is trouble, I have heard about her. Let Hugh see what he left behind," and Miranda spit.

They came out and Miranda announced. "I finally finished that outfit for her Dad, what do you think?" Gordon looked at his daughter and said, "That's nice, very nice. Good job, Miranda."

Hugh looked too, like he could have put a hole through April. Then he said, "April, could we talk for a while outside? Just you and me."

April said, "You know my parents well enough. We can talk in here."

Miranda and April went into the living room and sat down. Miranda on her recliner, Dad in his, and April sat on the couch with Ruby who would not let anyone else sit on the couch with them. Dad told Hugh to bring in chairs from the kitchen.

They sat there for a while and Hugh spoke up, "So how was the farm competition?"

"It was very busy. I barely had time to do much of anything. I didn't go out or date anyone," April wanted to drive the message home to Hugh.

"Well, that's good," Hugh said. "So, what was the outcome? Did you win?"

"I don't know. So far no one has mailed anything to me. Mom? Dad?"

They both shook their heads, "No".

"Yes. I just got back four days ago, and then I left for the race on the second day," April said.

"A race? I didn't know you were in a race." Hugh said to April.

"Well, I guess that is in part because you never wrote back to me when I wrote to you. And when you got into town, you never called me until yesterday," April said.

"Well, yes. I am not much of a writer," Hugh said.

The girl rolled her eyes and said, "You are too."

April clenched her fists and said quickly, "Will you excuse me? I must go to the ladies' room," and April got up and left fast.

Miranda came upstairs and she looked at her daughter just standing upstairs angry on the verge of crying. "Don't let him see you like this," she said. "You did nothing wrong. You trusted him. He never said anything to you?" She asked April. April just shook her head, "No".

"Here bite on this," and she gave April a small piece of sponge to bite on and concentrate on, so she would not be emotional.

They came back down, and Hugh started again. "Well, you see I met Sandra not too long ago. She came down to where I was, and well, we sort of hit it off. We started dating, and we have good new to share. We learned a week ago that Sandra is four months pregnant. We are going to be parents." April felt like she was punched in the stomach.

Gordon was quick to say, "Congratulations." Miranda and April followed. April was chewing on the sponge like it was to save her teeth. April could not and did not say anything. She wanted to puke. With that Hugh got up and said they had to go. Sandra got up acting like she was so far along her back hurt, and they left.

They were gone over an hour when April realized she still had his grandmother's ring around her neck. April had heard the news, but it had not sunk in. She said she did not want dinner.

She wanted to go for a ride. Her Dad asked if he could go along, and she said she wanted to be alone. April rode for about five miles and headed for Mr. O'Toole's cabin. She dismounted and knocked on his door.

It took a while, apparently he had been napping. "Oh, Darlin', come on in here," he was glad to see her. And he led her to a chair to sit down.

"I was not sure if I would be welcome," she told him.

"Oh, now. Why would that be?" he asked her.

"Well, because Hugh and I are no more, and never will be," she answered him.

"I know, Darlin', such a shame, such a stupid trap he has himself in. He was weak and lost a gem. I tell ya, a gem." and he hugged April.

For the first time, April broke down and cried. He sat her down and let her cry it out.

"I am sorry. Forgive me," she said through her tears.

"Nonsense, you sit here and get it all out of ye now," and she did for over an hour.

He made her some nice cold buttermilk, and she drank it slowly feeling better. She loved this old man so much, and it grieved her that he would not be in her family.

April told him as much and he said to her, "You 'n me, Darlin', we are family. You stole my heart long ago. I am no fool. I know a good thing when I see it."

At that point April reached up and took off the necklace that held his deceased wife's ring.

"Ah, he had the nerve to give you this ring, and did not keep his end of the bargain," he said.

April told him she had many opportunities to go out, date, and cheat on Hugh, but she did not. He did and he not only cheated, but he also got her pregnant. He is awful, disgusting Priesthood holder, the worst type to hold any title in the church.

"I know. I know, Darlin', such a mess. Me daughter is unhappy. She learned the truth last night and visited me. Hugh is not welcome to stay at their home. He is to take that woman somewhere else. They made it clear they love their son, but not what he did. To lay with the harlot of two counties and everyone knows what a thing she is. Nope she is not welcome in their home. This makes no sense to any of us," and he squeezed her to him from a sitting position beside her.

April told him she had not cried yet, until she came here. It made her sad because she loved Hugh's family. She had made up her mind a year ago that it was him and only him, and she clung to him in her memory thousands of times.

"You are a woman, but he is not a man. A man does not turn his back on commitment. He must have a weakness," he said.

"Yeah, he sure does. He used his little head, not the one on his shoulders," April said disgustedly.

Mr. O'Toole began to laugh at that line. He poked April with is finger and she laughed too. "You'll be all right, Darlin'. Go and talk to me daughter, she is more heartbroken than you are," he said.

"I will, very soon," and she got up to leave. She mounted her horse and reined him away.

As she rode home, Mr. O'Toole watched her go and he kicked at his porch floor. "What a damn shame. What a mess, to have the world in your hands and throw it away." He shook his head and went inside for a good cry.

April rode home hard, the horse loved it too. She had not been riding for some time. When she got back home April had to walk the mare to cool her down.

April asked her Mom to call Mrs. Marshall on a pretense of getting together. Miranda did.

"Hello, this is Hugh."

"May I speak with your Mother, I need to remind her of the luncheon tickets she purchased. They are here and were quite costly."

"Okay, I will get her. Hold on."

"Hello, Miranda. Yes, I completely forgot about those tickets."

April said, "It's me. I need to see you. Can we get together soon?"

Then Mrs. Marshall said, "I can swing by tomorrow and pick them up, if that is okay with you. Bright and early? Ha ha. I will see you then," and the phone clicked.

April told her Mother that Mrs. Marshall would be here tomorrow early. Maybe they could drive away somewhere and talk. Miranda said that was an excellent idea, to go away where they would not be seen. April knew just the spot.

Mrs. Marshall arrived at six in the morning. She had on sweatpants and a shirt. "No sense in causing alarm with dressing up," she said.

April said to her, "I thought Hugh was not allowed in your home, yet he answered the phone!" Mrs. Marshall answered her, "He had no right, and he was told about it. Our home is no longer his home. He was there to get his things. He filled the trunk and was taking clothing out when the phone rang."

They left and drove to a remote site at the Jones' farm, back behind the pond where it was secluded by trees. Not even the workers could see them there. April turned off the engine and turned to look at what would have been her Mother-in-law.

Already Mrs. Marshall was in tears, "I am so angry at Hugh. He messed everything up with you, with the church, and in our home. His father told him to leave and not come back."

April reached for her hand and squeezed it. "I don't know what to do," Mrs. Marshall said.

April squeezed her hand again and said, "Nothing. There is nothing you can do. You cannot change him or make him think right. He is acting on his own. All you can do is be happy. This is YOUR life, not his. I have a feeling in time Sandra will cheat on him, sadly that is her track record. I think she saw Hugh, what your family has, and felt it would be easy street for her. Now that Hugh has no place to go, I have a feeling she will not stick around too long," April said. And then April added, "Don't hold a grudge against the baby. It's not the baby's fault. I know you love children, and this is your first grandchild. You may have to fight for the baby, hire an attorney, and save it. But it's not the baby's fault what his Mother and Father did."

"April, I don't know how you have the ability and strength to be so positive and know the right thing to do when it is raining hell." Mrs. Marshall said to her.

"I pray a lot and right now more than ever. I depend on the Holy Ghost to help me," she said. "I am in debt to the Savior with every breath I take. I can never repay him for all the good in my life, neither can you. Don't dwell on negative thoughts. Think about all the good in your life. The good husband you have, and I know Trevor is worried about you. He looked frightened the last time I saw him," April said.

"Each day there is good in the world, sometimes it's just a lark on a limb of a tree, or a sunset. But beauty is all around you, as is good. Look for it and it will calm your heart. We have been counseled 'Do Not Fear' so many times in the scriptures. You would have more luck leading a horse to the water and making him drink than you would to have Hugh listen to you with common sense," April said.

"Yes, this upset me. It came out of nowhere. I suspected when he called me and abruptly hung up that something was wrong. No matter what, I choose to be happy," April told her.

"Well, Dear, I admire you immensely. I am in taters over this, and you are holding together. I will do just that, live my life and be happy. And you are right, sooner or later Hugh will come back. He is our son and I believe deep inside him he is dying, and he doesn't even know it yet. When it hits him, he will need us. I know he loves us. He told us in tears the day he left," she said to April.

"How can he say he loves you when he brought so much drama to your home? I feel that loving someone is pleasing that person or persons. Right now, Hugh is trying to use you, all," April said.

He wants what he had and will not get it," Mrs. Marshall said.

April then said, "Man did he fall far and fast, with that witch of two counties. I can only imagine what our Bishop will have to say to him. Well, it's his life. He chose it. For me, I don't know what to do with my life," April told her with a sigh.

Mrs. Marshall leaned over to hug her, "You don't need to do anything right away. Maybe this is not the time to act."

April looked at her and said, "I do. I am angry over this. I was not in any way ready to settle down, not even now. If I were a betting person, I know that this is not what Hugh wanted either. He is going to continue in the Marines, he must, he signed a contract. What is she going to do while he is away?"

"The first thing I want to do is go to the temple," April said. "I believe I need to and then I will spend a lot of time before I know what to do."

Mrs. Marshall said, "Please, I know it's a lot to ask, but if and when you go, I want to go with you, April. I love you and I am so damn mad at my son acting immoral, having a child out of wedlock, and well you understand. Hugh knows better. I know he does.

April said, "You know that a woman asked for John the Baptist's head on a plate, and she got it. Another woman cut Sampson's hair weakening him. There are evil women, and it is up to us to teach our girls/women better and teach our boys/men better. I was taught in Sunday School to know what I would do in any given situation, and that is a lesson I never forgot. For me, I don't have an off/on switch inside me. I cannot turn off the love I have for you and your husband, your father, or your son Hugh.

Yes, I am angry at what he did. I am not judging him, but he hurt me. Knowing I was away, and I was chaste and honest with him. He asked me to wait for him and I did. Now I am going to move on with my life, do things, and be happy. Maybe in two or five years, things will change. I hope.

"As far as the temple? Yes, I want you there with us," April said.

Mrs. Marshall asked April, "if in two or five years would you still wait for Hugh?"

April looked directly at her and said, "Can I trust him? Right now, my answer is I don't think so. I just pray to God that Hugh does not want to talk to me alone, because if he does, I will not be as civil with him as I was at my parent's house. He will be blasted. Right now, I am hurt, and my anger feels like it is oozing out of my pores. He needs to know that I did not hurt him or cheat on him! And I had opportunity to. Hugh hurt me and I will throw down my gauntlet and declare he shall never come near me again. I can't respect him."

Mrs. Marshall wiped her eyes and said, "I understand. I do," the two of them talked. They talked for over two hours and then they hugged a tearful hug. "I will see you and talk with you, Elaine. I will invite you to our events, and I will never stop loving you," April told her.

"Oh, April, I hope so. I am counting on it. For now, my heart is broken. My son, MY son did this."

April started the truck, and they headed out on a back road so as not to be seen. April drove over the hill to the back of the barn and there in the driveway sat Hugh with "her" in the car.

April stopped the truck instinctively, pulled out two fishing rods, and told Mrs. Marshall to follow her. They pulled the small fiberglass canoe out onto the pond and climbed in. Mrs.

Marshall's cell phone began to chime, and she pulled the phone out of her pocket. It was Hugh.

"Yes, Hello," she said.

"Where in the hell are you," Hugh demanded.

"First, don't you dare use that language or tone with me. I am not one of your fellow Marines. Second, it's none of your business. I do not answer to you."

Hugh was speechless, but then said, "I am sorry, but I did not want you with April."

His Mother answered Hugh, "You have not said who I spend my time with, you did not listen to us when we tried to council you about this woman, did you?"

"Come on, Mom. Where are you? Hugh asked.

"I am fishing up on the winding road near the Pines," she said.

By this time April had caught three decent-sized rainbow trout and put them on a line in the water connected to the canoe. Hugh jumped into his car and tore out. He was going to look for his Mother and would not find her. Mrs. Marshall would be home cooking pan-fried rainbow trout, one of her husband's favorite things to eat, long before Hugh came home.

They both pulled the boat onto the shore and April grabbed Mrs. Marshall's hand. "This may sound nuts, but we must forgive him. This is not our problem, but what he does will affect us both. Let us try to be accepting and follow that with kindness. I know that this is very hard to do right now, but it is the right thing to do. And always pray," and they hugged.

The very next morning April felt numb. This was way too much drama for her. She just wanted peace, and to focus. When her Dad came in with the morning mail, he plopped an envelope in front of her. She lifted the envelope up and it was from the Farm Competition Review Board. She looked at her Dad and asked him to open it for her. She did not want to know. Her Dad was very concerned April was really down in the dumps.

He tore open the envelope carefully and his face fell. He said, "WE are regretfully sorry that you failed the program. You are so sad, unable to smile, and are not happy, that we failed you."

When April heard that she said "Dad!"

"Dad? What do you mean calling me Dad?" he said poking her to make her laugh. "How about, I say April! April! April!" He had her now. She was laughing and falling off her chair. The pair of them were soon on the floor and Gordon did not stop tickling and poking his daughter. The two of them were laughing nonstop.

Miranda came in and she too was laughing. Life can grab onto you, and you take it too seriously. Miranda felt it was enough, "All right, you two," she said. Gordon stood up and poked his wife. "Don't start on me, Mister," Miranda said.

They all had to catch their breath and they were still chuckling when Miranda saw the opened envelope and letter lying on the table. She held the letter in her hands when April said, "Mom will you read this letter to me. Dad was teasing me."

"And he should have. I am glad he did. We don't see you smiling so much these days. Granted it's been a bit bumpy, but there is no reason you should punish yourself, feel so sad, and not smile," she said. "We are not enemies here."

Miranda held the letter and began to read, *"This letter is to inform you of the results of this year's competition for the 182 applicants.*

There were many comments for several of the competitors, but one competitor received more comments and had the highest grades.

IT IS OUR PLEASURE TO INFORM YOU THAT APRIL DI ANGELO IS THE WINNER OF THE FARM COMPETITION. Please contact our home-based number to forward the winner's check. Sincerely yours . . . .

Miranda leaned over to hug her daughter. "You did it! You won. Oh, April, all that hard work. It paid off and now you have every reason to simile."

April sat there with mixed emotions. It's true, she had many bad feelings in the past two days, but now she was trying to be positive. "But darn it anyway," she said to herself. She did not want to stay in this drama Hugh created. It was her life, and yes, he hurt her, but she was determined to be happy.

"Up, keep moving up," her Dad said winking at her.

April could not hold back and said, "I love you guys. I really do. Please let Nora know for me. Will you?"

"Why don't you drive over and tell them yourself," Miranda said.

April agreed. She finished her breakfast and headed out.

She saw Nora and Lena packing their things in the trunk of their car in their alley way. So, April pulled up behind their car and turned the engine off. She walked over to them and said, "Do you need some help?"

"No, we got it. We really should let this in the trunk, but when we get groceries or other things, it's in the way," Nora said.

"Holy Cow!" April said. "That's one big vacuum cleaner."

The Girl in the Mirror Book 4

"What's up?" Lena asked. April told them the results of the farm competition. Both women hugged and praised her.

"We need to get together and plan a picnic or something," they said.

April said, "Better yet, I am hoping to go to the temple and see the Patriarch soon. I would like for the both of you to come along. Both women's eyes were sparkling with excitement.

There were no other young people in their lives that wanted them. April was always so caring and considerate of others, and it was never a burden to her. She truly wanted them with her, and they were grateful. "We would love that, and just let us know when so we can plan," they told her.

"Well, I suspect that since Mom is the first counselor in the Relief Society, they will organize a temple trip. You know, to help those who can't drive to get there. I am sure we can almost, if not, fill the bus," April said. She felt full of joy because there was so much to look forward to.

April got in the truck and there was still something bothering her. There was a nagging feeling within her, and it was something she had to deal with soon. She was going home to pray. That was a good start.

At home April decided to call her Bishop. She did and his wife answered, "How are you dear?" his wife said to April.

"I am fine. I was hoping to meet with the Bishop. I have something I would like to discuss with him."

"Well, I know that he is home tonight, if you would like to come over around 6 'ish', then he will have time to speak with you," she said.

"I do not mean to barge in. I mean it's important, but not that important," April said.

"Now I learned at our graduation that you believe in service. So do we. I know for a fact our Bishop has nothing on his calendar tonight and we would love for you to come" she said.

"Truly I appreciate it, and I will be there at 6. Thanks again," April said, and they hung up.

April heard her Mom pull up and she began to pull the grocery bags from the car. April bound out of the house to help her, telling her about seeing the bishop that evening. Miranda's heart burst with joy. Her daughter knew how to handle things the right way.

"Would you like us to come along?" she asked.

"No, I will be okay. I need to clear some things with him," April answered.

The clock seemed to go so slow, April looked at it every 10 minutes. By 5 p.m. she was getting washed and dressed to leave. As her Dad came in for dinner, she was on her way out. She stopped him to tell him where she was going. He kissed her and said to be careful.

At the Bishop's home it was quiet. Mrs. Ramson opened the door welcoming her in. Bishop Ramson was in the kitchen calling, "Come in, come in. Are you hungry?"

April laughed saying, "No thanks. I am not hungry." And she realized in most every Mormon home they wanted to feed you or give you something to drink as if you were starving.

They went into the parlor, and he closed the door. Bishop Ramson sat at a desk while April sat down in front of the desk. "So, what can I do for you today?" he asked her.

"I have had a lot on my mind lately, and I need clarification, if you can help me. I also want to discuss a career choice with you," she said.

"Okay, how about we talk about what is on your mind lately?" he said.

So, April told him how her heart had been broken and although she was smiling on the outside, inside she felt like she was dying.

Her Bishop said, "It is not unnatural to feel sad or let down in an instance such as this. But you have kept civil, you have not met with him making demands or arguing. Keep your distance and in time things will settle down. Remember in the book of Mormon there were always times when Maroni had to flee trouble, but he was prayerful and kept away," he said.

"Yes, I met with Hugh's Mother, and we had a good talk, but I would like to go to the temple for my endowments," she said.

The Bishop was confused. "Are you planning on going on a mission?" he asked her.

"Well, sort of," she said, "I have been thinking about joining the military. To get away for a while, two years at least. Then maybe I will be in the right frame of mind. Right now, I am angry, and I need to focus that anger in the right direction. I felt the military's rigorous training would be right for me," she said.

The Bishop said, "Maybe you need to give this some time, and in a week or two you may see a different direction. The military is a rough, rugged place for a woman."

"Yes, just like me, rough and rugged. I have thought about this for over six months now and I believe this is right," April said.

I am hoping the Relief Society plans a temple trip so many can go. But I do want to get my endowments before I enlist," she said.

"Yes, you can, and should April. It is an honorable thing you have in mind, but I caution you that often women are not respected in the military by officers or by men in general. Keep safe and stay prayerful. There may be a Mormon group you could be assigned to," he said.

April said to him, "I'd rather not. I would rather be with nonmembers because in that way they will see my example and may want to know why I am the way I am. Why I keep to the right."

"That is to be commended, but it can be difficult, You have always been a good girl, even when you were very little, and came here with no one to guide you. You kept a prayer for God to keep and watch over you. So, keep it up always. If you do this, I promise you that you will be all right," with that he stood up and shook her hand.

"Do you have your Patriarchal blessing yet?" he asked her.

"No, I do not," she answered.

"Here is the telephone number of the Patriarch. Call this number and make an appointment soon. He is a good man and will help you."

April stood up and shook his hand taking the paper with the number on it and the Bishop hugged her. "God speed you home safe. We all love you and will pray for you," he said.

April left feeling more hopeful than when she arrived. It felt right.

She got home and then she talked with her Dad. "Honey if that is the path you choose than we support it. I am not saying we are happy with it. But it is your life, and you must do what you think is right for you, because if you don't you will always have regrets," he said to her.

The next day April called and made an appointment with the Patriarch. As luck would have it, he had room to see her that next week.

"Awesome," she thought to herself. She penciled down the date and time and thanked him. She danced a little circle in the kitchen and Ruby danced with her. She swooped her up and said, "I am going to miss you, Bubba. You have been my wingman in bed for years. And I sure am going to miss you, but not half as much as you will miss me. Maybe Dad will let you snuggle with him, but he snores," and she buried her head in Ruby's fur. She decided to sleep in the same shirt for the remainder of her time at home. When she did leave, she would let Ruby have it, so maybe that would comfort her.

When Dad came home, April had dinner ready. Mom had meetings. They sat down at the table and April told him about her date with the Patriarch.

Dad put down his fork and patted her hand. "That is so good, April. It will outline your life here and help you," he said.

Mom did not get home until late, 7 p.m. She was tired, and April made a nice cool drink for her. Miranda sat on her recliner. She drank her drink of cherry ice and said, "I am not hungry, but this sure hits the spot," and soon she was so tired she was ready for bed. They all had family prayer and headed to bed for an early start in the morning.

April helped with the pony rides and lessons. She made dinner for several evenings for her Mom who was planning the Temple trip, along with Pioneer Day in July and other things. April was worried about her Mom and felt the Temple trip would be so good for her.

Mom came into the kitchen and said, "We are taking a bus, we have so many people going and it would be less expensive for all of us if we took a bus."

April said, "I want to sit with you, Nora and Lena."

Mom said, "I think your seat partner has already been chosen. Judge Du Val cornered me in church and said YOU are his partner on the bus."

"Oh, boy," April said, "Can't wait!"

The day April went to see the Patriarch, she was not nervous. She said her morning prayers and was anxious to go. She felt to have a blessing that mapped part of her life with directions he could truly use. How blessed she was to have this, but then any worthy member of the church could go and have a blessing, and this was hers:

April Di Angelo, Your Heavenly Father has this Patriarchal blessing for you.

Precious daughter in the House of Joseph, privileged to come forth in this latter day, reserved for you to have opportunity during the period of your mortality to participate in the rapid days of growth.

Your lineage is that of Manasseh, but virtue of which if you are faithful to your responsibilities, you may claim the blessing of Abraham, Isaac, or Jacob and of Joseph, he who was proven as a youth in a strange land.

If you remember your lineage and apply your soul to the development of your talent your Heavenly Father will give you opportunities to lead, strengthen, unite, and save many of his children.

Precious experiences wait on your development and call. Be patient as you are polished and perfected with the difficulties and decisions which you will be called to make or endure. Let your trust be in your Heavenly Father. Pray unto Him regularly. Read his word as revealed through just and holy men. Harken to the voice of Latter-day leaders of the Priesthood for they teach the words of eternal life.

Be fearless, tactful, exact, and remember when you live the gospel principles you will have joy and peace no matter where you are or what you are doing.

When that morning comes when you kneel across the alter in God's Holy House with one striving as you are striving to be prepared for the responsibilities of marriage and of parenthood, you shall have sweet assurance of the nearness and approval of your Heavenly Father on your commitment. From that moment devote your energies to the perfection of your family. Let your husband preside over the kingdom of his posterity. Do develop to your fullest possibilities.

Be noble in character. Seek to be perfect in all your callings, and your Heavenly Father shall give you love that cannot fail; shall give you joy beyond your present powers to comprehend. I bless you that you may always have a cheerful disposition by which you shall minister in love to comfort and bring inspiration to others.

I bless you to come forward in the first resurrection if you are worthy. Be patient and careful in your callings. Remember to pray to your Father in Heaven before you choose any decisions. I bless you to know the difference.

You shall be called to make difficult decisions and I caution you to always be prayerful. Know that you have been blessed throughout your life. Never doubt the love, your Father in Heaven loves you. Be patient and know that is true. He will never fail you so long as you put forth your faith and trust him.

For the Temple trip, everyone was to meet at the chapel parking lot and board there. April was in the kitchen holding her little overnight bag. She did pack some money in her bag's pocket. Then she saw headlights come into their lane. The car turned around at the barn and stopped by the steps.

Judge Du Val stood up on his running board on the driver's side and hollered to her. "Come on. Come on, let's go."

April saw her Dad in the living room and asked, "Is it okay if I ride with the Judge to the chapel?"

"Sure go," Dad said.

April ran out the door, opened the passenger side, and hopped in. "Hit it," she said to him, and they both laughed.

As he drove along, he slapped her leg, "Are you alright?"

April looked at him and nodded "Yes", and said, "I am trying every day. It's not easy, but I am trying."

"Good," he said, and he squeezed her shoulder.

"I heard Hugh is having a real problem with Sandra. The Marines are telling him they did not sign him up for him to bring along a wife that they are responsible for. Housing is not plentiful, and Sandra does not want to live on base. On his salary they cannot afford to live off base where Sandra wants to live. Not sure what he is going to do and it's a hell of a thing to be distracted like that when he is trying to do well," and he shook his head.

April sat there thinking and said, "I don't feel sorry for him. He made these choices on his own. No one held a gun to his head."

The Judge looked at her, "Don't be so angry. It does not look good on you."

April waved her hand at him as in, "Go on."

"You and I are going to have such good talks side by side ALL THE WAY TO THE TEMPLE" he said. April rolled her eyes, and he laughed.

And then she thought about the bad situation Hugh was in and how good she had it and she did feel sorry for Hugh, just a little.

At the chapel it was a little chaotic. There were many people standing on the sidewalk, and some were still at their cars unloading. There were also more and more cars and trucks coming into the parking lot, and the bus was not there yet.

April saw Melinda Johnson. She was so nice. Her husband had been killed in an accident about four years ago leaving her with four children, one boy and three girls. The youngest was only three years old. Melinda was with child when the accident occurred. But she was out to church every Sunday with all the kids dressed neatly. They were all behaved and quiet.

When the Di Angelos went to church, they often were in the same pew as Melinda and her children. They all had a pencil and a piece of paper or one or two books to look at and share. When it was time for sacrament, Melinda would tell them and they all scooted up on the bench and sat with their arms folded, very reverent.

Melinda was an ultrasound tech at the hospital. She had to use the hospital's day care for the children who did not go to school. Only two were school age. The last two were barely five and the other three.

She owned her own home in town, and she often had Nora and Lena come clean or sometimes maintain the lawn. So, she had time with her children. It was not easy being a single Mother.

As the bus pulled in, April stayed by the Judge's side, and he pulled her hand to stay behind him as they boarded. He chose a seat near the middle of the bus on the right side. He slid in giving her the seat by the isle. April sat with him as Melinda boarded and she nudged the Judge in his side. "Did you notice how pretty she is?" April said to him.

"No, I did not. I am not in the market for a wife," he said.

"And why not?" she asked him.

"I like being on time for one, like tonight, your parents are late. I saw your Dad downstairs, but your Mom was not. He was waiting for her. I am not that patient. Second of all, I don't see me driving a minivan. That is so not my style. Third, kids are noisy and make messes, and I am a very clean person. Also, I like my music and quiet," he said.

April looked at him and said, "You have issues. I don't see that in her or her kids. They are a sweet loving family," she said.

"Are you trying to be a matchmaker for me, Dearie?" he asked her.

"Well, you are not even trying. I mean I was a mess when Dad and Mom took me in. You remember that don't you?" She asked him.

"I do remember, but you were only one, not four," he said.

"Oh, give me a break. You'd be so lucky to be with someone like her. She is a great cook. Ask Dad how he liked the coconut cream pie she made for him," April said.

"Oh, really, and he never invited me over for a slice. I will mention that to him," the Judge said.

Those two went back and forth almost the entire trip. It was a crab session. It was a good way for April to deal with the anger she had. If anyone could pester April, it was the judge. At the bus stop April went to the front of the bus to speak to Mr. Steven's wife.

"I am so happy to see that you came along," she said. "I really enjoy your company and sweet smile."

"Oh, go on," she said. "He said we should go, so here I am," she said to April.

"Well, I am glad, and I hope to see you inside too. I better get back to my seat. I am sitting with bossy boss," April said.

"I can here you two all the way up here," she said to April.

"Oh, no. That's not good!" April said.

Then she scooted up to where Melinda was sitting. "How are you?" she asked her.

"I am tired, but glad to be going to the temple. I have put it off for far too long," Melinda said.

April asked her, "I may be nosey, but are you going for an answer of some kind?"

"I am," she said. "How did you know?" she asked April.

"I didn't know. It just came out. It must be the Holy Ghost again," and they laughed.

April hesitated then Melinda asked her, "What?"

"Well, I was going to ask something kind of personal. So don't think I am being rude. Okay?" April said.

"Okay, go ahead. I have been asked so many things in the past year, and I doubt you could be rude to me," she answered April.

April then whispered to her, "Have you ever looked at Judge Du Val? I mean, he is single, he has a good job, and he is well respected."

Melinda said, "I know of him, but I do not know him. I do know that he thinks highly of you and it must be awesome to have someone like that care so much about you."

"Exactly my point," April said to her. "Imagine if he and you were a couple. He would feel that way about you and your children and help you."

"Oh, now. That is going too far. My kids are just kids. They play, make messes, and well . . . are kids. He is a strict, orderly man. I doubt he could handle all this," Melinda said.

"Well, the thing is, no one could. It would take him loving you. The rest would follow along," April said.

"Boy, are you ever confident and full of ideas," Melinda said. "I'd go out with him if he asked. I don't know anything bad about him, but I am not asking him."

April hugged her and said, "I hope you pray about this in the Temple. You are more likely to receive your answer. It's a good thing we are going." April winked at her and returned to her seat. Her companion had put a pillow at his window, and was nodding off to sleep.

April checked her watch it was almost 7:00 a.m.; they were up at 5 a.m.; they were at the chapel at 5:15 a.m.; the bus came around 6 a.m.; and the time seemed right. They had about an hour to go. She sat there quietly and looked around. Almost everyone was asleep but not Nora. So, April slipped out of her seat to sit by her.

"How are you?" she asked Nora.

"I am good. We left a little late, but we made it in time," and Nora smiled at her daughter. She marveled at her blonde curly hair. She truly was taking after her great grandmother who was

Chippewa, but had blonde curly hair and the same cheeks. Nora was sure April would look like her too when she was older too.

The two of them sat together chatting quietly for quite a while. April marveled at Nora's beauty. She had jet black hair, and she had not been in the sun much. Her skin was honey brown. April loved her dark eyes too. April was told why she was different, genetics from the past, and that comforted her. Yeah, she felt lucky. It was like she had three Mothers and two Dads.

April went back to her seat and the Judge was restless, he was turning in his seat. April leaned over and whispered in his ear. "You are to listen to me. You will meet the woman to take as your companion this day. Do not shirk from this blessing, sayeth I," and he poked her.

"Cut it out! Can't a man get any sleep?" he asked.

"Hey, you wanted me as a seat companion, I know of someone who is much quieter than I am if you want a different seat on the way home," she told him. He took the palm of his hand and wiped it down April's face as if to shut her down. She put his arm around her neck and leaned against him.

"I sure am going to miss being your number one," she said to him.

"Awe, for goodness sakes. Stop it. You are so far off target, it's not funny," he said.

"Oh, am I? Let's wait and see. She is like a trinket on the shelf. If you wait too long, then someone is going to pluck her off the shelf, and she will be gone you know," April said.

When they arrived at the Temple, everyone shook off sleep, straightened their clothing, and grabbed their bags. The Judge asked April who was going with her for her endowments.

"Probably Mom, Nora, Lena, Mrs. Marshall, and maybe Melinda. She might soon be like family," she said.

He leaned over breathing hot breath in her ear, knowing she hated that.

Miranda said, "You two are like little kids. Behave," and Gordon just laughed.

At the Temple they all pulled out their membership. Temple recommends that everyone had to be checked for the right date and so on. No cell phones, no cameras, and then they went in. The kids went to do baptisms, and the adults went their own separate ways.

April stayed with her Mom and the trio. Miranda asked Melinda, Are you with anyone?"

She said, "No."

Then Miranda asked if she would like to go with them, and Melinda said she would be grateful for the company.

April laughed to herself. "Am I wrong?" and she said that she was going to pray for the Judge to open his eyes. It was his time and if God thought she was right for him, then for Him to send a message to the Judge and wake him up. She had things she wanted to converse with the Lord too.

The Temple is a quiet, organized, and peaceful place. A place to re-discover yourself, for your soul to find rest and joy. It all becomes so simply clear, the meaning of life in the Temple.

After her endowments, April was now able to go through a session in the Temple. She did but had trouble staying awake, that is how she always reacted to sitting still.

Then she was able to go to the Celestial Room. She loved it. It was so serene and so peaceful in there. April knelt down and asked the Lord to help her. She prayed for her Mom and Dad to accept the decision that she felt was right, and to have the appropriate time for her to make that commitment. She prayed for Hugh, that he would find peace and sincerely apologize to his parents. She prayed for Sandra to want to change her life, become respectable, leave her past, and embrace Hugh's good family. He did not become good all on his own. She prayed Sandra would realize that. Then she prayed for the Judge to find a companion for eternity, and whoever that might be, let him know firmly because he was so stubborn and set in his ways. She prayed for his heart to be softened and realize when he sees a companion he understands. Yes, she prayed for a long time. At times she wept because of the close feeling she received from God. There is no other place in the world to feel that close to God as when you are in his Holy Temple.

April did not care to do any more. She wanted to stay a bit longer in the Celestial Room. Here it was so wonderful. She hated to leave. She saw her Mom and the four come through. They came to her, and April realized she was given a small glimpse of heaven - our family members will be with us and still be able to come and go.

Nora sat by her and said, "I am so grateful to be a member, and to have the Temple to come to. So I can contemplate things in my life, ask questions, and receive answers. I never knew until I came here to live near you, what a wonderful blessing this has been. I know now that families can be together forever."

April said, "I am so very glad you get it, because so many people do not."

Lena was with Melinda and Mrs. Marshall. They all looked bedraggled.

"What is wrong with Lena?" April asked.

"The man she had been seeing off and on, found someone else. She is hurt, not too badly, but now she is sort of bitter. I don't know why she feels she must have a man in her life. I don't feel that way. I had her as a companion just as I did when we were kids, and I am happy with just the two of us," she said.

"Well, I sort of know how she feels," April said to her.

Nora touched April's arm. "When you are ready to make a commitment to a man, you will know. You were too young to say you would wait for him. You had a different journey. You were busy with the farm competition. You two grew up knowing each other, but as we grow, we change. He is older than you are and in a different frame of mind. Don't hate him. He was impatient. It might work out for the two of them. Don't wish it not to, because if it fails, it is not because of your ill wishes toward them. April, you always had such a sweet, sweet spirit, hold on to that and blessings will come to you," Nora told her.

April kissed her on her cheek. She truly was a blessing to her. April was so grateful Nora and Lena were.

The group of women gathered and headed down to the cafeteria. April was in the line with them when someone caught her eye. She looked and looked again. She left her tray and walked over to the young man and tapped him on his back. The man turned, saw her, and they embraced. It was Hans from Poland! He was here on his mission! He told her that after she left, he and his family spent a lot of time with her parents. They impressed them so much, and they learned so much from April living with them. Family Home Evening, having prayers, and praying more than they ever did previously. He noticed a peaceful feeling like never before in his family. His Dad made arrangements to take the lessons from the missionaries, and they all were baptized within months after April left their home.

April's heart leapt with joy. How awesome! She begged him to bring his companion with him and sit with her family. They would be so happy to see him again. He agreed and when he came to the table where Gordon and Miranda were sitting with the others, he felt like he was home in Poland. He told the news to the table and Gordon reached over and shook his hand, so did the Judge.

Miranda cried, and he consoled her. "No these are tears of happiness," she said.

"So where are you serving? What area?" April asked.

"We have not been assigned. We are here in the Temple with our State Mission President Couple," he told them. "But when we do, I hope it's not too far from you folks," he said.

They all headed back upstairs. April looked up the winding staircase and thought how beautiful it was. As they walked along, the walls had large pictures of the Savior Jesus Christ and they were remarkable in their detail. No one was watching where they were going. They were just slowly walking along looking at the huge murals. Suddenly Melinda was bumped hard by someone and was pushed right into the chest of the Judge. The hit was so hard they both almost tumbled to the floor. Everyone apologized and the Judge helped Melinda and asked her if she was all right.

Something happened because it was as if he had seen a ghost. The blood drained from his face and his eyes got bigger as he supported Melinda. April saw it as did her Mom and Lena.

"Is he all right?" Lena asked.

Miranda said to let them alone, they would work it out. And you know, they did!

That night everyone was staying in the Marriot Hotel until the morning. The judge was overheard asking Melinda if she would like to go to dinner with him.

She said yes so easily it shocked her.

They had a nice time at dinner. They talked so easily and laughed. By the end of the meal, they both felt they had a good friendship. As they walked into the foyer of the hotel, the Judge asked Melinda if she would mind if he called her when they got back home. He enjoyed her company and thought he could take her out to dinner, or just spend some quality time together.

Melinda told him she would like that.

The bus pulled out about 11:00 in the afternoon, heading for home. The seating arrangements had all changed. April lost her seating companion as Melinda was sitting with the Judge. April took a seat with her Mom. They talked every now and then when her Mom asked her, "So are you feeling better now?"

"Yes, I am. I think I have things worked out. There is nothing I can do about Hugh but pray for him. I am working on my next thing, and it will come in time." April was being evasive. She did not want to tell her Mom just yet.

They got back to the church parking lot, jumped into their cars, and headed home. They were all tired.

Gordon said, as much as he had a good time, he was going to be all messed up come tomorrow morning. Having two days off in the middle of the work week was difficult. Thursday and Friday would feel like Monday.

They got home and there were some girls sitting on their lawn, "POH it's Shelly, Megan, and Kayla," April said. She had a lot of friends, but not many close girlfriends. Because of her rough work ethic, not many girls were like that. But these three accepted April even though they could not keep up with her.

"Hey, April, were you away?" they asked her.

"Yeah, I went to the Temple. I had some things to sort out," April answered them.

"So, you know we heard about Hugh, and that sucks," Shelly said.

"It's okay. Really it is," April said. "He is the one who changed his mind. I did nothing wrong."

"Don't tell me it does not bother you, Girl. I know that you were head over heels for him," Megan said.

"Yes, it does bother me, but there is nothing I can do about it. It's done," April said.

"Let's go and kick her butt. I know where she lives," Kayla said.

April then told them, "No, don't. That is not right. I was here a few days ago with my parents when Hugh told us Sandra was pregnant. She is not here. She is with him at the base arguing. She does not want to live on the base. Believe me, he has his hands full," April said.

"Serves him right, the pig," Shelly said. "You are too nice to have someone crap on you girl."

"We are not going to solve anything out here complaining. Come on. Let's go inside and have something to drink or eat." Then the four of them piled into the house.

Gordon loved to tease the girls. He saw them and said, "Oh boy, we have four cooks that are going to make our dinner tonight."

"Oh no," they said. "Not unless you like milk and crackers," And they laughed.

Gordon stood in the doorway trying to come up with something to say when one of the girls asked him, "Are you going to put us in jail?"

"I can if you want me to," he said and he reached for his hand cuffs and walked to Megan.

"Hey! I wasn't the one who said anything," she said.

They all began to scream and laugh when Miranda came into the room.

"Daddy, what are you doing to our guests?"

"I am arresting them. Just like they wanted me to," Gordon said.

"No, we don't. That's a lie. We didn't want to be handcuffed or anything," they said.

Miranda loved these girls, they were the shot of happiness April needed. This group had known each other since the fourth grade. They rode ponies here, did hair together, tried to get into the same classes, and were such happy girls.

When Gordon and Miranda went outside to sit on their swing, April quietly asked the girls what they planned to do for their education.

"I am going to nursing school," Shelly said. "I leave in September."

Megan said, "I am going to nursing school, too, but I want to be a sonogram specialist. I have a lot of the courses in nursing, and then I will transfer for the x-ray portion."

Kayla was not sure, she thought she'd like to be a hair stylist and go to beauty school but her Mom wanted her to go to dental school. She said if she could not get in here or at Pittsburgh, she did not want to go.

"What about you April? Did you decide?" they asked her.

"Do you still want to go to vet school or be that darn attorney?"

April leaned back and laughed, "Neither," she said. Then she held her fingers to her lips for them to be quiet. "I have decided to enlist," April told them.

"Enlist, what do you mean? Are you going away or what?" Shelly repeated the quiet "Shhh!" and they spoke in whispers. "Are you joining the Army?" one asked her.

"I think I will join the Navy, but opt for the Seal program," April told them.

"No, they all whaled, don't, please don't do it, you could be killed."

April smiled at her and shook her head.

"Oh yes, you could. My Dad's cousin was a Seal, and he was killed," Megan said. "Please, don't do it."

April sat there and said, "Look I love you guys, and I mean that. All of you could go to one of our D Farms, work, and earn your own way. I'd sign your papers myself. But this is MY life, and MY dream. I feel like I am so lost. I need something to focus on, I have so much anger inside of me, and I need to let it out. I am not ready for vet or law school. Right now, my concentration needs to be slapped to follow through. I am a mess, truly. And I do not want my parents to know."

Shelly said, "We still have a lot of summer left. Let's go dancing and party. We can take a trip, have fun, and that might help you a lot. We are all good friends, and we stick together through thick and thin. We have been there, so won't you give us a chance?"

April looked at her friends, "I will swim with you until I can't anymore. I will dance until I am dizzy, but I don't party because I do not drink, smoke, or do drugs. I stay away from things like that, and you all know that. A trip to somewhere, maybe, but when it's all said and done, I doubt it will change my mind. It's like this destiny inside me. I feel it is right."

"No, give us a chance," they all begged her, they threw pillows at her, and sat on her. April was laughing so hard that she could not breathe, and she lifted two girls off her at one time. "Man, you are strong, Girl," they said. "Come on. Let's go talk to your parents, and they did."

Miranda knew that something just was not right. She felt it in her bones. They invited Nora and Lena for a cookout one evening when Nora asked, "How is April?"

Miranda did not mince her words. She came right out with how she felt.

Nora agreed. She said, "April is distant, I can feel it, not in her words or her actions, but something is not right. It is as though she is covering up something. Something she did not want anyone to know, to protect them, or maybe herself."

"It doesn't do any good to ask her," Miranda said. "She always says 'I'm fine. Stop worrying about me. Really, Mom!' You know in an impatient voice."

"Then something is bothering her," Nora said. "Lena you and I are both like that when we have something to do. We just plow through."

Lena agreed, she remembered when she left her abusive husband. She told everyone she was doing fine, and not to worry. When all the while, she was packing her things and making plans to leave.

"Just let her go. Whatever it is, she will do it anyway," Lena said. "She is a determined person, and stubborn. When she has her mind made up, that's it."

Miranda said, "You are right, but most of her life she chose the right thing, the right way. So, let us all pray for her that the choice she is making or has to make is the one that God will want for her."

Nora added, "But sometimes God has his children go through things that are not so pleasant and it is necessary for them to learn how to handle themselves. To learn to handle their problems the way the Savior did." They all sat there shaking their heads in affirmative.

Gordon came to the table with more tomatoes he had cut inside, and Miranda asked him to check the burgers.

"Let's keep this to ourselves," she asked the other two woman and they said they would.

Two weeks of playing with no focus was making April miserable. She almost couldn't take it anymore. She was tired of dancing, of swimming, and traveling. She wanted to scream STOP!

Her friends meant well, but this was not helping. In fact, it was making it worse. April told them she had had enough. One more night of camping and then she was ready to go home."

"NO, we want to take you to . . . "

"Nope, I am done. I know what I must do and there is no sense putting it off."

Megan started to cry, "God, I wish you'd listen to us," she said to April

"God, I wish you'd all listen to me," April told them. "This is my life, my walk. I love you girls so much. Please be respectful for what I feel is right, FOR ME. Please?"

The girls knew April was right. She always was different than most girls. April loved to work and play hard. April was without a doubt a rough and tough cowgirl. She never shirked from any job or duty asked of her. Not matter what it was. She bore it like it was fun. When all the other girls complained, April kept working and smiling.

Their fathers told Shelly, Megan and Kayla being around April was good for them. Some of April's work ethic might rub off, because when there was work to do at their homes they disappeared. When April came and there was work, she worked. And if the girls disappeared, April went and found them and encouraged them to work too. She made them work. Yeah, she was an oddball, but when Megan went to Texas that one year on vacation with her parents, she saw a lot of girls like April. They hauled wood, threw bales, and roped horses in dust. Yeah, when she told April about Texas, April told her they are in California, too. I am one of them."

After two weeks of running with her friends and blowing four hundred dollars, each of the three was hesitant, and one wanted to come home. They dropped April off and each one got out and hugged her crying. Miranda witnessed this from her kitchen window. "Now what?" she thought to herself.

April lugged her duffel bag and tent onto the porch, and her Mom met her there. Throw the wash in the washing machine, and Dad will take care of the tent. It should be aired out. No?"

"Yeah, it should. I can do it." April opened the tent and hung it out over the two wash lines. Then she came in looking so suntanned brown. Her skin was as dark as any Native American, her hair was bleached with white strands in it, and she was smeared with dust.

"Go up and shower," Mom said. Dad is coming home in about twenty-five minutes, and we are having steaks tonight, baked potatoes, a salad, and our dessert is strawberry Jell-O with real strawberries in it. April trudged into the house in her bare feet, and up the stairs to shower. She laughed to herself. For Mom, everything was made better with food. No matter what the problem was, or how you felt, food was always her solution.

April put on an all-in-one jumper, shirt, and shoes. It was cotton and comfortable. She got out her flip flops and went on the porch. Mom was fussing with the table settings outside and April went to help her. They were not finished when Dad pulled up.

"Hey, what do we have here?" he asked.

"We are trying to set the table and the wind is not cooperating. April, put some decorative stones on and in the plates and cups.

"That should work until we need to use them," Dad said.

He quickly went in and changed, then came out to cook the steaks. No one could cook steak like her Dad. Soft, juicy, and just the way you wanted them – either rare, medium rare, or well done. Mom liked her steaks done. Dad liked his rare, a bloody mess, and April like hers barely pink, medium done.

They gathered the food, put it on the table, sat to eat, and Mom asked April to say the prayer. April bowed her head and said, "Father, we ask this in the name of Jesus Christ to hear our prayer. Those who made this dinner to be blessed for their efforts. May this food give us energy and to have patience to accept other's views and have understanding. We pray these things, Father, and thank thee for thy many blessing in the name of Jesus Christ, Amen."

"That was some prayer," Dad said. "Got something specific on your mind," and Miranda kicked her husband under the picnic table.

April put down her fork and said with a big breath, "Yes, I do. I have made up my mind what I want to do, and honestly, I don't know how to tell you. I am afraid of how you will take it," she said.

"What do you mean?" Dad asked her.

"Dad, I want to enter the military. I want to sign up with the Navy and see if I am Seal material. If not, I will just do my time with what they ask of me."

Gordon almost choked. He just looked at April, and her Mother began to cry.

"See, I just knew this would upset you both. And I am sorry, but I just feel this is right for me. I feel as if I am being called. No, not called, but pulled to go. Can you understand that?"

Dad has his hand on his wife's. "I do, but could you please explain this to us so we can understand you, April?" he asked of her.

"I will, but if I do I know Mom will be very upset with me and for that reason I can't. I would not do anything to upset her intentionally."

"Just say it, April. We need to know in order to understand," her Father said to her.

April took another breath, looked at her loving parents, and said, "I love you both so much, more than you will ever know. What I have done over the years has never been for me. It was for you both. I was dropped off here like a scavenging mouse. I had no home, and no belongings. I begged for food, and I stole food. I lied all the time to keep safe and you saved me. I remember Mom carrying me out of Flo's Diner on her hip saying everything would be all right. And it was, and I owe you both so very much that I just had to succeed."

"Everything I did, from riding in the Olympics, to skiing, skating in everything I did, I did for you. I would not ever let you down, my gratitude and love for you is so . . . I just can never repay you for your commitment and love to me. But this is my life now. What I have been through these past few weeks has torn my heart out. I hurt and I don't like that. I just can't get past it. I am so unhappy, not able to concentrate, and I am bitter. I am so ugly on the inside. I can't stand myself. I see your faces and I know I am hurting you, and for that I am sorry."

"In part because of how I feel about America, and because I love my country, I want to enlist, soon. I want to be a Seal, if I can make it. I am athletic, strong, and determined. I feel that if I do my part, God will surely watch over me and keep me in his care."

Dad put his napkin down on the table and looked directly into her eyes. "April, being a Seal is extremely dangerous. There are missions that never happen. Do you understand what I mean?"

"I do, Dad, but that is what I want to do. I need to do. I don't know if you can understand this, but I feel as though I am being pulled. That is why I wanted to go to the Temple, to get my endowments, so I would be ready to go. I discussed this in the Temple with my Father in Heaven, in his house, and I received confirmation to go. I truly feel it is meant to be for me. This is my calling," she said. "Even my Patriarchal blessing indicates this. I know both of you read it. Did you read what I read? How I wish you would please see my side of this. Please?" She asked them.

Miranda was not able to speak. She was so full of sorrow. "Mom, I don't want you to feel the pain that I do. I am not leaving you with anger or pulling away with spite. This is what I feel I am supposed to do. If you would just listen in prayer, I believe you would feel better about this," April said.

Dad said. "This was a good dinner," and he began to pile up the plates and take them into the house. No one had eaten, not really.

April felt as though she had let them down. She felt disgusted with herself. She did not help them clean up. She stayed away. It had to sink into them.

She went around to the side of the house where there was an alcove for the chimney. She knelt there and began to pray. Her words were tears, she never wanted to hurt the two people she loved the most. She pleaded with her Father in Heaven to help them understand. This was her mission, and she knew in her heart that it was right. It was the only thing she really knew, other than that she really knew her parents loved her.

As April prayed, she heard loud and clear, as if someone was standing in front of her, "Bring peace into your heart and all will be well."

She got up and went into the house and asked her parents to have evening prayer. April knelt, prayed, and she said that her heart was finally at peace. The joy of knowing the direction she was to take, for her heart was set to always do good in any job she would be asked. She prayed for the Holy Ghost to guide her and help her in all ways, to watch over her family, comfort them, and bring them unending joy.

As they got up, Gordon kissed his daughter, and Mom held her and did not want to let go.

That night, Gordon and his wife lay in bed talking. "I think she will be all right," he said. "She will be trained extensively and maybe she won't make it and just serve in the Navy."

"I need your faith," his wife said.

"No, you don't," he said. "You have great faith, and you will be called upon to use it. Oh, this girl of ours," Dad said.

The next morning when April got up there was a note on the table.

> *Dear Daughter, both of us have been selfish. We want to keep you with us forever. A lifetime with you is never going to be enough. Thankfully we have been sealed as a family in the Temple, for eternity. I believe in Jesus Christ's words. I pray while you are out there*

> *you will continue to read and gain knowledge from the Book of Mormon and the Bible.*
>
> *We want more than anything for you to be happy. We do understand how you feel. It was a horrible, hurtful thing that happened to you. But as your blessing said, you will go through things like this. With faith you can have joy in even bad circumstances. This is what we believe you are trying to tell us. So, with a lighter heart than we had last evening, we want you to know you have our blessing to follow your calling as you described to us. Know this, as you serve, we serve with you. There are so many family members who will be praying for you during your time away. We hope you allow us a chance to get them all together to wish you well, safe trip, and to come home safely.*
>
> *Please, let us talk. Love, Mom and Dad.*

They did talk and they did have a nice sit-down party with all of the family. They paid for Grandpa and his wife to join them sending them tickets. There were sixty people to wish her well and to give richness to her life. This made a memory of those who loved her while she would be away. They would be on her mind every now and then.

One of those people was the Judge and she came to him asking, "May I come into your office to have a will made for me and my parents?"

"Sure," he said, "Come in either tomorrow morning or later in the day, and we will take care of all of that for you."

At the Judge's chambers that following day, April waited for the Judge to come out of a hearing. He came in wearing his big black robe and laid his robe carefully across a chair. He rubbed his hands together and went to April half picking her up to hug her. "Okay now," and he pressed a button on his desk. "Missy, will you come in here, please?"

Missy came in with the documents that were prepared ahead of time. She could not look at April. Missy could not hold back her tears.

"It's all pretty standard. All your possessions will go to your parents, including your company, unless you specify anything." he said. "No, that's fine," she told him.

"Okay then, sign here and on the next two pages. They are marked with highlighter tabs."

April signed where indicated and stood up, "Is that all?" she asked.

"Nope, it's not" he said. "Come over here." He pulled a chair right in front of him, tapping his fingers on the seat. April was sitting so close to him their knees touched.

"I would have put you on my desktop like I did when you were little, but you have grown too big for me to do that," and he winked at her.

"Now, I want you to listen to me, and be smart. Do what they tell you, exactly what they tell you. Not what you think! If they tell you to run, don't blaze a trail, stay with your unit. You are capable and smart, but your heart may get you into trouble. Think consequences when you are out there."

"I love you, and you know that. I will pray for you and write to you. But if you don't make it back, I will be madder than hell.

Do you hear me? It will be your fault if I fall away, get drunk, and die," and he laughed, but April was not. Her eyes were filling with tears, and she could not talk.

"What's the matter?" he asked her.

April could not look up. She murmured, "I love you, too. More than you could ever know. You have always been there for me. You listened to me, picked me up, and you have cheered me up. You have been my second Dad without the glory. For me, it will make my heart happy if you settle down with someone who is as kind, smart, and funny as you are. You deserve that.

April stood up and hugged him in a hug that lasted for a few minutes, not seconds. Both had tears and could not say anymore. He walked her to his door, she opened it up, turned to him, and they hugged once more for the last time.

The day before she left, she stopped to see the Captain who had heard about her decision. "You have made a wise choice. You are in your prime. Don't listen to those who tell you, you can't. You know you can. We are proud of you, as are many in this community. You have served us well. Now go and serve your country well," and they both hugged.

A month before April had signed papers with the United States Navy with a contingency to try out for the Navy Seals. The recruiter commended her and that was that! April knew she was locked in, no changes for her. She was committed.